"With candor, sympathy, and a deft touch of suspense, Michelle Buckman has written an engrossing and touching story of Maggie McCarthy, a girl whose struggles with family, friends, sex, and popularity will resonate with every teenager, boy or girl. Maggie's faith in God is no crutch—it's the real deal, genuine and truthful, even when it hurts. This is one novel I'll give to my own teenagers to read."

—RICHARD LEWIS, author of *The Flame Tree* and
The Killing Sea

"*Maggie Come Lately* is a provocative unfolding of sixteen-year-old Maggie McCarthy's perilous journey toward self-discovery when forced to deal with mankind's darkest side. Like a master artist, author Michelle Buckman chips away at stereotypical notions while slowly unveiling the hope, faith, and rich familial bonds that guide us and sustain us."

—JODY EWING, author of *One Way: Bumps and Detours on the Road to Adulthood*

"Michelle Buckman's *Maggie Come Lately* has real characters in real problems with real faith. A page-turner with an important message that is anything but preachy, *Maggie Come Lately* is one to be read and shared for many years to come."

— BARB HUFF, author of the ON TOUR series

Maggie Come Lately

MICHELLE BUCKMAN

TH1NK
P.O. Box 35001
Colorado Springs, Colorado 80935

Published in association with Yates & Yates, LLP, Attorneys and Counselors, Orange, California.

TH1NK is an imprint of NavPress.
TH1NK and the TH1NK logo are registered trademarks of NavPress. Absence of ® in connection with
marks of NavPress or other parties does not indicate an absence of registration of those marks.

ISBN-13: 978-1-60006-082-3
ISBN-10: 1-60006-082-X

Cover design by David Uttley, The Design Works Group, www.thedesignworksgroup.com
Cover image by Getty
Creative Team: Nicci Hubert, Laura Wright, Reagen Reed, Arvid Wallen, Pat Reinheimer, Bob Bubnis

This novel is a work of fiction. Names, characters, places, and incidents are either the product of the
author's imagination or are used fictitiously. Any resemblance to actual events, locales, organizations, or
persons, living or dead, is entirely coincidental and beyond the intent of either the author or publisher.

Unless otherwise identified, all Scripture quotations in this publication are taken from the *King James
Version* (KJV).

Buckman, Michelle.
  Maggie come lately : a novel / Michelle Buckman.
    p. cm.
  ISBN-13: 978-1-60006-082-3
  ISBN-10: 1-60006-082-X
  1. Teenage girls--Fiction. 2. Motherless families--Fiction. 3.
Popularity--Fiction. 4. Friendship--Fiction. 5. Child sexual
abuse--Fiction. I. Title.

PS3602.U28M34 2007
813'.6--dc22

2007000239

Printed in the United States of America

1 2 3 4 5 6 7 8 9 10 / 10 09 08 07

FOR A FREE CATALOG OF NAVPRESS BOOKS & BIBLE STUDIES,
CALL 1-800-366-7788 (USA) OR 1-800-839-4769 (CANADA).

To teenage girls everywhere — live your faith, love for life.

PROLOGUE

SHE KNEW INSTINCTIVELY that Maggie was leaning against the door. She didn't care. She had to take a shower. The baby book said so: *"When the baby's crying makes you too tense, place him safely in his crib and take a shower. It will relax you and drown out the noise of his crying."*

She closed her eyes and tilted her head back. Hot water rained down her face, slid over her skin, and splashed at her feet. Steam rose around her. The sound of the water blocked out Billy's whimpers. In the confines of the shower, she was alone. Billy was in his crib. Tony was on the sofa where he'd fallen asleep watching a dinosaur movie. Her daughter, Maggie, was supposed to be playing dolls, but she didn't care what the little girl was doing, as long as there were no small hands pulling at her, no small voice pleading for attention. Maybe Billy would cry himself to sleep and she could slip into bed after her shower, just for a short nap.

Weariness dragged at her.

She scoured her skin with a pale blue washcloth, washing away the drudgery, then lathered her legs and picked up Frank's old double-edged razor to scrape away the shadow of three days' stubble. She loved watching it disappear strip by strip. Sweeping one hand along her bared skin, she reveled in the idea of being a teenager again. Again? She was only twenty. Dreams of high school filled her mind: spending time with her friends, getting ready to go out on the town during those years before responsibility, before feeling trapped and helpless in motherhood before her time.

She pulled the razor around her kneecap and started again at the bottom. One, two, three strips. The fourth pass nicked her skin right at her ankle bone. She watched the blood ooze out and seep down her foot, mesmerizing her. It didn't hurt. She plugged the drain, then dropped to the bottom of the tub and propped her foot up against the side, watching it, thinking.

Frank had suggested she go back to the doctor, but what did he know? He was seven years older than she was. He hadn't missed out on high school, the part of life everyone else told stories about for years afterward. He couldn't understand what was going on in her head. He expected her to push herself out of this morose hole of postpartum depression. He couldn't understand it was quicksand that sucked ever harder, despite her thrashing lunges toward normalcy.

She told him she'd been back to the doctor, but she hadn't. What she wanted was to wake up and discover her world the way it used to be—life outside this house, outside of motherhood and marriage. Was this all there was? Laundry and dishes and dirty diapers? She remembered dancing and parties and kissing in the moonlight. She remembered life. What could the doctor do to bring that back? He couldn't change what she had become.

The baby was screaming now. Wincing at the noise, she squeezed her eyes shut and forced herself to ignore his pleas.

The water was rising in the tub, hugging her feet, her buttocks, edging up her body, cloaking her in warmth. The cut didn't sting like she expected. She'd cringe at a needle. She'd suck at a paper cut. But her foot, bathed in the warm water, didn't hurt.

Maggie pounded on the door. "Mommy, can I come in?"

Water still showered down, pelting every part of her. "Go away. I'll be out in a few minutes."

A thump. Maggie was sulking against the door, she knew.

"Let her," she mumbled. Even as she said it aloud, she regretted it. She loved her daughter, her redheaded baby with wide green eyes and a dimpled smile full of tiny, perfect teeth. She loved all three of her kids. But she wanted more. Somehow she'd lost sight of who she was, of who she was supposed to be when she grew up, and she didn't know how to get that vision back. It was like wandering around in a cave with a flashlight that was losing battery power, its light diminishing to a narrow beam cast into nothingness.

The blood was slowing. She looked at the razor. It moved of its own will, perhaps.

More blood. More peace to draw on.

She watched the blade as if it were in a stranger's hand. One hand to the other wrist. Away from the arguments with Frank. Away from the problems, the bills, the reality.

Pain seared through her as red gushed from her wrist. It made her sleepy to see it pouring out, blending into the water, running off her skin, rushing away.

"Mommy? Mommy!"

She sighed and made an effort to answer over the noise of the shower. "What?"

Maggie's voice sounded small, far away, muffled against the door. "Don't be mad at me, Mommy. I'll be a good girl."

She couldn't take her eyes off the red turning translucent in the stream of water. The water on her face warbled her words. "I'm not mad at you."

Maggie's voice rose a notch, hopeful, questioning. "I love you, Mommy."

Her lungs ached with shallow, inadequate breaths. *I love you, Maggie. I love you, but it feels so insufficient, so inconsequential. Who am I?*

Gradually, the blood ran slower. Her limbs hung heavily, too heavy to raise. Her chin hung low, as if in mockery of the haughty air she'd so often displayed, of the look she'd given her mother when she'd announced she was pregnant with Maggie at sixteen. She didn't feel haughty now.

"Mommy, I want you to hold me."

She could only turn her eyes toward the door. The love emanating from the little body on the other side drifted to her in a haze and brought unexpected warmth, followed almost immediately by a bone-deep chill as if the love had been sucked away. With sudden clarity, she realized where she was, what she was losing—the very meaning of existence: love. The thought came as her life ebbed away.

Her voice dissipated to a whisper. "I'm so sorry."

Four-year-old Maggie crumpled into a ball, knowing with the strange instinct of the very young that her life had just shifted and a void had appeared. The path before her would be walked alone.

Chapter One

MAGGIE DROPPED HER book bag on the floor and slumped against the kitchen counter. "Happy birthday to me." The kitchen looked exactly as she'd left it that morning before school. Fluorescent green plastic bowls, the ones she'd splurged on at Wal-Mart last month, sat on the counter with dried-up milk cementing scraps of cereal to the edges. The pan from last night's pork chops soaked in a sink of murky water—the suds replaced by globs of oil floating on the surface. A ragged dishcloth hung over the tap. Lime green monkey place mats—she loved monkeys—sat askew on the heavy oak table. A clay napkin holder that Tony had made in fifth grade sat in the center with one limp paper napkin collapsed upon itself.

No miraculously clean kitchen. No cake or flowers in sight. No balloons. No presents. Not that she wanted balloons or flowers, really, but something to commemorate turning sixteen would've been nice.

During the first years after her mother's death, her father made an attempt to keep things normal. He bought her a birthday cake and hung streamers all over the house—at least on her fifth birthday. But maybe that was only because back then her grandmother was checking in on her and her brothers. Meemaw had said that the three of them were her last ties to her daughter and that they ought to live with her because she had no faith in their daddy's raising them properly by himself. She said he had no notion of what to do with three babies. But her father stood his ground, and Meemaw eventually gave up and returned to Arizona. Since then her existence had faded into birthday cards, Christmas presents, and her annual letter, sent on the anniversary of the suicide to remind the three of them what a wonderful mother they'd had.

Some kind of wonderful.

Billy sauntered through the kitchen door and dropped the mail on the table. "Look, my skateboarding magazine finally came." He slapped the magazine on the counter in front of her, pulled a mason jar out of a cabinet, and filled it to the top with apple juice.

"How many times do I have to tell you not to drink the entire jug in one sitting? Save some for the rest of us. I can't get any more till next week."

He gulped it down, left the jar and the jug of juice on the counter, snatched up his magazine, and kept going. "I need some help with my math homework later, but I gotta go to Brad's house to practice soccer first. Later." The back door slammed behind him, rattling the tiny metal chimes hanging from the eaves of the porch.

Over the past couple of years, life had moved to a new level where her brothers no longer needed her in the sweet, loving way they had when they were little. They seemed to need her more nowadays, but in a detached, demanding way. Sure, Billy still sought her help with homework once in a while and sometimes even asked her advice about things, but the hugs she used to get regularly now came fewer and farther between. She wondered how long it would be before he didn't need her at all, like Tony, who expected just as much from her but no longer gave any affection in return.

She sighed as she poured herself a small glass of juice and placed the jug back in the refrigerator before moving to the table to sort through the mail. Most of the envelopes were bills, but one was a card. "From Meemaw, of course." She tore it open and ran her fingers over the rose embossed on the front. A grown-up card, not some kiddy picture like years past, as if she finally just matured today. Meemaw didn't realize she'd been a grown-up for as long as she could remember, responsible for her brothers and the house and everything else her father couldn't handle.

A fifty-dollar bill lay inside. She gasped. *Fifty dollars!* Meemaw usually sent ten, which the boys spent long before it arrived every year. So, in truth, did she. But fifty dollars changed the game completely. She wouldn't spend it without really thinking through the purchase.

There was a verse inside about her sweet sixteen, but the scrawled note caught her attention first:

Margaret Ann,
Today you are sixteen, a momentous occasion in a girl's life,
an official declaration that you are no longer a child, but a
woman. Step wisely, dear granddaughter, for on her sweet
sixteen, your mother, my sweet daughter, conceived you.
Love and Blessings,
Meemaw

Maggie's hands trembled. She hadn't thought of her sixteenth birthday in those terms—her mother pregnant with her. Had she been scared? Scared to tell Meemaw? Scared to tell Daddy?

The back door creaked open, admitting Tony and his friend Webb. Webb was in the tenth grade like her, and a year older than Tony, but since Webb lived at the top of the hill, the two boys had been friends forever.

Tony peered into the refrigerator, his long brown hair flopping into his face. "What is there to eat?"

"Saltine crackers."

Webb leaned against the wall. He wasn't growing his hair out like most boys his age. It was just the right length, to his collar, and sleek black and shiny, not wavy red knots of hair like hers, or scraggly like Tony's greasy mop. She noticed he had a bit of fuzz growing on his upper lip and wondered when he would shave it off.

Tony still had his head stuck in the refrigerator. "Crackers? I need some real food."

"That's what was on sale this week, so that's what we've got."

"Hey, Webb, how about a bologna sandwich?"

"Sure. Whatever."

"The bologna is for lunch, Tony. Crackers or nothing."

He plopped the meat on the island and opened the pantry looking for bread.

"I said no. Put it back."

"What's it to you?"

"We have to get a new washing machine. I told you that. So we're cutting back on groceries. Now eat crackers or you can wear your clothes dirty the rest of your life, 'cause I'm sure not washing them by hand."

"I'm hungry."

"Fine. Eat all you want. Just don't cry to me when your clothes don't get washed."

Webb leaned forward and slapped his arm. "C'mon, man, let's go to my house."

"Whatever," Tony said, following him out the door.

"Don't forget you have to practice guitar," Maggie hollered after him, "and you have that English paper due."

Maggie watched them go, watched Webb go, and fingered the card still clasped in her hand. *My mother pregnant at sixteen, and I haven't even been kissed.*

Chapter Two

THE PHONE RANG. It was a stranger's voice, stiff, a telemarketer, undoubtedly reading from a script. "Hello, Mrs. McCarthy. We at the Foundation for the Physically Impaired aren't asking for a donation today, but just thirty minutes of your time. Do you have thirty minutes to help these unfortunate people, Mrs. McCarthy, most of them poor, innocent children, who are relying on kind people like you in this hour of need?"

"I'm not Mrs. McCarthy."

"Oh, I apologize. May I speak to Mrs. McCarthy?"

"No, you can't. She's dead."

The voice hesitated. "Oh, I'm so sorry." The script voice dropped a notch and lost some of its crispness. "To whom am I speaking?"

"Her daughter, Maggie."

"Well, Maggie, perhaps your father would be willing to help our cause."

"I doubt it. I take care of most things."

"Wonderful. You do sound very mature," the voice said. "Could you help our cause? Could you spend just thirty minutes delivering pamphlets in your neighborhood?"

"Lady, I'm sixteen. I just turned sixteen today. Why does everyone expect so much?"

Maggie hung up and stared at the phone. Her back ached with the effort of shouldering all her responsibilities. Depression hung around her like a wall of cotton, making it difficult to move, muffling her breaths as if it could physically suffocate her.

She stared at the dirty dishes littering the counter, not wanting to wash them but not knowing how to ignore them. She felt old. She reached her arm into the nasty cold water to release the stopper, turned on the tap, then stared out the window while she waited for hot water to reach the faucet. Outside, on an ancient azalea bush near the window, an Argiope spider, its huge black and yellow body spread out in glory in the middle of the intricate work of its webbing, hung like a sign announcing that fall had arrived. Nearby, oblivious to the danger, Monarch butterflies danced on the warm afternoon breeze, carefree. *Oh, to be a butterfly, soaring!* Maggie thought of how all the earlier butterflies of the summer would have perished after laying their eggs, but these, the autumn butterflies, would fly all the way to Mexico and back before laying their fatal batch of eggs in the spring. What made them different?

She was sure she was born to be caught in a web, not to fly free. Wasn't there something that would help her break out of this rut?

As steam rose from the flowing water, Maggie turned her attention back to the dishes. She rinsed the sink and refilled it, trying to recall a time when she must have been carefree, when she had done nothing and enjoyed it, but she couldn't remember ever feeling that way. Even in childhood, she'd been in training for this. Her games had been holding doll-babies and cleaning up after them, making pretend lunches, and washing away the leftover scraps of sand meals.

She picked up a bowl and scraped the sticky cereal from the plastic surface. What would she have done differently if she'd been given the chance? The first thing that came to mind was tag. She would have played tag. Dropping the first bowl into the water, she watched it drift to the bottom of the sink where it disappeared beneath the cover of soapsuds, then she raised her eyes to the yard outside again. Tag. But even tag would have emulated what she'd become, someone racing around trying to catch the faintest scent, the merest touch of a normal teenager's life: like Tony with his friends, always on the go, getting invited places, being involved in everything around him. She wasn't invited anywhere except to Dixie's house. In tag, she would've always been It. And she never would've caught anyone.

Hide and seek would've been better. She would've hidden, and no one would've even bothered to try to find her. She would have won every game.

What Maggie wanted to do was get away from herself. Her mind crawled around inside her skull looking for an escape hatch. She wished she could find the button to shut herself down, to step outside who she was and run away, but that would make her like her mother, and she'd vowed to God she would never take the easy way out. Maggie's constant prayer was to not lose sight of what it meant to live. *Please, God, guide my path.* She prayed the words her father had taught her, as she'd done almost daily since the time years ago when she told him she was terrified of ending up like her mother.

In her heart, she hoped God would change her life so that she would wake up without a care in the world except getting dressed for a party and having some fun.

She looked out the window again, realizing she would need to take the initiative to change things, to create a new path for herself. *God helps those who help themselves.* It was something Meemaw had said on the phone once. She knew it wasn't a biblical phrase or anything, but it made sense. God might open the door to new opportunities, Meemaw had explained, but she had to be willing to step through and take advantage of change.

The idea welled in her. The time had come to redirect her life. The question was how. And who exactly did she want to be? A normal teen. But what was normal—popular? Beautiful? Could she ever be either of those?

The dishes didn't take long. They never did. It was just the irritation of having to do them and knowing that no one else would pitch in, not even on her birthday.

As she dried her hands, the phone rang again. She stared at it for two rings, wondering why she should even bother answering it. She'd already talked to Dixie after school and knew she was off shopping with her mother and little sister.

On the fifth ring she picked up. It was her dad. "Honey, I need to talk to Tony."

Great, no "happy birthday" here, either. "He's not home. He's up at Webb's house."

"Well, call up there and have him call me back at the office, will you?"

"Can't you do it?"

"Sorry, I've got another call waiting, and I don't have time."

"But Dad, he's at Webb's house, and Webb never answers the phone when he sees our caller ID."

"Then walk up there and give him the message."

"Dad—"

"Thanks, Mags. Bye."

No problem for him to ask, she thought. *He doesn't have to climb the hill.*

She wished they weren't so broke all the time; then she and Tony would have cell phones. Well, Tony would, anyway. She didn't have much reason for one.

As she stepped out the front door into the fresh air, she breathed easier. She really didn't mind the walk up to Webb's. Being outside was much better than being stuck in the house cooking or cleaning.

She paused on the front porch to slip on her shoes. The weather was typical for a South Carolina September — hot and humid, with high temperatures during the day that wouldn't let up until almost Thanksgiving — but today a slight breeze flitted through the elm tree that shaded the house. She closed her eyes a minute to concentrate on the feel of the air against her skin and on hearing the sounds around her. A dove cooed overhead, a cardinal twittered on a nearby branch, and the Garlens' dog, Smokey, yapped incessantly one block over, probably at Mr. Smith's cat stuck in a tree. The Garlens were an old retired couple who lived a few houses down on the road that ran perpendicular to Maggie's house. They were friendly to everyone, and the very best at decorating their yard for Christmas. Mr. Smith lived around the corner from the Garlens, in a tiny brick ranch between a couple of colonials. Maggie didn't know him like she did the rest of her neighbors. He kept to himself. But she did know he considered the cat his family. Maggie thought it was the most beautiful cat she'd ever seen — a long-haired calico with wide yellow eyes. She wished Smokey would leave the pretty thing alone. She whistled a couple times until Smokey showed up at her side and sniffed her pockets for a treat. "I don't have anything today, boy," she said. She patted his head, and he trotted off.

She breathed deeply as she listened to a frog croak in the nearby stream and leaves rustle in the breeze. Some of the depression eased its hold from around her heart. She could lose herself outdoors in all the sights and sounds.

She loped across the yard and stopped when she reached the pavement. There at the far end of the street to her right was a man sitting in the shade of a tree—a man she didn't recognize from the neighborhood, though he was too far away and cloaked by shadows to be sure. She watched him a moment as he stared back at her from under a ball cap. He had a beard. That much she could tell, but she couldn't recall a bearded man living in the neighborhood.

Seeing him watch her made her feel uneasy, but after a minute she decided she was being ridiculous. Who would scope out their neighborhood for anything? One thing was for sure, if he intended to steal something, he wouldn't find anything of value in their yard—unless he wanted to cart away the old grill from the back porch.

She jogged down the road away from him, slowing to a walk as she reached the bottom of their small hill and began climbing up the long, steep grade toward Webb's house. The houses thinned out along this stretch and gave way to a thick stand of trees. The old hardwoods had been cut down ages ago, when the area was first developed, but pines had grown in their place and now towered like a small forest on ten or so lots that had never sold. It was a tiny refuge on a hillside, an oasis in Maggie's eyes.

She paused halfway up and thought about following the trail through the woods to her thinking spot, a little clearing with a huge boulder where she liked to sit when she needed to put life back into perspective. The woods were cheerful this time of day, with squirrels scampering from tree to tree, Smokey or some other neighborhood dog nosing about, and Webb's tabby cat prowling through the underbrush. Maybe she could stop on the way home after she'd delivered the message. It would still be light for hours, and she loved to walk through the woods to watch how the sun filtered through the treetops.

At the top of the hill, where Hillside Road met Pinewood Road, stood the Dwellers' house, where Billy was playing with Brad and a half-dozen other boys. Brad's father, Mr. Dweller, was one of those perfect fathers everyone loved — always ready to wrestle or play basketball or whatever the kids asked him to do. He coached Billy's soccer team and helped with Maggie's church youth group.

Maggie didn't like him, which was silly, really. He was a typical balding middle-aged man, outgoing, and a great friend to Billy. Billy loved going to the Dwellers' to practice soccer or whatever with Mr. Dweller and Brad, and joining them to go camping, fishing, and all the other things their own father never seemed to have time to do. But a month earlier, she'd seen Mr. Dweller standing inside his glass storm door in his bathrobe, and as she walked by, his bathrobe fell open. She knew it was probably an accident. How could it have been anything but accidental? Still, it gave her the creeps, and she'd been avoiding him ever since.

Sure enough, he was in the yard wrestling with the boys. Two were on his back. Billy was pinned to the ground under him. She thought of yelling out, telling Mr. Dweller to get off her brother, but she didn't want to talk to the man, and Billy would only grumble that she'd embarrassed him; all boys wrestle. She watched them for a moment before she moved on, but her spine tingled with the same sinister feeling she got when she thought of her beautiful woods shrouded in darkness—something that frightened her for no valid reason. Anyone else in the neighborhood would tell her she was nuts for feeling that way.

She turned right onto Pinewood Road and jogged past a couple of brick two-stories before slowing to a walk again at the driveway of Webb's brown split-level house.

She didn't bother with the front door. The boys were never in the main part of the house. Instead she circled around back to the basement entry, rapped once, and entered. If she waited for them to answer the door, she'd be there all night.

The door opened into a dark den with an unused brick fireplace against one wall and old flowered love seats facing each other in front of it. Newspapers stood stacked in one corner by a shelf of haphazardly placed books and knickknacks, and a pile of odds and ends spilled out of the opposite corner. The room was musty and smelled like a boys' locker room. Maggie rubbed her nose to ward off a threatening sneeze.

Through another doorway, she found Webb and Tony . . . and Sue. Perfect Sue Roberts with the straight glossy blonde hair, long legs, and great body. She might be something to look at, but Maggie didn't know how Webb tolerated her. Sue lived in the neighborhood and had been all right in elementary school, but nowadays she acted superior, even though she was a dunce when it came to math and science.

The three of them were slouched on Webb's yellow and red bed, their backs resting against square orange pillows leftover from a previous generation's bad decorating scheme. In the corner, a television flashed with some video game that had all three of them enthralled. Sue sat between the two boys with Webb's arm draped casually over her shoulder, his fingers just inches from her ample cleavage, which was bared to the world by the deep V of her pale blue shirt.

Maggie recognized the shirt. She'd seen one like it at the mall and had wanted to buy it, but of course she hadn't. She thought of the money Meemaw had sent and wondered if she dare blow it all on one item.

She averted her eyes. "Tony, call Dad."

As she turned heel to leave, Sue piped up. "Whoa, a personally delivered message. How sweet. Is she trained to fetch too? Get me a soda, will ya, Maggie?"

Maggie took a deep breath and kept walking. She heard Sue's words behind her: "I can't believe she's your sister, Tony."

Maggie slammed the basement door and blinked away tears in the bright sunshine. Something had to give.

Chapter Three

MAGGIE LOOKED TOWARD Dixie's house at the far end of the lane, tempted to seek her out, but she knew Dixie would still be off shopping with her mother, so she trudged back down the road toward the Dwellers' house. The other neighborhood boys had left, but Billy and Brad were still there, practicing their soccer kicks with Mr. Dweller. The only thing Billy loved more than skateboarding was soccer. She sighed, knowing she wasn't likely to see him at home anytime soon, so long as Brad and Mr. Dweller were willing to kick the ball around.

As she turned left and headed down the hill, Mr. Dweller caught sight of her from the side yard and started toward her. She picked up her pace. *Billy might like you, but I don't. It's bad enough the nights you help with our church youth group. Leave me alone!*

He continued across his yard, following her as she paced herself down the hill, resisting the urge to run as she looked over her shoulder. He crossed the road. Was he motioning toward her?

"Hey, Maggie, how're you doing?" He reached into his mailbox, which stood on the corner adjacent to his house.

With a sigh, she turned back around and loped a ways down the hill, her mind playing whiplash. *He's a nice guy, best friends with every kid in town, and everyone at church loves him. He's just a middle-aged man with a beer gut. Why am I so creeped out?*

She left the road and took the path through the woods to her thinking rock. It was serene, a place where she could contemplate life. She balanced on her boulder and closed her eyes, basking in a small patch of sunshine, but soothing thoughts wouldn't come. There was something rustling around in the woods. Not squirrels. Something bigger. Probably Smokey looking for another cat to send up a tree.

When she opened her eyes to the soft afternoon daylight, she realized it was still early enough that she could get her homework done and look at the sales ads in the newspaper for a washing machine before worrying about supper, though what she really wanted to do was talk to someone, to not have to think for a while.

She trudged out of the woods to the bottom of the hill where she saw Kimberly, a five-year-old neighbor, waving out her front door, her blonde curls bouncing around a dimpled face that was still as round with baby fat as the rest of her body. "Maggie! Maggie, come here. I've been waiting for you."

Maggie passed her own house and hurried up the tiny slope to Kimberly's front yard, noticing with a glance that the strange man had left.

Kimberly ran across the grass and clobbered into her. "I have a surprise for you!"

Kimberly's mother, Renee Graham, waited in the doorway, then led them all down the hall to the kitchen, where the table was set with homemade, crayon-colored paper place mats, cups of milk, and a huge chocolate chip cookie with pink icing squirted all over it in an undecipherable scrawl. "I made you a birthday cookie," Kimberly squealed as she clapped her hands and danced around. "I've been waiting all day for you to come home."

Maggie smiled and hugged the little girl. She'd first started helping with Kimberly when the little girl was barely a month old, initially just holding her or entertaining her while Mrs. Graham worked in the yard or around the house, but now she often baby-sat her for weekends at a time. Kimberly was like the little sister she would never have.

"We would've baked you a cake, but we figured you'd have that with your family, and you can't eat but so much cake in a day," Mrs. Graham said.

Maggie nodded, not wanting to admit that she didn't expect any cake at all. She was sure Mrs. Graham couldn't imagine a birthday without cake. It made her wonder how her own mother would have celebrated the day with her. Would she have had a cake waiting when Maggie got home? Or would she have been a businesswoman, too busy to bake, and more prone to buying one from the Food Lion down the road? What would her mother have given her for her birthday?

For the millionth time, Maggie cast the questions aside; her mother had given her a lifetime legacy, a forever birthday present of selfishness when she took her own life—abandonment in its most glorious form.

She gritted her teeth until her head ached every time she thought of her mother's suicide, but she wasn't going to let it ruin her birthday, not with Kimberly grinning at her. She shook the thoughts away and concentrated on the glee emanating from the little girl. By the time she left the Grahams' house, she felt much better. At least someone cared about her, even if it wasn't her father or brothers.

She went out the Grahams' back door and cut through the backyard. At the edge of her yard, she ducked under a crape myrtle, right into a cobweb; its silver threads clung to her hair. Fear of spiders rushed her to the back door, through the kitchen, and up the stairs to her room to brush out her tangle of red curls. As her heart slowed, she pulled the wild mass into a ponytail and breathed a sigh of relief.

In the ensuing silence, her room hung around her like a fortress of green familiarity. Her yard-sale room, she liked to call it. She'd picked out everything in it—quilt, nightstand, four-poster bed, and brown dresser—from a church yard sale. She still had the same white baby lamp on her dresser that she'd had before her mother died. A poster of monkeys hung on the wall above her bed, and a stuffed monkey sat propped on a ladder-back chair by the window. The wall facing her bed was covered in photos, none of them of her mother. She'd had one but replaced it with a photo of her best friend, Dixie, when she was ten, when her resentments flared. Back then Dixie had kept her blonde hair in pigtails that were so short they poked out of the sides of her head like puppy dog ears. Her face was round with chubby cheeks and big blue eyes that smiled like her mother's, but she was built like her father, short-waisted with thick legs and fleshy shoulders. Not that her father had looked like that toward the end of his life. He'd withered away to nothing before he died two years ago. Dixie without a father and her without a mother. They were a pair, but it was different for Dixie. Her father hadn't killed himself. He loved Dixie with his whole heart and cried himself to sleep with Dixie in his arms the day before he died, crying not for himself but because he knew he was leaving her with so much life to face without him there to help. He'd known how Maggie had pined for a mother and resented her mother's suicide for years, and didn't want to leave that same kind of void in Dixie's life.

Maggie moved to her nightstand and slid her small stack of library books out of the way to open the nightstand door and stare at the picture of her mother, her auburn hair blowing in the breeze and her eyes winking at the camera, not toward the baby in her arms. "I'm just a bundle in her arms," Maggie whispered to the air, "an afterthought. She's thinking about something in that picture, but it's not me."

She flopped backward onto her bed.

Something crumpled beneath her. Rolling over, she saw it: an envelope with Billy's sloppy twelve-year-old print across the face — *To Maggie*. She tore the envelope open and unfolded the sheet of paper. It was a sketch of a boy on a skateboard doing a flip on a ramp with two words scrawled at the bottom: *Happy Birthday*. No cute line like *Don't get flipped out just because it's your birthday*, or *Flipping out that you're sixteen*. Just *Happy Birthday*. Being from Billy, that was enough. Tony wouldn't have two words to say to her, but Billy still loved her enough at twelve to show it once in a while. He'd actually drawn a picture just for her. It was silly, she knew, but tears sprang to her eyes. A birthday cookie and now this. She smiled for a minute. Then stopped. Anyone else would think it was stupid. *It was stupid.* A cookie and a drawing. What a birthday. She flopped back on the bed again, her eyes settling on the print of Jesus on the wall across from her dresser. "Jesus, why can't I be like a normal sixteen-year-old with lots of friends and parties, a car and a cell phone? Is that asking too much?"

She hugged her squishy monkey beanie pillow and imagined herself looking like Sue, walking through the school hallways with boys pausing to look at her and friends waiting for her at the doorways, instead of just Dixie and sometimes Clarissa. She thought of actually going to a party.

She thought of Webb putting his arm around *her*.

Praying for popularity seemed too trivial, too self-centered. She knew God didn't care about her being popular. She thought of the prayers at church on Sunday for homeless people, for little Jackie Harris at church who'd been hit by a car and lay at death's door, for Mr. Nelson's heart surgery, and for the doctors who were traveling on a mission trip to South America. But it didn't keep Maggie from getting back to what was in her heart. *Please, God, you must have some purpose for me. No one at school even acts like I exist. I want to be somebody. I want to be normal.* It didn't sound as selfish that way.

She lay there envisioning being popular, until she heard a car in the driveway. Her father, home from work.

"Maggie! Maggie!" Her father's voice sounded urgent. He probably needed supper quickly so he could go back to the office for a couple hours, as he often did.

With a sigh, she stood and headed toward the kitchen, considering what might be the fastest thing to cook. Something that required few pots and pans, because she had no desire to be in the kitchen any longer than necessary. But first she wanted to ask him if he knew who the man with the beard might be.

When she pushed the kitchen door open, she stopped in shock. Her father and brothers stood around the counter with a pizza, a store-bought cake, and a helium balloon with a monkey on it. "Happy Birthday!"

She couldn't believe it. She tottered into the room in a daze. "You got me a cake? And pizza?"

They gathered around the table munching pizza, the boys jabbering to their father about seeing a movie at the theater, a video game, and some trick Billy had seen in his new magazine and tried on his skateboard. She captured them in her mind like a Polaroid snapshot: her father's suit disheveled from a day at work—his tie gone, his white dress shirt unbuttoned at the collar, his eyes almost closing to two slits as he smiled at the boys' stories; Tony nodding and chewing with his long hair falling around his face and his jeans hanging around his hips; Billy laughing, his mouth an open circle full of food, his wide nose turning red the odd way it did when he was excited. Sometimes she seemed outside of their male circle, but tonight it was okay.

The pizza disappeared in twelve minutes.

Her father reached into a nearby drawer for a lighter and lit the sixteen candles on the cake. "Make a wish," he said.

Maggie watched his blue eyes twinkling in the candlelight and thought about the card from Meemaw and how her mother had become pregnant with her on her sixteenth birthday. Did her father remember? Did her father look at her and see her mother as he first saw her all those years ago? She had her mother's features, but even in the hall photo, the difference between the two of them was obvious—her mother posed with one hip cocked out, her head tilted slightly, her eyes sparkling, her chin lifted ever so slightly, a coy smile that hid a secret playing on her lips. Beside her image, Maggie's school photo appeared flat and lifeless. Her mother had possessed that self-confidence, that suaveness and worldly air that Sue had. How did a person get that way?

Maggie closed her eyes. It was okay to ask God for something personal when it was a birthday wish, wasn't it? *Please let sixteen be a great year. Let me become more like Sue. Let me be pretty and popular and—*

"Are ya writing a book or what?" Billy said. "Blow out the candles already."

—and let Webb . . . She couldn't even put that into words in her mind. It was too preposterous to even think.

The candles sputtered out, lifting her birthday prayer up on a wave of smoke.

When Dixie called a while later, Maggie understood why her father had come through with a cake. "So how did it go?" Dixie asked.

Maggie pictured Dixie perched on her bed in one of her father's old shirts; that's what she always wore to bed. She said it was like being wrapped in his arms and she hoped she never outgrew his size because she wanted to wear them to bed forever. She would be sitting cross-legged, her poker-straight blonde hair hanging around her cheeks, which were still as chubby as they were at six, ten, and twelve, even though the rest of her had slimmed to a healthy fleshiness. Her athletic legs would be smooth from just having been shaved because she took her shower at precisely eight o'clock every night; she hated sharing the bathroom with her little sister in the morning. Undoubtedly, she would have a bowl of popcorn in her lap and a glass of milk on the nightstand. Dixie was the only person Maggie knew who could drink milk with popcorn.

"How did what go?"

Dixie munched in Maggie's ear. "The birthday surprise."

"You knew?"

"Of course."

Then it clicked. "You put them up to it, didn't you? I knew they wouldn't have thought of it on their own."

"Of course they wouldn't, Mags. They're guys. Did you find my present?"

"Your present?"

"Yes, it's under the bed. I left it there the other day when you were gone to the grocery store. Open it."

Maggie squatted down and reached for a dark shape shoved under the edge of her bed, a box covered with monkey wrapping paper. She tore into it, expecting monkey pajamas or a monkey T-shirt or something, but instead it was the same style shirt Sue had been wearing that afternoon, except in a deep emerald green.

She grabbed the phone again. "I love it. You shouldn't have, Dixie. I know it cost a fortune. I saw it at the mall. I can't believe you bought this for me!"

"I knew you'd like it. It'll look hot on you."

"Well, I doubt that. But I sure love it."

They talked for another thirty minutes before hanging up. Maggie turned to the mirror, the new shirt pressed to her chest. "Watch out, Sue. Change is coming."

Behind her in the reflection, the portrait of Jesus looked on.

Chapter Four

AN HOUR LATER, she collapsed on her bed in her pajamas with her red hair splayed out around her and read *Teen* magazine. The house was quiet. Tony had gone back to Webb's house, and Billy, after she'd helped him with a couple difficult math problems, had shut himself away in his bedroom, probably to read comic books. She'd thought of offering to play a board game with him, but she didn't really feel like it. Today was her birthday, after all, and she just wanted to laze around. The television droned on in the background for a while, but even that eventually fell silent. She needed to turn on some music.

Rolling over, she jumped in alarm at seeing her father in the doorway.

"You scared me."

"I'm sorry," he said, entering the room and taking a seat on the corner of her bed. "I was watching you, thinking about how quickly sixteen years have gone by. You're not a little girl anymore."

Had he just noticed? "No, Daddy, I'm not. I haven't been for a long time."

"Your mother would be so proud of you. You're so beautiful and smart, and you take care of us. I want you to know how much I appreciate everything you do, Maggie."

She was surprised by his comment, but it wasn't enough to completely erase her recent feelings of aggravation. She'd rather have help than belated appreciation. Still, it was a step in the right direction. "Thanks for saying so, Daddy. Sometimes I wonder if anyone ever notices all the junk I do around here."

He attempted to smooth down a wild curl. "You look so much like your mother. It's spooky. I wish she were here to see you."

She could have been, Maggie thought. *It's her own stupid fault. She took her life for no reason.*

But her father was here, and she was seeing him as if she hadn't seen him every afternoon. So often, his brows were knitted in concentration and his mind was elsewhere, but tonight he was relaxed, focusing just on her, and she did likewise, noticing the tiny laugh lines around his eyes, the spattering of gray in his scruffy brown hair, and the five o'clock stubble on his face. She remembered running her hands over his cheeks when she was little, loving the sandpaper feel of them against her baby-soft palms. All he'd been to her throughout her childhood welled up in that moment. Her eyes watered, and she laid a hand against his cheek. "I love you, Daddy."

His eyes glazed with tears too, and he pulled her into a hug. When he finally released her, they both had to wipe at their eyes.

"We always wanted you, you know. Right from day one, we knew you were a blessing from God. I couldn't wait to hold you in my arms. And now, here you are all grown up. Before I know it, you'll be taking off, won't you? Leaving me here to fend for these boys on my own."

"I'm not going anywhere, Daddy. Not for a couple years."

He nodded, but she knew he was thinking of her mother, and how they'd run off and married at Maggie's age. Maybe he was just realizing what that must have done to Meemaw, seeing her daughter go off with this boy she didn't like, belly swollen with child — all her well-laid plans for her daughter to go to college, to achieve something big, gone up in smoke.

"I'm not my mother, you know."

He nodded again. Then laughed. "I realize that every night at supper time. You cook a lot better than she did. Believe me, when I say grace, I'm truly thanking God for your cooking skills."

Maggie smiled.

"But you have your mother's ways about you. The tilt of her head. The way you smile — right there, like that. That far-off look you get when you're dreaming about something."

"I do?"

"Yes, and even more so the older you get. Watching you grow up has been like capturing her in childhood. I didn't know her when she was a little girl."

He reached into his pocket and pulled out a dark blue velvet box. "I know you probably had your mind set on something really cool for your birthday, like an iPod or a cell phone or something, but those things will have to wait. I've had this planned for a long time. I wanted to wait till we were alone. It wouldn't mean as much if your brothers were gawking at you. You know how they can be. I want this to be between you and me . . . and your mother."

He placed the box ceremoniously into her hands.

She'd never had a moment like this with her father before. He'd kept a secret in his heart, a special moment planned out just for her. She wanted to linger over it and make it last. She ran her fingers across the blue velvet and then slowly raised the hinged top.

She had expected a simple cross and chain, or maybe a bracelet of some sort, but inside was something totally different—an antique choker made of miniscule round disks, each one with an open star in the center. The links met in the middle with two hands that clasped a heart. Tiny blue cuffs made of turquoise chips encircled each wrist of the gold arms, one of which was adorned with a small bracelet. The choker was beautiful in a funky way. Mesmerizing.

Maggie fingered the links but couldn't find a clasp anywhere.

"Let me show you." Her father released the latch, hidden within one hand. Maggie lifted her hair up as her father settled the necklace around her neck and slipped the latch back into place. "It's called the Claddagh emblem, created in remembrance of the Irish who immigrated to the United States to escape the famine in Ireland."

"I've never seen anything like it."

He leaned back. "Your mother and I couldn't afford much of a honeymoon, so we went to Charleston. We were supposed to get a hotel room for the night, but then we went walking through City Market. I'll have to take you there sometime. It's a long building open on both ends. Reminds me of a flea market, but not junk for sale. The booths are full of jewelry and specially woven baskets, pottery, rugs, knitted sweaters . . . all kinds of craftsmen's work. Anyway, your mother saw this necklace and had to have it because it matched her wedding ring, so instead of getting a hotel room, we bought the necklace and slept in the car." His smile had gone crooked, whimsical, and Maggie knew he was back in that car with her mother, a young man with no idea what was ahead of him.

"It's a symbol of love and friendship." He touched the golden hands, his fingers brushing her skin. "Your mother loved it. She was really into her own eccentric style. I don't know if it's something you would wear or not."

"Absolutely, Daddy. It's wonderful."

He reflected on her a moment, the whole of her, her face, the necklace, the two together, and his face relaxed into a satisfied smile. Then he sat up straighter and dug into his pocket again. "Now for this. That was of your mother's choosing. This one is an heirloom."

He held out a square ring box. "You might remember this. You used to try it on. I put it away when your mother died, knowing it should be yours at some point. I know she would want you to have it today."

He opened the box and let Maggie pull out a sterling silver ring she'd forgotten about, but now remembered with a jolt. Two fine strands made up the band and met where two hands held a crowned heart, much like the design of the necklace.

"This was Mom's wedding ring?"

"Yes, but it goes back much farther than that. It was my mother's, and her mother's before that, and so on for generations."

"Your mother gave this to Mom?"

He nodded. Sadness pulled at his face. "It really tore me up when it came back with her personal effects. She never took it off, except for you because she knew it would be yours someday. You see, tradition requires that the ring pass from mother to daughter. I didn't have any sisters. My mother almost gave it to a niece, but she didn't want it to leave our lineage, so she held onto it until I married. Since I was the oldest son and the first married, she gave it to your mother as a wedding present, knowing that someday it would be passed on to you.

"My great, great grandfather gave it to his bride, Fiona, as a wedding present. It had already been in the family for several generations, but, like me, he didn't have a sister, so his mother left it to him. I don't know the names of the ancestors before him, but from Fiona, it went to Colleen, then Mary Katherine, then Anna—my mother—then to your mother, and now to you."

Maggie turned it this way and that, examining the detailed workmanship.

"Go on," her father said, "try it on."

Maggie slipped it on her right-hand ring finger and held it up, splaying her fingers like a model to show it off.

"Perfect fit, isn't it? I knew it would be." He took her hand and looked at it more closely.

"I'll treasure it, Daddy." She meant it for her father's part in it, if not for her mother, but just sliding it on her finger had opened a small crevice in her hardened heart. Could she think about her mother in some new light? Could she come to love her instead of hating her for leaving Maggie alone to handle life?

"Your mother loved it because it is so very Irish, and she loved expressing her Irish heritage. She loved everything Irish, especially your flaming red hair."

"She wouldn't have been so delighted if it had been on her head."

"Oh, don't count on that. Your mother never let anyone put her down for anything that expressed who she was. She held her head up with pride through everything. It wasn't easy being pregnant at sixteen, but if anyone made a comment, she put them in their place. She was proud to be your mother. You need to remember that, Maggie. Be proud of who you are, because there's no one like you anywhere."

That was easy for him to say. Her mother had had friends. At least Maggie assumed she did. In her photos, she looked like the kind of girl who would have been popular.

"Did she have a lot of friends?"

"She did when I met her, but not so many later on. It was hard with her having babies to take care of while her friends were going to movies and parties. I should have seen what having a family was doing to her. She was so young. But times were hard and we seemed to just struggle through one day at a time. I wish I had paid more attention to how she was feeling. I didn't realize she was so depressed. I was buried in work, and . . ." His voice trailed off. It was too much to dredge up.

Maggie couldn't watch her father break down in front of her. As badly as she needed to hear what brought her mother to suicide, she couldn't do it today, not on her birthday. She hugged him. "You've been everything to me, Daddy, and these"—she put her hand to the choker around her neck and flashed the ring—"these mean the world to me. I couldn't have asked for a better birthday present, not from you or Mom."

He embraced her tightly. "I'm glad. I wanted it to be special for you. I want you to know how much your mother loved you, and how much I love you. What happened with her had nothing to do with you. She would never have wished you away, I promise that. If you could have seen how she lit up when she looked at you. Please remember that, and that I love you with all my heart. You'll always be the number one girl in my life."

She knew that was true. He didn't say it often, but it was there, a feeling between them. "I love you too, Daddy."

When he left the room, she sat rubbing the ring, thinking about her mother. She tried to wrap her mind around what her parents' lives must have been like, but it was hard to see beyond her own perspective, her own motherless life. What if she'd been in her mother's place? What if she found out today that she was going to have a baby? What if, instead of looking forward to grad-uating in two years and moving on to independence, instead of being free from running this house when she turned eighteen, she had to face the prospect of being here forever, of doing nothing but taking care of her brothers, washing their stinky clothes and fixing their supper?

Maybe she didn't have it so bad. And maybe she and her mother had more in common than she thought. She lay back on her bed again and held the ring up to the light, thinking more about her mother, until her father stuck his head back in the door.

"By the way, now that you're sixteen, it's time . . ." He hesi-tated. "Well, let's just say I'm bringing someone home tomorrow for you to meet."

Chapter
Five

THE NEXT MORNING, Maggie stood before the mirror trying to get up the courage to wear her new emerald green shirt and choker to school. She switched from the new shirt to one of her ordinary T-shirts and back again three times. Growling with frustration, she pulled the T-shirt off once more and pulled the new shirt on. The V-shaped neckline showed as much cleavage as a bikini top. Could she really go to school like that?

At least the jeans couldn't be debated. She only had four pairs, and there was nothing especially stylish about any of them.

She would try on the jewelry, just to see how they looked together. She reached for the Claddagh choker and moved to the mirror to figure out how to insert the clasp into the tiny arm. Finally it clicked into place, and she backed up a pace to examine her figure in the new shirt. It hugged her in all the right places and made her green eyes stand out.

She tried out different expressions in the mirror, trying to look like her mother did in the hall photo. She tilted her head and smiled. How did her father see her mother there? She turned sideways and tried it again, but she just didn't see it. Maybe it was her hair. She never wore her hair down. All those curls embarrassed her. They may have been cute when she was five; she looked like Shirley Temple or Curly Sue. She could have played Little Orphan Annie with ease. As a teenager, it made her feel like an undergroomed poodle. But maybe . . . With a snatch at the ponytail scrunchy, she released her hair to cascade around her face. She frowned. "Nope, no way," she said, and took the brush and pulled it back into a ponytail. What did all those actresses do with their hair when they grew up and it wasn't cute anymore? She had a strong suspicion that all their curls were fake and that they had normal, straight hair forced into curls just for film.

Maybe what she needed was makeup. After all, she was sixteen.

She reached into the top drawer of her dresser and pushed pencils, paper scraps, and other junk aside until she found what she was looking for: lipstick. With tentative strokes, she brushed some onto her lips, and then rummaged through the drawer again. She used to have blush somewhere. Dixie made her buy it at a Mary Kay party. Where was it?

"Maggie!" Her father's voice rang through the house.

No time left.

"Coming!"

One more glance in the mirror. She didn't need blush anyway. Her cheeks were rosy, almost too red, and dotted with freckles that no amount of foundation or blush would hide. She'd just have to stick to her *au naturale* routine.

She turned sideways and smiled at herself. Maybe there was something there today. A twinkle. An inkling of her mother. The beginnings of who she wanted to be.

She pulled the ring from her jewelry box and slid it on her finger. As if it were magical, it elevated her spirits. She reached for her tennis shoes, then stopped. Instead, she pulled out a pair of clunky navy heels she wore to church with her one Bohemian skirt. Looking at her reflection again, she was amazed; the shoes actually rocked with her jeans.

Her father nodded and followed her as she grabbed up her book bag and headed to the car. "You're wearing the necklace."

"Of course, Daddy. And the ring." She flashed it in his face and dove into the passenger seat before he could comment on the shirt and lipstick in front of her brothers.

Billy stopped smashing papers into his book bag and leaned over the seat to glance at the ring and nod. "Where'd it come from? I like it."

Tony scowled. "What is it? Two hands holding an apple?"

"It's not an apple; it's a heart with a crown on top, just like this one on the necklace. And they're heirlooms, you dope. Daddy gave them to me for my birthday."

Tony scowled. "Don't ever give me an heirloom then. I want video games."

"They used to be Mom's."

Tony's face paled as the scowl faded. He leaned closer and touched the two hands on the choker. "This was Mom's?"

"Yes. So was this ring. Daddy bought the necklace for her on their honeymoon, and the ring has been passed down to the girls in Daddy's family for generations."

He turned and stared out the window. "She sure had weird taste."

Maggie sighed.

Billy reached toward her. "Let me see." He lifted the choker in his fingers and rubbed the tiny hands. "It even has little bracelets on the arms. I like it. It's all good."

Maggie smiled at his slang. He was an all right brother.

The thing eating at her was how her classmates would react.

Dixie met her at their usual place on the corner of the school lot under an old oak tree. Her eyebrows shot upward. "Wow. You turn sixteen and *bam,* you're gorgeous."

"It's the shirt you bought me, silly."

"Ain't I good? It's perfect. Where'd that come from?" she asked, reaching for the choker.

"Daddy." Maggie told her the whole story as they walked toward the front entrance.

"That is totally cool. It's bound to bring a lot of comments. It's so incredibly . . ."

"Funky?"

"Well, yes, but in a good way."

As they moved through the halls, Maggie got a couple glances, but no one stopped in their tracks until Sue. She took one look at Maggie's shirt and rolled her eyes at Heather and Tammy, her primary sidekicks. "Well, there goes wearing *that* shirt ever again. Does it look like that on me?"

Heather and Tammy laughed, as if on cue.

School had been in session for less than a month, but the routine had already fallen into the same rhythm as her freshman year. The same girls hung out in the hall, insulting everyone else. The same guys were jocks. The same kids cut up in class. The same girls acted ditzy. Maybe change was impossible in high school.

Clarissa, a skinny girl with mousy brown hair, slid by Sue and caught Maggie by the arm. "Oh, Mags! The shirt! It's much better on you than Sue's blue one is on her." She stuck her tongue out at Sue. "And that necklace. Where'd you get it?"

"It's an heirloom," Maggie said, thinking it sounded important and expensive, and maybe it was. But she didn't say it to impress Clarissa, who was one of the more down-to-earth girls at school, a free agent who talked and sat with whoever met her whim of the day. She possessed an inner strength and honesty that shone in her face.

Sue gave a flip of her hair and turned away. Clarissa pulled Maggie and Dixie farther down the hall, chattering the whole way.

A couple boys did double takes in the hallway, their gazes falling to her low neckline, and Mitch Kinsley told her she looked nice, but he was only a freshman and not worth impressing.

No one else commented about her shirt or the choker until history class. Mr. Baire, a short man with thick glasses and a shuffling step, moved between the desks, returning quizzes to the students. As he set Maggie's test down, his eyes settled on her cleavage, and she cringed. Was the shirt that revealing?

His eyes bore into her. She felt like sinking beneath her desk or covering herself with her textbook.

He pointed at her chest. "May I?"

The choker! He was staring at the choker, not her cleavage.

The only thing worse than being a nerd was being a nerd to whom a teacher drew attention, especially in a nerdy class like history, taught by a nerdy teacher like Mr. Baire. Maggie stared down at her desk. She could feel every eye in the room on her. She felt her soul curl up under their stares, but stopped herself from cringing. *Isn't this what I wanted?* She looked at the ring on her finger. Proud, like her mother. She sat up straighter, her hand going to the two golden hands, and raised her eyes to meet Mr. Baire's. "Sure."

"Oh, a ring too."

She held up her hand so he could see it more clearly.

"Amazing. A Claddagh! Where did you get it?"

"It's a family heirloom. My daddy gave it to me last night for my sixteenth birthday."

"Do you know what it symbolizes?"

"Love and friendship?"

"That's somewhat right. Many immigrants brought jewelry fashioned with the Claddagh symbol as one of their few treasures from Ireland, especially during the famine of 1845, when all else was lost. But you're wearing the ring upside down."

Never one to pass up a chance to catch some nugget of history and cram it into their heads, he shuffled to the board and drew out a crude example of the symbol.

"The Claddagh ring is a traditional Irish wedding ring dating back to the seventeenth century. It's called the Royal Claddagh because of the crown on top of the heart, and though it's often worn by people today merely as a symbol of friendship, its meaning is much more significant. The heart represents love, of course. The hands represent friendship. The crown represents loyalty and lasting fidelity. A woman should wear it on the right hand, with crown and heart facing outward, to show her heart doesn't belong to anyone. When she finds love, she turns the ring around, with the heart facing inward. When she commits to love, she moves the ring to her left hand as a wedding band."

He looked around at the kids' faces. So did Maggie. The guys were all bored. Asby Jones was rolling up little pieces of paper as if they were joints. Sid Watkins was playing dot to dot with Henry Harding. But the girls were listening. So was Sam, a boy who sat in the back row and rarely spoke, but listened intently, with his big brown eyes taking in everything that happened around him.

Mr. Baire continued. "Let me tell you how the ring came to be. It's an interesting legend.

"It started with a young Irish fellow named Richard Joyce, who was kidnapped by a band of pirates and sold to a Moorish goldsmith. In the late sixteen hundreds, King William III demanded the return of all slaves, including Joyce. Apparently, the goldsmith was remarkably wealthy and offered to give Joyce his daughter's hand in marriage, along with half his wealth as a dowry, if Joyce would stay put rather than return to Ireland, but Joyce refused. He had become a master goldsmith himself by that time, and had a truelove back home, with whom he vowed to reunite."

Asby groaned and inhaled on his fake joint.

Mr. Baire walked over, snatched it out of his mouth, and kept talking.

"Back in Ireland, his truelove had never given up on him. When he returned, he presented her with the Claddagh ring as a symbol of their enduring love, and they were married."

In the back row, Heidi Siddons put her hands to her heart and sighed.

Asby cussed.

"Never to be separated again," Mr. Baire added, staring at Asby. "When people fled Ireland during the famine, most had few possessions of any value to take with them, except their Claddagh rings, and so these were often the only inheritance they had to pass on to their children, which is why the rings are often associated with famine immigrants. Unlike most inheritances, these rings are traditionally handed down from mother to daughter, so it's quite unusual that Maggie was given hers by her father."

Maggie almost swallowed the words, but they broke loose and rose into the room, revealing a secret that she rarely discussed with anyone. "It was my mother's, but she died when I was four." She paused, but no one reacted. No one could absorb that simple sentence and understand all it implied, all it had wrought in her life. She was her father's daughter, and that had to sustain her. "The ring was passed through seven generations or more on my father's side, only passing to a son if there weren't any daughters. My grandmother gave it to my mother when she and my dad got married."

"Ah, you're a lucky girl to have received such an important piece of your Irish heritage. Cherish it."

After class, two girls stopped by her desk to look at the ring, and by the time she got to the door, Sean Black was waiting. Sean didn't hang out much with the other guys. He wasn't into sports or student council or anything. He worked after school and had a girlfriend named Becca, who was practically glued to his side, even though she lived in the next town and attended Southern High. "Can I see it?" he asked.

Maggie held out her hand, wondering if he wanted one for Becca.

"My mom is Irish," he said as he looked more closely. "She'll get a kick out of that story. Cool ring."

He sauntered off down the hall. Dixie grabbed her arm. "Well, look who's Miss Popular. Maybe I need to get some jewelry."

"Popular because Sean spoke to me?"

"Like, everyone in class was looking at you."

Not the way I want, though. Not as a friend or an equal. "They're just chalking it up to another strange thing about me, that's all."

"Nonsense. It's better than being invisible, which is our usual status."

Maggie debated that—strange versus invisible. Neither was what she wanted. Why did people think she was weird? What would it take for them to treat her like she mattered?

But maybe Dixie was right; at least people were noticing her today, and speaking to her, like a magical first step toward popularity.

The tardy bell was going to ring at any moment. She pulled at Dixie, and they sped down the hall to their next class, her mind working on who her father would introduce her to that night. In her heart, she secretly hoped it was a boy, maybe the son of a client or someone he'd met out at the college when he was taking night classes last month. It seemed almost too old-fashioned to believe, but what else could he have meant? Optimism burned in her veins as she imagined it all as God's doing. He was going to answer her prayer—first with people at school talking to her, and tonight with her father bringing home a prospective boyfriend.

Chapter
Six

MAGGIE HAD BEEN trying to envision her father's surprise guest all afternoon. Brown hair? Blond? Tall? Short? Every image came back to Webb for comparison.

She had carefully placed the jewelry back into the velvet boxes and changed into an old T-shirt as soon as she got home, so she could clean the house. She turned on the radio and scrubbed the bathrooms as she listened to Kelly Clarkson, Carrie Underwood, and others, with visions of a handsome male visitor dancing in her head.

At four o'clock she stuck a roast in the oven, lucky to have planned a meal for Friday night that would feed an extra person if need be. She had no idea whether or not this guest her father was bringing home would be joining them for dinner.

She cleared junk piles off the kitchen counter, threw away a pile of sale ads, and collected all the dirty socks and discarded dishes from the family room. She vacuumed and dusted, then stood back to take it all in. It needed something. Her gaze stopped at the mantel and settled on the candles Dixie had convinced her to buy at her mom's candle party. She'd never lit them, hesitant to use them since they were so expensive, but this seemed the perfect time. Maybe they would make the house smell less like boys.

She wasn't sure what time her father would get home. Most Fridays he quit right at five o'clock and came home with a movie rental for them to watch together, but occasionally he didn't straggle in till nine. On those nights, he didn't have much to say. He would pull off his coat and tie and head upstairs to put on a pair of boxer shorts and a T-shirt. Sometimes he went straight to bed without eating the plate of food she'd stuck in the fridge for him.

Tonight, since he was bringing home this mysterious guest, she was sure he would arrive early.

Billy showed up at five-thirty, covered from head to toe in dirt.

"What happened to you?"

"Football."

"What? Were you the ball?"

"Very funny."

"Go take a shower."

"I know, I know. Dad already told me. Company tonight."

Her mouth fell open. She couldn't believe Billy knew their father was bringing someone home. That made it all the more serious.

Tony came in the front door a short time later, kicked his shoes off his feet so that they spun halfway across the room and landed by the sofa, then plodded up the stairs.

"Don't make a mess. I just got the house cleaned up."

"I didn't make a mess," he shot back over his shoulder. "I took my shoes off. Aren't you always telling us to take our shoes off at the door?"

Maggie grumbled to herself. Tony was so obtuse sometimes it wasn't worth the wasted breath to argue with him. She collected his shoes and set them neatly by the door.

Daylight still poured in through the windows, so the flickering light of the candles didn't have much affect on the atmosphere, but the room smelled of blueberries or something fruity, blending with the savory scent of roasting meat.

She pulled the roast out of the oven to check its progress. Perfectly browned. Time to put on the rice. She pulled a huge bag of white rice from the pantry and measured out one cup. Rice was a mainstay in their house. It was inexpensive, easy to cook, and filled the stomach.

She jiggled the measuring cup and looked to see if she had enough, then poured the grains into a pot. As she added precise amounts of water and salt, she smiled. There was something very orderly about cooking—combining ingredients to make something scrumptious, and timing different segments of the meal so that everything came together at the same moment, no matter how discordant the preparations and cooking times.

Next, she searched the pantry for a vegetable. Peas. They were easy, needing only minimal heating in the microwave. If she cooked them on the stove, she tended to leave them on too long, and if the shells separated, Billy wouldn't eat them.

The table was set properly with everything including spoons, which they wouldn't use, and napkins at every plate, though she knew Billy would use his sleeve without giving the napkin a second thought.

Finally everything was ready, but her father wasn't home. She circled through the family room to the front door and stared at the road. No car. Not that she could see far enough past the trees to know if he might be coming down the road, but it made her feel better to try. She paced back to the kitchen, peeked in at the roast again, and then back to the family room, out the front door, and down the driveway. He had to be coming.

His car was nowhere in sight. And if she saw his car, she didn't want to be caught standing in the driveway, waiting so anxiously for him.

Something made her look the other way, to the far right, at the end of the road. The man was there again, sitting under the same tree, staring down the road toward her.

She shivered and ran back to the house.

The water had quit running noisily through the pipes, which meant Billy was out of the shower, and Tony had his stereo blaring, which meant he was doing something other than playing a video game. It would be too much to hope that he was combing his hair or brushing his teeth.

There wasn't much else she could do, so she turned off all the food and went to her room to brush her hair into a fresh ponytail and apply a touch of lip gloss. She thought of putting the new shirt back on, but she lost her nerve and settled for a striped T-shirt, then turned and looked at the portrait of Jesus across the room. *Oh please, Lord, all I want is to be normal, and to have someone love me. Dixie says we're invisible. I'm not invisible to you, am I? Don't let me be invisible to the world.* The prayer rumbled around in her head, but the only reply was the steady tick of the clock on her nightstand. *I know . . . in your time, not mine. That's what they preached in youth group last week, but it sure is hard to wait.*

Twenty long minutes later, and many trips from the kitchen, across the family room to the front window, her father's car finally rumbled into the driveway. Maggie held her breath as she watched him emerge from the car and walk toward the front door.

It wasn't a boy with him. It was a woman.

Maggie's heart practically stopped. Why was he bringing home a woman?

She was pretty in a middle-aged way. Her dark hair was cut short with just a bit of curl to it that softened the angular lines of her face and jaw. Her dark suit coat added to the width of her shoulders and her short skirt emphasized her legs. She had a purposefulness to her brisk steps that reminded Maggie of the school secretary who waddled down the hall in short, wiggly steps when she was on a mission with no time to waste. This lady was too thin to waddle, but her sense of urgency was evident.

Maggie didn't know what to make of the situation. Her father had never before in all the years of her life brought a woman home. Maggie leaned against the wall, glanced around the room, and steadied herself to meet this woman. She was sure from the roots of her hair to the tips of her toes it absolutely could not be a *date.*

"It must be a work associate," she explained to the walls.

Billy rose from in front of the television and joined her at the window. "Who? The lady?"

Tony clomped down the steps. "I heard the car. Time to eat?"

Maggie nodded. "It appears so, along with some lady."

Tony didn't have time to respond before their father ushered the mystery woman through the door. As he made introductions all around, Maggie could see by his twinkling eyes that he was pleased all three children were greeting him and his guest.

"Andrea, these are my children, Maggie, Tony, and Billy. Kids, this is Andrea Ford."

As her father introduced them, Maggie watched the woman's steady expression. Her eyebrows seemed posed in a constant state of inquiry, as if she spent so much time studying the people around her that her forehead was forever locked into a question mark.

Andrea Ford. Maggie repeated the name a couple times, wondering what her presence meant, as Andrea swept into the room ahead of them all and perused the interior in five seconds flat. "How sweet, Frank. You've done well decorating, considering your lack of female input. It feels very homey."

Maggie wasn't at all sure she meant the comment as a compliment.

Andrea took it all in with a wave of an arm. "I'm sure it's difficult to manage it all on your own."

"Oh, Mags takes care of most of it."

"Yes, bless you, Maggie. Frank has repeatedly pointed out how much you do for him and your brothers. He's very proud of you."

Maggie raised her eyebrows and turned to her father. He'd been talking about her to this lady? But her father's attention was narrowed in on Andrea, watching her every reaction to his home.

As Andrea reached for a family photo, it was more than Maggie could stand. "Supper is way done. Let's eat."

"About time," Tony said, and he led the way to the table.

Maggie had already cut the roast and returned it to the oven, along with the peas to keep them warm. All she had to do was pull out the food-laden platter and vegetable dishes and put them on the table.

Andrea was finding things in the kitchen to bring into conversation. "Such a bright color scheme, and monkeys too. How extraordinary for a kitchen theme. . . . Oh, what adorable photos on the refrigerator, especially this one of Billy playing soccer. Home photos are so endearing, even if they aren't professional. . . . And these others must be cousins or something—living up north from the looks of all that snow. I didn't know you had relatives there. . . . What an adorable napkin holder. Did one of you make it?"

Billy delved into his pottery-class story while Maggie rushed around the kitchen getting everything into place. After she placed the last of the food on the table, and their father said grace, Maggie offered Andrea first dibs on the roast beef. She wanted to make it clear who did the cooking in this house.

"Oh no. I couldn't possibly eat that. Tell her, Frank," she said, touching their father's arm. "I never eat meat, especially beef."

Billy, who had snatched a piece and was already chewing, was quick with his opinion. "You wouldn't want any, anyway. It's dried out and chewy as day-old bubble gum."

Not my fault. I wasn't the one holding up supper. "Well, we have rice and peas."

Andrea's smile was fake, indulgent. "You're too young to worry about joints, obviously, but you'll see as you get older that you need to avoid white foods like white rice, white bread, and potatoes. They'll stiffen you in an instant. You see, the starches in white foods alter the insulin levels in the blood stream and trigger arthritis because they are processed so quickly by the body, much like white sugar triggers hyperactivity in children."

Aren't we smart? thought Maggie. "I can see where someone your age might need to worry about that."

Andrea's smile stayed fixed, but her eyes narrowed. "I think I'll have a few peas."

"They're good," Billy said. "In school they go mushy and the shells come off, but Maggie fixes them just right with lots of butter on top."

Andrea's spoon stopped halfway to her mouth. "Butter? Really?"

Maggie watched her, daring her not to eat them.

Andrea ate only three forkfuls before she laid her utensils down. She spent the rest of supper ignoring the food as she floated from topic to topic, as if they were all mingling at a party, asking Tony about his classes at school, asking Billy about soccer.

"Frank tells me you're quite the soccer player, Billy," she tossed out.

"He's excellent," their father interjected. "He practices more than any kid on the team—all year long. Wears me out in the backyard every chance he gets."

Maggie stifled a laugh. She loved her father, but he wasn't the type to spend an afternoon playing soccer with Billy. Maybe on an occasional Saturday, but only after cutting the grass, trimming the bushes, and doing whatever other fix-it-up chores he assigned himself.

Andrea smiled sweetly at their father and listened as Billy jabbered about his save in the last game, then she shifted tactics. "How did you learn how to cook, Maggie?"

"Some experimentation. Some just reading cookbooks. Mostly my neighbor, Mrs. Graham."

"Really? She gave you cooking lessons?"

Maggie had no desire to share her life with this lady, but her father was watching. "I've been baby-sitting her daughter for five years. During the summer when I'm out of school, she takes a temporary job while I watch Kimberly. I have to have supper fixed when she and her husband get home, so she leaves me detailed instructions on how to make whatever they want cooked. First I cook it at her house, then I bring Kimberly over here and cook it for us too. Not much to it."

"She keeps us well fed, that's for sure," her father said as he pushed his chair away from the table. "You children will excuse us," he added, and escorted Andrea to the family room.

Tony made a point of lagging over his third helping of roast beef until Andrea had left the room. "This is just plain weird," he said.

"Is she a, well, you know . . . a girlfriend or something?" Billy asked.

"Or something," Maggie replied as she pushed the kitchen door closed. They were all keeping their voices especially quiet, below the rise and fall of their father's voice in the family room as he and Andrea talked and laughed.

Tony shoved the last bite in his mouth and talked around the hunk of meat. "You'd think he would have warned us."

"You'd think," Maggie said as she gathered dishes from the table.

Tony swallowed. "I figured he was bringing home one of his poker buddies."

Maggie stopped in her tracks, plates in hand. "Daddy doesn't play poker."

"Sure he does. Every third Friday. Why do you think he gets home so late? There are four of them in the office that play together."

The stereo came on in the family room, the static rising and falling as the tuner scanned over channels then settled on light pop. Maggie was glad for the background noise. It would mask their conversation. Still, she kept her voice subdued. "Daddy? Poker?"

"Well, sometimes it's hearts or spades or euchre or whatever. But cards, anyway. You know how he loves cards."

That was true. He did love playing cards. They often played cards together as a family, the four of them gathered around the kitchen table, munching on pretzels, drinking Coke, and poking fun at each other through an hour-long game. He'd grown up playing cards with his brothers during long summer nights at his grandmother's house, a little shack on the bank of the Pamlico River, and it was his way of bringing those memories back to life. His brothers had all moved away except Uncle Matt, and he traveled so much they rarely saw him. When he did come over, playing cards was a ritual part of his visit, and they all looked forward to it, even Tony, who had become more and more reticent about the usual family functions.

How long had her father been playing cards after work without Maggie realizing it? "Every third Friday? I thought he had meetings."

"Yeah, well, you're so thick you don't see that no one would get caught dead in a striped shirt like that, either."

Maggie looked down at her T-shirt. She liked the bright blue and white stripes. "Like you're an expert on fashion now?"

"I don't live under a rock."

Was she that dense?

Billy was searching the cabinets. "Where'd you hide the Little Debbies?"

"Ask Mr. Fashion," Maggie said and slammed the dishes into the sink. "There were four left last night, but I think the rat got into them after school." She turned around and leaned against the counter, ignoring the sting of her brother's words for more immediate matters. "Anyway, we still haven't figured out about Andrea. What's up?"

Billy turned to look at her. "It's all good. Maybe she'll take over the cooking and cleaning, and you won't have to scream at us about our stinky clothes all over the place." He grinned and punched her on the shoulder.

Maggie sighed. Billy didn't have any memories of their mother. He had been an infant when she died. But still, Maggie couldn't believe he would give in so easily to the idea of a woman in their house. It felt so . . . invasive.

"It doesn't bother you guys having this woman come in here and criticize our house and our food?"

Tony laughed. "Your food, and I can't say she was too far off the mark there."

"You're unbelievable."

He shrugged. "The way I see it, it's a miracle he hasn't brought someone home before now. It's been twelve years, Maggie. It kinda creeps me out, but I can see where he needs somebody. *I* need somebody."

"Right, like that's happening."

"You haven't got a clue."

She shook her head at him. He wouldn't confide in her nowadays, but there still wasn't anything Tony did that she didn't know about. He spent all his afternoons at Webb's house, and there wasn't anything going on but video games.

Billy had given up on finding Little Debbies and settled for a glass of chocolate milk. He dumped two huge spoonfuls of chocolate into his cup and stirred, the spoon clanking noisily against the glass. "Everybody needs love. That's what Brad's daddy says."

Maggie quirked one eyebrow. "Brad's dad said that to you?"

"Sure. He says we've all got to love one another. That's what Jesus wants."

Tony was drawing circles on the table with his fingertip, half listening. "Sunday school. That's not the kind of love we're talking about, bro."

Maggie still couldn't believe Tony was being so nonchalant about it. "So you don't have a problem with this?"

"What if I did? It's his life. We're just his kids. Get a grip, Mags. It happens every day to kids at school. Difference is, we don't have a mama here to scream over daddy having a girlfriend, which is what most of our classmates have to deal with."

With that, Tony stood and left the room, paused in the family room to mumble something to his father, and left, the front door shutting firmly behind him.

Maggie didn't want to be left alone. She didn't want Andrea showing up in the kitchen and forcing her into small talk when she had this huge ache in the middle of her stomach. "Billy, if you stay and help me with the kitchen, I'll challenge you to a game of chess or backgammon."

"Make it both and it's a deal."

She grinned. "Deal."

After making short work of the kitchen, they passed through the family room with a wave and a quick explanation, and fled up the stairs to Billy's room. Billy won both of the games, hooting and hollering as he played his final moves, but Maggie didn't tell him to lower his voice. This was their home, and she wasn't about to change their noise level just because some lady was sitting in the family room with their father.

Maggie was almost sorry when the games were over, but she needed to be alone to think. She tucked Billy in, as much as he would tolerate—which meant half a hug before she left his room—then changed into pajamas, crawled into her own bed, and stared at the ceiling, wondering how her life had tilted so out of whack. That morning she'd thought she was going to meet a fantastic guy, and now she was facing life with some woman having her claws in her father.

She lay awake for what seemed like hours, too restless to let sleep overtake her whirling mind. Tony returned home. His steps paused momentarily in the family room, then he tromped up the stairs to his room and began strumming his guitar.

An hour later, she heard the final murmurs of her father leaving the house with Andrea, the door clicking shut behind them, and the ensuing silence as the strains of music from Tony's guitar ceased. She lay there awhile longer, until she heard Billy snort and moan as he tossed in his bed in the next room. She imagined him curled up in a ball, unable to find his covers in the dark, so she eased out of bed and down the hall to his room. Sure enough, the sheets and bedspread were in a knot at his feet, so she pulled them over him and kissed his forehead. Even after his shower that evening, he still smelled like dirt and sweat, and a little like spicy sausage; but it was a good smell, his smell, and it made her smile. Sometimes he seemed more like her son than her brother. She picked up his dirty clothes, put his books back in his book bag, and laid out clean clothes for the morning.

She stopped at Tony's doorway and listened to make sure he was asleep before entering. He'd scream at her if he knew she checked on him, but she'd been doing it all her life, making sure his legs weren't dangling off the side or that his pillow hadn't landed on the floor out of reach. As she suspected, one foot hung off the side. She pushed it back onto the bed, and he rolled over with a sigh. She adjusted his blankets and laid her hand on his shoulder. He could be a pain, but her heart still swelled with undeniable love for him.

Her bedroom seemed lonelier tonight than ever before.

Back in bed, she stared at the ceiling until a car drove by at a snail's pace, rattling slightly as if the bumper were loose. She imagined that it belonged to the bearded stranger and that he was out on the prowl for something.

She turned on the small lamp on her nightstand, plumped up a couple pillows behind her back, and picked up the novel she was reading for English class, *Wuthering Heights*. But she couldn't concentrate. Her mind wandered from the car to the events of the day. Tony's words rose to mind again. Was her shirt really that lame? Were all her clothes lame?

She would worry about that on Monday.

Her eyes fell again to the book in front of her. She'd barely gotten through eight pages when she heard her father's car in the driveway. With a sigh of relief, she glanced at the clock and knew he would fuss at her for still being awake. She reached over, turned off the light, and shoved the book to the floor.

As he ascended the staircase, she closed her eyes and played like she was asleep, but he entered her room and sat on the edge of her bed. "Give it up, Maggie. I saw your light on."

She blinked in the dark.

"So what did you think of her?" he asked.

She didn't know what to say. It wasn't often she found herself at a loss for words with her father, but she could hardly tell him the truth—that she thought Andrea was a horrible woman, and she couldn't understand why he'd brought her home. "I don't know, Daddy. It's hard to say after such a short visit." Could she say what she was really feeling? "What do you think, Daddy? I mean have you been *dating* her?"

He didn't answer right away. His gaze steadied on her face, and Maggie guessed he was trying to read her thoughts.

"I thought after all this time, you would be okay with it. I'm not a monk, you know. I loved your mother with all my heart, but life goes on."

She knew by the way he was looking at her with that soft expression and steady eyes that he was at the same time gauging her reaction and pleading with her to understand. He broke eye contact and stared off across the room at the window and the trees beyond. "I figure you'd understand now." He took her hand in his. "Even though you don't talk about having a boyfriend, I know there is someone you have your heart set on. I see it in your eyes when you think no one is looking."

Maggie blushed.

"You're not a child anymore. You're sixteen, a woman by all rights. Your mother had you when she was your age. You must understand how things are between a man and woman."

Maggie bit her lip. She wasn't going to make it easy for him. He didn't understand what he was asking of her, letting some strange woman into their lives.

"I've waited a long time, Mags. You've got to see it from my perspective."

Tears welled in her eyes.

"Just give her a chance, will you?"

How could she express everything that was crashing together in her head and her heart? He was her father; he belonged to her, not to some strange lady. Andrea didn't strike her as the type of person to leave room for a teenage girl in a relationship. She was too take-charge, too in-your-face and demanding. But how could she say no to her father, who had waited so long to find love again?

It took all her strength to bring herself to speak. "I'll try, Daddy."

He wiped her tears away and kissed her cheek. "That's my girl." He pulled the covers up around her. "Now get some sleep. It's late."

She turned to her side, hid her face in the pillow, and muffled her sobs.

Chapter
Seven

MAGGIE HEADED UP to Dixie's house early the next morning. She was halfway up the big hill when she heard a car and automatically stepped off the road to walk along the grass. At the bottom of the hill, a ditch ran beside the road, but at this stretch, the ditch flattened out. Twenty feet of grass and a tangle of weeds grew with wild abandon among scraggly bushes and thorns before they fell away to the thicket of trees that held Maggie's special thinking place. The outer stretch used to be mowed regularly enough that trees had never taken hold, but no one bothered with it anymore, and a few pine and oak tree sprouts could be seen forcing their way up through the underbrush. The only clear spot through the brush was the narrow trail that she and other kids kept flattened with steady foot traffic.

She wasn't quite to the path when a car slowed behind her. She turned, expecting it to be Kimberly and her mother, or another longtime neighbor pausing to greet her, but then thoughts of the bearded stranger set her heart to pounding.

It wasn't the bearded man. It was Mr. Smith, the man with the cat, who lived around the corner from the Garlens. He slowed down and came to a stop alongside her. His blond hair was slicked to one side. The morning sun shone directly into his face, making his eyes squint into two unreadable slits, and his lips, so thin they were almost nonexistent, pulled across his teeth in a strained smile. He rolled down his window and leaned his elbow on the ledge, his fingers gripping the upper edge of the window frame. "Have you seen my cat?"

"Not today, Mr. Smith. She sure is a beauty, though. I hope you find her."

"I'm worried that dog messed with her."

He was wearing a pink button-down dress shirt. He always wore some kind of button down, never T-shirts, as if he were on the way to a business meeting no matter the time or day.

"Smokey wouldn't hurt her. He just likes to bark a lot."

"We'll see," he replied, and sped off, leaving her blinking in the bright sunlight.

She looked up and down the road, trying to remember when she had seen either Smokey or the cat. "Smokey!" she hollered. "Smokey! Come here boy." In the distance, she heard an excited bark. She hollered once more and waited. In less than a minute, he was at her side, dropping a ball at her feet and licking her hand. She rubbed his ears and kissed the top of his soft golden head. "You're a good boy, aren't you? You wouldn't hurt Mr. Smith's cat, would you?"

In reply, he licked her nose.

She laughed. "Thanks. I could have done without a nose cleaning." There was no sense in hollering for the cat. For one thing, she didn't know its name, and for another, she knew from experience a cat wouldn't come running quite the same way as a dog. A cat had to have a reason, or it wasn't likely to bother responding to a human for anything.

Maggie patted her leg, and Smokey trotted along beside her to the top of the hill. When he spotted Brad playing ball with Mr. Dweller, he trotted off to join them.

"Bye, Smokey," she called, then continued on her trek to Dixie's. It was still early, but she knew Dixie would be up. Her mother made her clean the upstairs every Saturday morning, and Dixie always rose at dawn to get it done so she wouldn't be tied down for the day.

Mrs. Chambers came to the door still clothed in beautiful silky black pajamas covered by an old pink terrycloth housecoat that hung from her shoulders, open like a cape around her. It was at least a decade old, a memento of some earlier place in her life that she clung to it like a toddler dragging around a ragged teddy bear.

Maggie loved the way Mrs. Chambers dressed, from her casual clothes and pajamas to her evening attire. She always looked sophisticated without looking stuck up or imposing. Maybe it was more like subtly sexy, but in a good way, like she wasn't dumpy or promiscuous, but someone all her own. Or maybe it was the way she wore her clothes, the way she carried herself. She was tall and thin, like a model. Her blonde hair was really short, up to her ears, and her blue eyes sparkled with warmth. She was like a pixie with a twinkle about her that made Maggie feel privy to some kind of magic, some secret about life and happiness that Mrs. Chambers was on the verge of sharing. Maggie felt good when she was around her.

Mrs. Chambers waved her into the house. "What brings you up here so early?"

"I have to talk to Dixie."

"Of course you do." She closed the door and hollered up the steps. "Dixie! Maggie is here!" She leaned on the railing.

"Something about a male guest last night, I hear. How'd it go? Was he cute?"

Dixie came flying down the steps in a pair of boxer shorts and a white T-shirt. Her seven-year-old sister, Cindy, came to the door of the family room to see who was there, then went back in and flopped down in front of cartoons. Cindy wasn't required to do anything except clean up after her parakeets and sweep the front and back porches. The baby of the family always seemed to get the easy track through life.

Dixie was flushed from exertion. "Tell us, tell us! I kept thinking you'd call last night. I was afraid to phone in case he was still there, and then I fell asleep watching a movie. What happened? Is he gorgeous? Did he stay all night or something?"

"You don't know the half of it," Maggie said. "That's why I had to come up here to tell you. It wasn't a boy at all. It was a woman."

Mrs. Chambers wasn't one to miss out on the good stuff. "Oh my. This definitely calls for a cup of tea. Come on in the kitchen, girls."

She had them set up with cups of tea and banana nut muffins in a matter of minutes, while Maggie settled in with her tale of all that had transpired the night before. "She was horrible. Totally horrible. Saying all that stuff about my cooking and the house. I can't believe Daddy brought her home." She sniffed. "I can't believe he's *dating* her."

Mrs. Chambers concentrated on the teapot in the middle of the table and sipped her tea in silence. She rarely spoke without thinking through the consequences. Dixie didn't share her reticence. "You should have told him the truth, Mags. You should have said you think she's an old bag, and what does he think he's doing bringing home some lady like that."

Maggie, comforted by her friend's sympathy, took a bite of her muffin. "Maybe I should have, but he was holding my hand and trying so hard to be understanding, getting my approval and all. It's hard to speak my mind when he looks at me that way."

Mrs. Chambers set her cup down and wrapped her hands around it. "I hope we know each other well enough, Maggie, that I can share my thoughts with you."

A jolt went through Maggie. She knew what was coming. Mrs. Chambers had always treated her like a daughter, and Maggie had never minded. She'd sat beside Dixie through talks about drugs and sex and problems with friends. Dixie and Maggie had practically been joined at the hip from kindergarten forward, so it would've been hard not to include her in whatever discussions affected Dixie because ultimately Maggie was woven into the scheme of her life. But this time the topic was focused on her alone. Dixie wasn't joined to Maggie's family like Maggie was joined to Dixie's. Dixie didn't regard Tony and Billy like brothers, or look to Maggie's father for advice.

Dixie's father had passed away two years earlier, after a yearlong battle with cancer, and he was still alive enough in her mind that no one could take his place. No one needed to; Mrs. Chambers managed to act both as mother and father. But Maggie loved her own father in a way she was sure she could never love any woman, mother or not. She and her father were joined in ways that no one else could fathom, by a love that ran deep and forgave all differences and blemishes. Still, Mrs. Chambers filled a void that she only noticed was there when this kind of discussion came up, getting to the heart of personal matters that Maggie's father didn't dare broach.

She spoke with quiet authority. "Your daddy hasn't ever brought home another woman. Isn't that what you said?"

"Yes, ma'am."

"Well, if you were him, do you think that after waiting twelve years, you would bring home a woman who was horrible?"

Maggie hadn't considered that. "No. But she was horrible. She was . . . I don't know. Abrupt. Something. Just mean."

"There must be something about her that is exceptionally wonderful for your daddy to decide that this woman was worthy of being introduced to all of you."

Dixie leaned forward. "Does she have big boobs?"

Mrs. Chambers frowned.

"No, she doesn't have big boobs. But she's pretty, I guess. She has a nice figure, black hair, but scowling eyes."

Mrs. Chambers shook her head. "Maggie—"

"Okay, okay. I guess she was nice to the boys. She asked about school and junk like that. And she seemed to hang on Daddy's every word."

"Ah. A man loves a woman who will listen."

"I listen!"

"It's not the same. Would it matter if Dixie sat here listening to you all day versus if Webb sat and listened to you for five minutes?"

Maggie blushed and glared at Dixie. "Did you tell her?"

Dixie was wide-eyed. "First I've heard of it. You and Webb?"

Mrs. Chambers laughed. "You girls are so transparent. Dixie, how could you not know she has a thing for Webb? Her whole face lights up every time she's around him. She's been that way since she was twelve years old."

"You and Webb?"

Maggie shrugged. She hadn't ever confided her feelings to Dixie. They'd known Webb forever and had ridiculed him and

Tony for so long as being lazy idiots that Dixie would have thought she was cracked. Instead, Maggie pretended to sigh over some of the boys at school to keep Dixie from guessing the truth. "He doesn't even notice me. He's hooked on Sue. How can anyone compete with that?"

Dixie made a funny face. "I know. Sue has boobs."

Mrs. Chambers took another muffin. "Contrary to popular belief, the world does not revolve around how big a girl's breasts are. They are mammary glands. God gave them to us to feed babies. I don't understand this constant predilection for them, or the insinuation that having large ones makes any girl more attractive than someone with small ones." She touched her own modest bust line. "I'm perfectly happy with my figure, thank you very much."

"Oh, Mama, be real. It's like being pretty or ugly, fat or skinny. It all matters. You're always preaching first impressions and all that."

"So here we are, back to the core of our problem." Mrs. Chamber's voice was gentle but firm. "You've had one brief interlude with Andrea, and you're ready to write her off as not being worthy of your consideration, even when your daddy has waited all these years before deciding she was the one he wanted to bring home to introduce to you and your brothers. We may not go to the same church, but I happen to know he's a very faith-filled man. I know he holds Jesus in his heart right there with you and your brothers, and he's not about to set any of you aside for the sake of a woman. In fact, it sounds to me like your opinion is very important to him. He made a special effort to talk to you about her afterward, to get your approval. I think you ought to at least give him the benefit of the doubt and trust that maybe there's more to Andrea than the first impression implied. She may be a very thoughtful woman with your best interests at heart."

Maggie hung her head, duly chastised. "You're right. I guess I'm not being any better than the people at school who judge me that way, figuring since I'm not popular I must not be worth their time."

Mrs. Chambers laid her hand on Maggie's arm. "I don't think anyone thinks that. Everyone just has their own comfort zones, and they tend to stay within them. If you and Dixie are intent on mixing more with other kids, the effort is going to have to be on your end, not theirs. You're going to have to join the activities they're doing and invite them into your space."

Obviously Dixie had confided in her mother about how invisible they both felt, but Dixie had never shared her mother's take on the situation with Maggie. It was a new perspective she had never considered. "I hadn't thought of that. But we can hardly bust in on their parties uninvited."

"Have you ever asked? Have you ever heard them talking about a party and said, 'Hey Asby, we heard about your party. We'd love to come.'"

"Mama, not Asby Jones. He pretends to smoke joints in class right in front of the teachers."

"Well, that wasn't a good choice was it? You know what I mean. I guess I've raised you up well enough to hope you'd choose the right parties to attend and not get into drugs and spiked punch."

Mrs. Chambers had offered them an entirely new way of facing their dilemma. Both dilemmas. Maggie sipped at her tea and thought it over. Whose space could she finagle her way into?

Certainly not Sue's. Or could she?

Chapter Eight

SEVEN-YEAR-OLD Cindy wandered into the kitchen as Dixie headed back upstairs to finish her chores, while Maggie sat at the table looking through the classifieds for a washing machine. Mrs. Chambers bustled around the kitchen, fixing Cindy a bowl of cereal and a glass of apple juice, then she took a seat beside Maggie. After a few minutes, she shook her head in despair. "Honey, I think you'd really be better off finding a new one on sale. Maybe there's one in the sales flyer this morning." She pulled a brightly colored flyer from the stack of papers. "You're lucky Cindy hasn't gotten around to cleaning the birdcage yet."

Cindy looked up from the comics. She was a miniature of Mrs. Chambers with a thin, heart-shaped face and a bubbly personality. "Okay, okay. I'm going," she said. She pushed her chair out and huffed up the stairs with a handful of discarded papers and a plastic bag she pulled from under the sink.

Mrs. Chambers spread the advertisement out on the table and leafed through it. "There's one. See? It's a bit more expensive, but you won't be buying someone else's problem."

"Wow. That would be nice, wouldn't it? Start out with a new one. It would last a lot longer too. And look." Maggie pointed. "It has a gentle cycle. We really need one of those. And a spin-only cycle. Ours quit doing that ages ago. Something went wrong with the switch."

Mrs. Chambers pushed back her chair and carried the breakfast dishes to the sink. "Are you sure your daddy expects you to do this? Maybe he wants to be the one to buy the washing machine."

"Shoot, he doesn't handle any of this stuff. He gives me money to budget, and I take care of it. He probably doesn't even remember how to work the machine."

"Does he know you're buying one?"

"Well, sure. He asked me this morning if I'd taken care of it yet."

Mrs. Chambers settled back into her chair. "You are really remarkable, you know that?"

"Because I'm picking out a washing machine?"

"Because you *can* pick out a washing machine. Because of everything you handle."

"It's not that hard. We do what we've got to do."

She nodded. "I guess we do." She stood up again. "As it turns out, I've got to go to this store this morning, so how about we round up my hardworking girls and all head out that way? I'll bet we could find ourselves a milk shake somewhere on the way back home."

"Really?" Maggie breathed a sigh of relief. She wouldn't have to work out borrowing the car or anything. "I'd love to have you and Dixie help me buy it. I have to go home to get my pocketbook, though, and get the money. That one is a bit more than

I planned to spend, but Daddy should still be home. I'll see if we can afford it. Can you pick me up at my house in twenty minutes?"

"Sure."

Maggie stopped in at Webb's house on the way home. It was midmorning now, so she knew she would find the boys in their usual positions.

Sure enough, Tony and Webb were both reclined on the bed with game controls aimed at the television screen. At least Sue wasn't there.

Maggie watched for a few minutes, waiting for a break; but Tony's turn went on forever, and she wanted to let him know she wouldn't be around and to get his own lunch. "Guess what? I found a washer. Mrs. Chambers is taking me to get it."

Tony spoke around the toothpick wedged between his teeth. "Why do ya come up here telling us that junk, Maggie? We don't care about some stupid washing machine."

She stood to go. "Of course you don't. You only care that your clothes are clean, and you don't even care about that enough to put them away in your drawers."

He mouthed her words and bobbed his head, mimicking her. Webb laughed.

"You're both idiots," Maggie said. "You don't have any responsibilities, but I do. I have to think about stuff like this. You're both fluff, just like those dumb girls at school who don't think about anything but makeup."

"Wouldn't hurt for you to think about makeup, Maggot," Tony said, his eyes never leaving the television screen.

"Maggot? Maggot!" she screeched. "You just wait, Tony

McCarthy. From this point forward, you're washing your own clothes. I don't care if they rot on your bedroom floor."

"Ah, Mags, don't get freaked. Just get out of my face about the washing machine."

"Oh, don't worry. I'm out of your face. There's a certain point that I don't think even Jesus would expect me to keep doing what I do for you. In fact, maybe if you have to go to school wrapped in your bedsheets like a toga, it will put you a bit more in touch with the Lord." She headed toward the door. "And get your own lunch. I'm eating out with the Chamberses."

Webb stared at her as if he couldn't believe she'd yelled at Tony. He'd certainly seen her let loose before, but not any time recently. She had a lot of Irish temper in her, but, for the most part, she kept it in check.

She shrugged. She didn't care that Webb had seen her get mad. What difference did it make? She'd been sweet as sugar around him for at least a year now, and he never saw her as anything more than Tony's unwanted appendage.

Why was she so hung up on him, anyway? He had nothing going for him. He was smart, but he didn't pay attention in school, so his grades weren't as high as they would be if he studied. The only class they had together was math, and she saw him doodle instead of watching the examples on the board. How lame was that? And he didn't have a job. He didn't even have any goals in life beyond beating the next video game. He might be dreamy looking with those gorgeous eyes and that hot body and that wavy black hair that just begged to be touched, but there were plenty of boys with more to offer. She was worthy of better than him. At this point, he could rot on his bedroom floor along with Tony's dirty socks.

Still huffing with anger, she strode from the house, down the road, past Billy playing at Brad's house, and headed down the hill before she remembered she ought to let Billy know where she would be.

She jogged back up the hill, slowing as she reached Brad's yard, and walked across the grass to where the boys were playing catch with Mr. Dweller.

Mr. Dweller caught the ball and shuffled it to his glove so he could greet Maggie with an outstretched hand. "Maggie, what a nice surprise."

She shook his hand without really thinking about it. "Hello, Mr. Dweller."

"Clark. Call me Clark like the rest of the kids. You're the only one in youth group that doesn't call me Clark." He dropped her hand and slid his arm around her shoulders. He pulled Billy into his other arm and gave him a squeeze. "We're all friends here, aren't we boys?"

"Sure, Clark."

Maggie glared at Billy for calling Mr. Dweller Clark, but he just grinned.

"Wuz up, sis?"

Maggie felt uncomfortable under Mr. Dweller's arm. She had to make an effort not to pull away. "I just wanted to let you know I'm going to the store with Dixie and her mom to get the washing machine, so you and Tony will have to take care of yourselves for lunch. Daddy will be leaving soon."

"No problem," Mr. Dweller said, giving her shoulders a hug. "He can have lunch with us, right Brad?"

"Sure."

He released Billy and gave him a swat on the bottom. "That's my boy."

Maggie forced herself to smile and eased out of his clasp. "Great. See you later, then, Billy. Be home by four, okay?"

"Okay."

Mr. Dweller tossed the ball to Brad. "Take over a minute, champ," he said, and followed Maggie as she crossed the yard. "I know your daddy is proud of the way you take care of your brothers. You're very grown up for your age."

"Thanks."

"I wish you'd let me help you. All you have to do is ask. You never ask for help, though, do you, Maggie?"

"I can handle it."

"But I like helping people. You know that. Everyone knows that. All you have to do is ask Clark Dweller. He's the man to help any kid that asks."

"Guess I'm not really a kid."

He paused. "No, you're a little lady. Look at you. Yes, quite a little lady."

She stopped and looked at him. He stopped too. "Good-bye, Mr. Dweller. Please send Billy home at four o'clock."

"Sure thing, Little Lady." He nodded and grinned. "I like the sound of that. Little Lady. I do believe I'll have to start calling you that. Our little nickname. What do you think?"

"Thanks," she said, "but my name is Maggie."

She left him standing on the curb and jogged down the hill. No matter what anyone said about him, she didn't care that he volunteered to assist with youth group, organized the camp-outs, and cooked at every church dinner. She didn't like him.

By the time she got home, her father was heading out the door, but she told him about the washing machine, and he got her extra money he had stashed away in his room. "Here you go. I trust your judgment." He kissed her on the top of her head. "Don't forget to be back at four o'clock. We're going out to dinner tonight."

Mrs. Chambers arrived moments later. Maggie grabbed her pocketbook and ran out to the car, wondering how her family was suddenly rich enough to buy a brand-new washing machine *and* to go out to supper all in the same week.

The washing machine was perfect. With Dixie, Cindy, and Mrs. Chambers clustered around her, she told the salesman she'd take it. He rang it up and told her to drive around to the back to pick it up.

"The ad says there's free delivery this weekend, as long as it's within the city limits."

"I don't think so. Maybe your mother—"

Mrs. Chambers waved her hands at him. "Oh no, I'm not her mother. I'm just a friend. You're dealing with her, I'm afraid."

He looked from one to the other.

Maggie put her hands on her hips. "Well, I need that free delivery. I don't have a truck to put it in, and even though I'm pretty independent, I don't think I can heft a washing machine."

The salesman pulled a sales flyer from a messy stash under the counter and read the fine print. "Okay, yeah, you get your free delivery. How about Tuesday morning?"

"Sure, like I can skip school for a washing machine to be delivered. Come on, Mister. Give me a break. Can't you arrange to have it delivered this afternoon?"

"I'm afraid that's impossible."

Maggie pursed her lips, but kept her temper in check. "Look, it's not impossible. Just call back to that dock and tell somebody to load it up and get it to my house. I'll be there in an hour." She snatched the receipt from him. "One hour. That's two o'clock. Can you handle that?"

Mrs. Chambers winked at him, sending pixie magic floating through the air. "You'd better do as she says. Irish temper and all. You don't want to get her riled."

He looked Mrs. Chambers up and down with a smile. "All right." He nodded. "Two o'clock."

Mrs. Chambers fluttered her eyelashes. "Thanks."

"No problem." His eyes didn't leave Mrs. Chambers's face. "You just come back and see us again real soon."

As they walked away, Dixie poked her mom. "You were flirting with him."

"No I wasn't. I was just convincing him to do the right thing. A little sugar can go a long way, you know."

Dixie laughed. "And it didn't even take big boobs."

"Of course not. It only took a wink and a smile."

Maggie sat in the rocking chair on the front porch, catching the afternoon sun while she waited for the deliverymen to arrive. The afternoon breeze felt good flowing across her skin. She closed her eyes and pretended she was on a porch at a beach house with a breeze coming off the ocean. She pretended there was salt in the air and the tainted smell of fish and shrimp, and waves pounding to the rhythm of her rocking. She was so into her dream that when something furry brushed against her skin, she jumped with fright and landed on the armrest instead of the seat, giving herself a good bruise in a bad spot.

There, curling around her ankles, was Mr. Smith's cat.

"Where did you come from?" she asked, picking her up. The cat looked thin, and her fur had lost some of its glossiness since she'd seen her last. "You look starved," she said. She carried her into the house and opened the pantry. There weren't many cans stashed on the shelves, so it only took a moment to find what she wanted—a can of tuna. She needed two hands to open it, so she set the cat on the counter and reached into the utility drawer. Everything went into it, so she had to carefully poke among the spatulas and sharp knives, pushing aside the meat thermometer and a plastic baster that didn't work very well because the meat juice ran back out before she could get it from the bottom of the pan to the top of the chicken. Along the back edge, behind a nutcracker no one ever used because she only bought canned nuts nowadays, she found the metal can opener, pulled it out, and went to work. As soon as it pierced the can, the smell of tuna pervaded the room, and the cat tiptoed across the counter to stick her nose in the way.

"Wait a minute, sweets."

With a couple of turns, the lid peeled off. There was no keeping the cat out of it, so she lifted the cat in one hand and the can in the other and carried them out front to the porch. "There," she said, setting them by the rocker. "Eat up, but don't you dare tell the boys. They'll make me eat my words about wasting food."

Maggie sat in the rocker again, watching the cat with satisfaction as she licked the can clean and then sat back on her haunches to lick her paws, as if she'd somehow gotten them dirty by eating the tuna. When she finished preening, she looked up at Maggie expectantly.

Maggie stood and scooped her up. "C'mon. I'll take you home

to Mr. Smith in case you've lost your way."

She walked leisurely down the road. Mr. and Mrs. Garlen were in their yard working in their flowerbed, but their dog, Smokey, was nowhere in sight. Maggie waved as she passed, and they called back a greeting. The rest of the street was quiet. She turned the corner. No one was out on Mr. Smith's street. As she plodded up his short cement driveway, she noticed his station wagon wasn't there, but he seemed like the type who would park in the one-car garage.

The porch was bare. Not even a plant or a chair on it.

Maggie rang the doorbell and heard it chime inside. No one answered. After a minute, she peered through the front plate-glass window to the living room beyond. There wasn't much to see. A chair sitting by an unused fireplace. Some books set in a row across the mantel. A standing lamp. No evidence of Mr. Smith's being inside.

She set the cat down on the porch. "Oh, well. I got you over here anyway. Stay here and wait for your daddy," she said. As she turned to leave, the cat sprang off the porch, ran across the road, between two other houses, and disappeared into the Taylors' backyard, just missing getting hit by an old green Cadillac that sped toward her, past Mr. Smith's house, and on down the street. *The bearded stranger?* Maggie didn't see the driver's face and didn't recognize the car.

She almost knocked on the door again, in case Mr. Smith was at home after all, so she could at least tell him the cat was okay and ask him if he knew who might own that Cadillac. But as she raised her hand to knock, she caught sight of her watch and decided she'd better get back in case the deliverymen arrived early. Mr. Smith wouldn't know who the man was anyway—he rarely talked to anyone.

She stuck to neighbors' yards on the way back, away from the road, but it didn't matter. The Garlens were no longer outside, and neither the stranger nor the green car was anywhere in sight.

The deliverymen didn't get there exactly at two, but they weren't far off the mark. Two stocky guys dressed in blue collared uniforms stepped down from the truck. The driver was dark and short and called *Diego*, according to the name tag sewn on the front of his shirt. His face was scarred with pockmarks and a deep slash that hadn't healed well across one cheek. His assistant was taller, with thin wisps of carrot-red hair showing under a Panthers ball cap. He smiled wide enough to show off one gold-capped tooth before pulling out a cigarette, which he clenched in his lips but didn't light.

"We got a delivery for McCarthy. That you?" Diego asked.

"Yes sir. I'll show you where it goes." She led them through the garage to the mudroom, Diego at her heels, his buddy two steps behind.

"You'll have to move the old one out of the way first," Maggie said.

"That ain't our job."

"Well, I can't move it."

"So get your folks to move it."

"That would be a little hard since there's no one here but me."

Diego cast a look at his buddy, *Johnny* by his name tag. "There's no one here but her."

Maggie shivered at the realization, at his implication.

Johnny pushed by Diego to get to the washing machine. "You look like my kid sister. She used to have hair just like yours."

Maggie touched her hair as Johnny reached behind the washer to pull the plug and undo the hoses.

"So what did she do about it? Her hair, I mean?"

He looked at her like she was nuts. "Do about it?"

"You know, how'd she fix it? I can't do anything with mine."

He went back to working on the hoses, talking out of the side of his mouth, around the unlit cigarette still dangling there. "She didn't do nothin' about it. It grew long and wild and hung all around her face till she died when she was ten."

"Oh."

Johnny pushed from behind till the machine was in the middle of the floor, blocking Maggie into the corner.

"Gee, I'm sorry. I didn't mean . . . ," she stammered.

He maneuvered around the side, pinning Maggie against the wall. Her body trembled as he pulled the cigarette from his mouth and shoved it into his shirt pocket. She became aware of how big he was and how helpless she was. "I guess she'd be about your age now." His breath smelled like an ashtray. Maggie stared up at his pale blue eyes. His foul breath flowed over her face. His nose was full of little hairs, but his eyelashes were so fair and thin they were almost nonexistent. His lips were like two pencil lines across his face. His body was hard and muscular beside her, from all the lifting of washing machines, she logically surmised, even while her heart raced with fear. She was alone, and she'd been dumb enough to say so to them. There was nothing she could do to stop them from doing anything they wanted.

How could I be so stupid? I worry about a stranger and a green Cadillac, yet I let two men into the house when I'm here alone!

His gaze took in every freckle on her face, the green of her eyes, and the curls of red hair that had escaped from her ponytail to dangle across her forehead and along her cheeks. His ashtray breaths wheezed in and out of his wide chest.

Maggie closed her eyes. *Please, Lord, protect me. Send angels to guard me and spare me.*

When she dared to open her eyes, he'd turned away. "Drunk driver hit her. I never got to say good-bye."

Maggie, limp with relief, caught herself on the wall and sucked in a long, slow breath to calm her nerves.

He grabbed one side of the machine. "Pick up that end, Dogface. You think I'm doing this all myself?"

Diego stepped up and heaved his end until they had the old machine moved into the garage, away from the laundry room entrance; then he opened the back of the truck and moved the new boxed machine into the empty space. Maggie moved to the corner of the garage and watched from there. With the box pulled away, Johnny hooked up the water and plugged the new machine into the outlet.

Diego stood close by, supervising his efforts. "We ain't supposed to hook it up and all, you know. That costs extra, but seeing how you're alone an' all, we's doing you a favor."

"Shut up, Dogface," Johnny said.

They finished up after a few more minutes and gathered the cast-off cardboard. Diego slammed the huge truck door and climbed into the driver's seat, while Johnny retrieved a clipboard from the seat of the truck and showed Maggie where to sign to verify delivery. "We can't carry off the old one. There's a fee for that, you know, or I'd do it. You'll have to carry it to the dump."

"Sure. Thanks for hooking it up."

"No problem," he said, heading back to the truck.

"I'm sorry about your sister."

He turned and looked at her. "When's your daddy getting home?"

She thought about what time it must be. *Two twenty?* "Two thirty," she lied. "What time is it now?"

"Just about that. You get inside and lock up, ya hear?"

"Sure, Johnny. Thanks."

He nodded and joined Diego in the truck.

Maggie ran inside, locked the door, and collapsed on the laundry-room floor until her heart quit pounding.

She was working on a second load of laundry when her father arrived with Andrea at four o'clock. He hollered for her as he moved through the house, his voice coming closer as she yelled back, "In the laundry room."

He poked his head in the door. "Hey, look there, you got the machine. How is it?"

"Great. It holds more than the old one, and it's quieter too."

"Where are your brothers?"

"Not home yet. But I told them to be here at four. They'll be along soon."

Andrea stepped around him to inspect the machine. "Looks nice. I like the controls. They look easier to use than mine."

Maggie waited for the derision to come. Based on the previous night, Andrea was bound to find something wrong with it.

"How'd you get it here?" Andrea asked.

Maggie rolled her eyes. "I had it delivered."

Andrea nodded. "By men."

Maggie gritted her teeth. Andrea was so bossy, such a know-it-all. Maggie knew it was wrong, but she couldn't bite back the words that boiled up. "No, little green elves delivered it."

Her father turned on her. "Maggie!"

"Sorry, but what a dumb question. Of course men delivered it."

She knew where the conversation was headed. She'd already spent an hour and a half chastising herself for her stupidity — telling those deliverymen she was alone, letting them trap her in a corner, making herself so vulnerable.

She was surprised when Andrea didn't say so to her. Instead, she turned on Maggie's father.

"What were you thinking? Leaving her alone while she had a washing machine delivered by two men? Are you nuts?"

"I didn't know she was having it delivered today."

"It's your job to know. Look at her. She's sixteen! She could have been raped or killed. What were you thinking?"

"By two deliverymen? Now that would make for a fine business practice. I think the cops would have a paper trail there, don't you? She's fine. What're you so worked up about?"

"Maybe they just scoped her out this time. They could come back later. Just because she came through unscathed doesn't change the fact that you put her at risk."

Andrea's words were echoing everything Maggie had been imagining since Johnny and Diego left. Anything could've happened. Maybe if she hadn't looked like Johnny's dead sister, it would've happened. She wouldn't let Andrea be right, though. Maybe they were two nice guys and she was just being paranoid. All her anxiety of the afternoon and all the angst of the evening before came crashing down on her. She whirled on Andrea. "Quit fussing at my daddy. You have no right. You're not my mother. I've been running this household for ages, so don't come busting in here thinking you're going to start putting me in my place or telling my daddy that I need a baby-sitter." She crammed a handful of clothes into the dryer.

"It's okay, Mags. She's just concerned about you."

"It's a statistical fact that girls—"

Maggie's hands were shaking. "I don't care about your statistics and your studies and your diets and your opinions. We've all lived perfectly happily by our standards for years, and we don't need you telling us what we're doing wrong."

"Mags . . ." Her father trailed off and silently pleaded with her, his expression saying everything that needed to be said.

"I'm sorry, Daddy. I was really going to try to like her for your sake, but she's . . . Oh, forget it."

Tony chose that moment to slide into the garage on his bicycle, followed by Billy on his skateboard.

"Wuz up?" Billy asked, jostling in front of Tony to join them in the laundry room. "Awesome. A new washer." He opened the top and watched the clothes swishing around.

"Yeah, really cool. It's laundry." Maggie fled down the hall and up the stairs. She had no desire to spend supper with any of them. She wanted to crawl under a rock and be by herself to lick her wounds.

Even with her bedroom door closed, she could hear voices rising and falling, mingling in conversation. They wouldn't care that she'd shut herself away.

She turned on her radio and stretched out on her bed with her eyes closed, but she could sense the portrait of Jesus staring at her until she opened her eyes and looked at it. "Why her, Lord?" She hissed the words at Jesus. "Why, if Daddy needs a girlfriend, does it have to be her?" Her emotions crashed, and she sobbed. "So what if Andrea was right? So what if I could've been raped by those guys? I wasn't. And I don't need her sticking her nose in my life."

The portrait continued to hang there with no change of expression. Jesus' eyes were filled with love, but the silence stretched onward.

"I can take care of myself," Maggie told Him. "I always have."

A short time later there was a knock on her door. Maggie thought it was her father. "Come in."

Andrea poked her head around the door. "It's me."

Maggie huffed and sat up, her eyes narrowed to two angry slits.

"Look, Maggie, I know we've started off on the wrong foot. I don't mean to be bossy. I guess it comes from growing up with three little sisters. They tell me I've always been bossy, and as much as I pray about it, I can't seem to get over it. But I'm trying, really."

Maggie picked up her monkey pillow and plucked at his painted-on eyes. She had nothing to say to Andrea.

Andrea stepped fully into the room. "I just don't want to see you get hurt. You're such a beautiful young thing, and I see so many girls—"

Maggie raised her eyes just enough to evoke an unspoken *shut up.*

Andrea cleared her throat. "Okay, you're right. We'll save that talk for another time, when we know each other better." She sat on the corner of the bed. "Do you think you could join us for supper if I promise to be on my best behavior?"

Maggie didn't respond.

"Please? For Frank's sake? He was so looking forward to tonight. I know he doesn't take y'all out very often, and he has a special evening planned for us."

She didn't want to disappoint her father. He was all she had, her only lifeline. She couldn't risk pushing him away. It might mean pushing him straight into this woman's arms. Nothing could be worse than that. Then she would truly be alone in the world. She couldn't count on her brothers. She rolled off the bed and stood up. "Okay. For *Daddy.*"

"Great. Well, change your shirt and get ready. We'll be leaving shortly."

There she goes again. Maggie gritted her teeth and looked down at the orange T-shirt. "What's wrong with what I'm wearing?"

"Nothing, if you're hanging around the house, but it would be nice to see you in something a little dressier for supper."

"We're not rich, you know. We make do."

"You mean to tell me you don't have any tops that aren't T-shirts?"

"Of course I do."

She nodded and left the room.

Maggie thought there might be steam pumping out her ears like some cartoon character. Who was this lady to tell her how to dress?

She opened a drawer, flipped through the stack of shirts, and pulled out a blue one with a round collar and short sleeves like a T-shirt, but the material was heavier and it didn't have any pictures or words printed on it.

"I'm doing this for you, Daddy," she mumbled as she changed.

Chapter
Nine

A WEEK PASSED. Andrea visited two more times—briefly on Monday to deliver an invitation to some event, which her father kept to himself, along with a bouquet of fake flowers she placed on the mantel to "brighten up the place," and again on Tuesday evening to take a walk around the neighborhood with her father, the two of them arm in arm under an umbrella in a slow, drizzling rain. Afterward, Andrea hauled their scratched-up old coffee table out to the garage and replaced it with a square sea chest and an antique-looking chess set. Maggie was sure Andrea placed the game on top for looks, not use, because when Billy asked her to play, she said no.

On Thursday her father returned home late from work and went to bed without eating the plate of food Maggie had saved for him. She wouldn't even let herself imagine that he'd been out to dinner with Andrea.

On Friday night at seven o'clock, he left the house on a date—the first one he officially announced as such. Tony and Billy seemed oblivious. Billy parked himself in front of Nickelodeon, and Tony sat in his room strumming his guitar, irritated that

Webb had gone to his grandmother's house for some family dinner. Maggie didn't know what to do with herself. Dixie was coming to spend the night, but she had to baby-sit until nine o'clock, which left two hours to waste. Doing homework on a Friday night seemed pathetic, not that she could have concentrated on it anyway. She tried to talk her brothers into playing cards, but neither was interested.

Maggie couldn't understand how they were able to ignore the fact that their father was out on a date. She sat on the sofa for a while with a book in her lap, staring more at the reruns Billy was watching than at the book. Finally, Dixie arrived. The two of them dashed upstairs to listen to music and flip through the stack of magazines Dixie had brought along, which was just enough diversion to keep Maggie from thinking about her father and what he was up to with Andrea—until all her angst came rushing back when she saw an article titled "My Mother's Boyfriend."

"What do you think of this?" she asked Dixie.

"My mama wouldn't dare," Dixie replied.

"You don't think she'll ever date again?"

"No way. At least not yet."

"That's what I thought too."

"You mean . . . Is that where your daddy is?"

"Yes."

"The same lady he brought home the other night?"

"Yes."

"Why didn't you say so?"

Maggie shrugged. "What's to say?"

"Do you still hate her?"

"Would you like someone who was dating your mother?"

"I guess not."

"Ditto." She confided everything that had happened so far in her dealings with Andrea.

Dixie played the peacemaker. "Sounds like she's trying to be nice."

"Then I'm not telling it right, because she's not. Well, she probably is trying just so she can get to Daddy, but it's not working on me. I don't want her here."

Dixie thought about it a moment. "Well, maybe they're having a horrible time, and your daddy will take her home and never call her again."

Maggie grinned. "I sure hope so."

The next day, the girls dragged themselves out of bed midmorning, ate breakfast, and gathered up Dixie's things. Dixie had to do her Saturday chores, so Maggie decided to go along to help. Her father had arrived home in the wee hours, and she couldn't bear to look him in the face. She was sure the long date could only mean one thing, and she didn't want to see it in his eyes.

The girls were just reaching the entrance to the path into the woods when Billy and Brad dashed out full steam and nearly ran into them.

Billy was flustered, his face red, his words tripping over one another. "Maggie, come here. Follow me. You've got to see this. C'mon."

Maggie and Dixie exchanged bewildered looks, ducked under a branch, and hurried after him, but Billy stopped in his tracks to push Brad back toward the road. "Go get your dad."

Brad took off at a run, out to the road and up the hill, his sneakers pounding the pavement in his rush.

Billy snatched Maggie's arm and tugged her into the cool cover of the woods, toward her thinking rock. Ahead of them, the morning sun slanted through the trees, eerily spotlighting the boulder like a stage.

There was something on the rock.

Maggie pulled back and stopped. She didn't want to see it. She knew it was going to be something gruesome, right there in her special place in the middle of a beautiful day, and she would never be able to sit there again.

"Come on!" Billy said, tugging at her again.

Dixie forged forward. "What is it?"

"You've got to see," Billy said.

Maggie took a few more steps. She wasn't sure she could look. She felt her stomach roiling.

It was something with fur. Golden fur. Large.

The closer she got, the more certain she became. She didn't have to look at the collar. She didn't have to look in his lifeless eyes.

It was Smokey. His body was stretched out on the rock.

She ran forward, ready to hold him and cry over him, but as she approached, her feet became lead. If he were just dead, that'd be bad enough, but it was much more horrible than that. His belly was sliced down the middle, like the frog she had dissected in biology, and his entrails were pulled out.

Billy stood off a bit. "Disgusting, huh?"

Dixie flicked Smokey's tail with a stick. "Who would have done this?"

Maggie tried to put it together in her head. Someone had killed Smokey and laid him out on her rock, then pulled his guts out. It was intentional. Planned. Whoever did it left him there for a reason. "How did you find him? How long has he been here?"

Billy backed up another step. "We were working on our fort,

you know, the one up there near Brad's house. We came looking for big branches we could nail on for a railing. I remembered there was some over here. Then we saw him."

"You didn't see anyone?"

"Nope."

"Didn't hear anyone?"

"Nope."

Dixie wrinkled her nose. "He doesn't stink much yet, so it can't have been too long."

Maggie covered her mouth and swallowed the bile rising in her throat. "That means he might still be close by."

"Who?"

"Whoever did it. Maybe we interrupted him."

Billy's eyes widened. "What're we gonna do?"

"Let's go tell the Garlens."

She took Billy's hand, and the three of them started back down the path, the leaves and twigs crunching beneath their hurried steps, until Mr. Dweller came running toward them with Brad leading the way. For once, Maggie was almost relieved to see him.

"We're going to tell the Garlens."

"Let's go see," said Mr. Dweller, "then we'll decide what to do."

They followed him back into the woods, their steps more surefooted with an adult in their presence. The boys rushed ahead, anxious to show Mr. Dweller their discovery, but Maggie remained back a pace, observing Mr. Dweller's reaction. He didn't look shocked. He stood before the dog with his arms crossed over his chest and his face devoid of expression.

"He was looking for something," he said.

Dixie stepped closer. "Huh?"

He pointed to an organ lying on the ground. "The stomach."

Brad poked at it with a stick. A cloud of flies rose from the bloody goop. "I don't get it."

"Me either, son." He leaned closer. "He hasn't been dead long."

Maggie nodded. She was trying to figure out why Mr. Dweller wasn't more grossed out. Maybe it had something to do with being a guy and a grownup, but there was still that creepy feeling she had about him.

As if he had read her mind, he looked straight at her. "So what do you think, Little Lady? Some kind of sicko, eh?"

She wouldn't let herself look away. "Yes, some kind of sicko."

He started toward the path. "You boys come on home with me. Maggie and Dixie can go tell the Garlens."

"But we found him," said Brad.

"Yes, but Smokey was Maggie's friend, not yours; isn't that right, Maggie?"

Maggie waved Billy to follow. "Billy, you come with me."

Mr. Dweller shook his head and took Billy's hand. "No, I think these boys have been disturbed enough over this. They need to come home with me and get it out of their heads."

She wanted more than anything to yell at him and demand he let Billy go, but his sense of authority stopped her. Dazed, she watched them head up the hill to Billy's house until Dixie poked her. "Come on. We have to tell the Garlens."

The girls sped down the hill, slowed when they saw Tony coming out of the garage on his bicycle, and stopped to tell him what happened.

"I'm gonna check it out."

"No, don't go," Maggie pleaded. "Whoever did it might still be hanging around."

"I'll get Webb."

"Oh, that's great protection," she replied, wondering how Webb would react. He'd often played ball with Smokey, even though he wasn't his dog, but she doubted he'd get emotional. Teenage guys were like that—they pretended to be above feelings or something.

The Garlens took Maggie and Dixie back up the hill in their SUV. Despite the girls' explanation, the elderly couple failed to comprehend that Smokey wasn't fit to be lifted into the back of the car and carried home, and Maggie couldn't bring herself to describe him in much detail. Instead, she suggested they at least take a shovel, in case they decided it was more appropriate to bury Smokey in the woods.

The four of them processed silently into the woods, Mrs. Garlen gripping Mr. Garlen's arm for support.

Tony and Webb were already there, leaning over the carcass with pale faces. Maggie couldn't remember ever seeing either of them struck dumb.

Mrs. Garlen gasped and hid her face in Mr. Garlen's shoulder.

Mr. Garlen looked like he might vomit. He eased his wife off his shoulder. "The boys will help me bury him, won't you?"

Tony and Webb nodded. "Sure, Mr. Garlen."

"You girls take my wife back to the car."

"No, dear, I'm staying here," she said. "The girls can go home if they want."

Maggie and Dixie didn't reply. They stood rooted in place like two more trees witnessing the final act of a gruesome play.

The three guys took turns with the shovel, digging a grave about twelve feet away at the edge of the clearing, where the trees formed an irregular circle around the boulder, and the ground was soft from the recent rain. Digging was easy except for the tree roots, but Webb chopped through them with the tip of the shovel and dug with fury.

Moving the dog proved a bit more difficult. In the end, Mr. Garlen took him by the front legs, and the boys took him by the back legs. Together they swung him step by step to the grave, then dropped him into the shallow hole with a soft thud. Mr. Garlen scooped up the entrails with the shovel and dumped them in alongside.

They worked silently, unnerved by the sight of the dog, each lost in thoughts about what maniac could have done such a deed, and why. Maggie tried to keep her eyes averted from the dog's torn body, but it was like a magnet, pulling at her.

Webb hacked at a root, then paused to lean on the shovel. Even the birds normally twittering in the trees had fled. Only the buzz of flies and bees droned over the carcass.

Maggie held her breath, feeling the somber weight of death like a presence.

In the pause, the sound of a branch snapping brought them all to attention. The same question flitted across every face. *Who is that?*

They all listened intently. At first, nothing. But then leaves rustled again as footfalls approached from farther up the hill, toward Pinewood Road. The girls took two steps closer to the Garlens. The boys stood helplessly looking at each other.

"Did you boys tell anyone else what happened?" Mr. Garlen asked.

Tony shook his head and stared into the trees.

The shuffling noise advanced toward them. Slow, careful steps. A crunch, then a pause. Another rustle, and a pause.

"I bet it's the creep that killed Smokey," Webb hissed.

"What should we do?" Tony asked.

Mr. Garlen took the shovel from Webb and raised it into the air like a baseball bat. "I'm going to bash him over the head."

Mrs. Garlen grabbed at his arm. "No, dear. It's probably just another dog or something. Put that shovel down before someone gets hurt."

Mr. Garlen shook her off and braced himself.

Maggie and Dixie clutched at each other's hands and backed away from the sound, into the shadows surrounding the clearing.

They could see him, the dark figure of a man emerging from between the trees.

Mr. Garlen took a step toward him and motioned the boys to get behind him. "Who's there?"

The figure stepped into the clearing. "It's me, Clark Dweller."

Mrs. Garlen stepped forward. "Clark? What're you doing here?"

"I took the boys home, then decided to walk back down here. There's a narrow path from our house that the boys use when they're working on their clubhouse. That's how they came upon the dog earlier. I got to thinking about it. I think we ought to call the police."

Mr. Garlen lowered the shovel and leaned on it, his face ashen. "The police? About a dog?"

"Yes." Mr. Dweller's gaze moved from the bloody boulder to the hole in the ground. "He was laid out here like some kind of sacrifice."

Dixie tried to take a step forward, but Maggie held her back. "No," she hissed. "Stay here."

Mr. Dweller heard her. His sights settled on the girls for a moment before turning back to Mr. Garlen. "Whoever did this might have something worse in mind. This is like a calling card, a warning, or a plea for help."

Mr. Garlen's furrowed expression said he thought Mr. Dweller was nuts. "Sure, I'm going to call the police and report that my dog was killed and they'll come rushing out here."

"Like in the movies," Mr. Dweller said. He pointed to the dead dog. "You know, the murderer leaves a warning because he really wants to get caught, to get help."

Mrs. Garlen pulled a tissue from somewhere up her sleeve and mopped the tears from her face.

"Well, it's a bit late now. We've all but finished burying him."

"I brought my cell phone. Call."

Maggie watched the two men, their faces turning red with tension.

"You call if you think it's so important."

"It can't be me," Mr. Dweller insisted. "It has to come from you."

Mr. Garlen sighed and took the phone. After a moment, he spoke. "Look, my dog was killed, laid out on this big rock in the woods and cut open. I just thought somebody ought to know in case it's some wacko doing this in other neighborhoods too."

A pause.

"There's nothing to see now. I've just buried him."

A pause.

"Hillside Road," he said, then rattled off his name and address.

A pause.

"Sure. Bye." He handed the phone back to Mr. Dweller like a sharpshooter returning a gun. "Satisfied?" Then he turned to the boys. "Let's finish up." He began shoveling dirt on top of the dog while Mrs. Garlen's sobs rose louder and louder.

Maggie stepped forward, put her arm around Mrs. Garlen, and led her back down the path toward the car. When she turned to make sure Dixie was following, she noticed Mr. Dweller's attention directed at Tony.

"Tony," she yelled, "when you get done, go get Billy and both of you come home. We need to talk to Dad."

For once, he didn't argue.

Maggie was in the family room explaining it all to her father when Tony got home. Billy wasn't with him.

She tensed. "Where's Billy?"

"Mrs. Dweller said they were all playing a game and that Billy was fine. She said she was running out to the store to get their favorite foods to take their minds off Smokey, and she would bring him home after they ate."

Maggie glared at him. She wanted her little brother here, with her. She needed to hold him and talk to him about what happened. She headed toward the door. "I'm going to get him."

"Leave him, Mags," her father said. "He's fine. He's better off playing with Brad right now than moping here with us, thinking about Smokey."

Maggie bit back the snappish comment she had for Tony and marched off to the kitchen. She would make the chocolate cake she had originally planned for Sunday and then call him home.

After the cake came out of the oven, she took her father's car to pick Billy up. He dragged himself out to the car, sullen and quiet.

"I wish you hadn't seen Smokey like that," Maggie said. "It's a horrible thing that happened."

Billy didn't respond. He stared out the window.

"I made chocolate cake for you."

"I'm not hungry. I want to go to bed."

Maggie pulled into the driveway, parked the car, and turned to feel his forehead. "You don't have a fever."

"I'm just tired."

"What happened up there at the Dwellers'?"

"Nothing. We played a game and talked."

"About what?"

He frowned. "Just junk."

"Tell me, Billy."

"You know, stuff like he does in Sunday school, about how God expects us to love each other to help us get through bad stuff like Smokey."

Maggie tried to find fault in that, but couldn't. "God didn't want Smokey to get killed, you know. Even the sparrow that falls from the sky . . ."

He sighed. "I know." He reached for the door handle. "Can I go to bed now?"

"It's not even suppertime yet," Maggie said, realizing she hadn't even eaten lunch.

"I'm tired. I don't feel like eating. Not after . . ."

Maggie felt her heart breaking. Why had Mr. Dweller been the one to talk him through this instead of her? "Sure. Go to bed."

Dixie phoned an hour later. She said the news had spread around the neighborhood within hours. Webb had marked the grave with a big rock so that all the kids who used to frolic with Smokey could say their good-byes, but none were likely to visit his grave anytime soon; the woods had become off limits for almost every kid in the neighborhood, and pets had all been called indoors.

Andrea joined them for church on Sunday and announced she planned to make a big Sunday dinner afterward, so Maggie jumped at the chance to have lunch with the Chamberses when Dixie arrived to invite her. They took off up the hill together.

Mr. Smith pulled up beside them, rolled his window down, and peered at them with a thin-lipped, beady-eyed expression of mistrust and accusation. "Did you girls hear about that dog?"

Maggie shivered, though she wasn't sure if it was from the mention of Smokey or Mr. Smith's malicious tone, so patronizing, with his slicked back hair and his oh-so-neat button down, this time pale yellow instead of pink.

"Yes sir," she said. "My brother was the one who found him."

He stared off toward the woods. "My cat is still missing." He looked back at them, his eyes shifting from one girl's face to the other. "Have either of you seen her?"

"No sir," Maggie replied, tentative enough about his obvious anger not to say the cat had been coming to her door recently. "Not since last week, but we'll keep an eye out."

He frowned, making his thin lips practically disappear. "You know what she looks like. I've seen you talking to her."

"Yes sir, Mr. Smith. She's beautiful. What's her name?"

"Cleopatra."

Maggie nodded. Maybe he wasn't angry. Just worried. She would be too, after what happened to Smokey. "Queen of the Nile. That suits her. She moves like a queen, all regal-like."

He nodded. "That's her. My beauty." He eyed Dixie up and down like he had Maggie, then rolled up the window and drove away.

Dixie made a face, her tongue stuck out and her nose wrinkled up. "What a creep. He wears his hair like somebody from the fifties or something. And that nose. It's as big as a house. Yuck."

Maggie linked her arm through Dixie's and pulled her back to a walk. "You shouldn't judge somebody by appearances," she said, even though she'd been thinking along the same lines. "Look how people at school have judged me all these years because of my ugly hair."

"You don't have ugly hair."

"Right. Want to try it on for a day?"

"Funny."

"I was being serious."

"I wonder where his cat is."

Maggie hadn't seen the cat since she fed her tuna the day the washing machine was delivered, and that had been a week ago. Who had she seen in the neighborhood since then? The bearded man. "Do you know anyone in the neighborhood with a green Cadillac?"

"What?"

Dumb question to ask Dixie. She probably didn't know what kind of car her own mother drove. "You don't suppose whoever got Smokey got Cleopatra too, do you?"

"I'd say that's what he's worried about."

"I would be too," Maggie said. "If I had a pet, I wouldn't let it out of my sight."

"Let me loan you a couple of noisy parakeets that constantly knock seeds all over the floor and see what you'd think about opening the cage and letting them out of sight for good."

Maggie swatted her and laughed. "You don't mean that."

"Sure. 'Freebird' has become Mama's favorite song lately."

"You're a riot."

"And you're a carrot," Dixie said as she took off at a run, out of Maggie's reach. "A carrot-head anyway!"

Maggie chased her, laughing all the way.

At the top of the hill, they paused, their laughter changing to gasps for air from their run. Maggie pushed playfully at Dixie, but stopped when she saw Mr. Smith's car ahead of them. He had turned left on Pinewood, away from Webb's and Dixie's houses, his car barely moving, the taillights burning red as he touched the brakes to peruse the area. They watched him yell out the window to Brad, who shook his head and went back to kicking his ball, as Mr. Smith continued to roll slowly along the road in his car, away from all of them. At the far end of Pinewood, he stopped to speak to Sue, probably on her way to Webb's house. Maggie sneered as Sue tossed her silky hair over one shoulder with a snooty air.

A sheriff's car pulled into sight, paused while the driver looked at Mr. Smith and Sue, then headed toward the girls.

"He must be going to talk to the Garlens," Maggie said. She nudged Dixie, and they hurried away in the opposite direction, toward Dixie's house.

Dixie glanced back at Mr. Smith again. "Maybe you're right. It's not his fault he's ugly. I guess I do kinda feel sorry for him. No family. Just a cat. He can't find her, and there's Smokey mutilated in the woods."

Mutilated, thought Maggie. *What a horrible word.*

Chapter
Ten

THURSDAY WAS BILLY'S soccer game, and this week was Maggie's turn to run the concession stand alongside Miss Irma. Maggie would rather have run it with another teenager, but Emily Jackson had been making up the schedule for as long as anyone could remember, and once she sent it out, it was set in stone. A body better not miss her scheduled concession duty for anything less than a trip to the emergency room. Legend said that some mother years ago didn't show up on her day, and when Emily Jackson heard that the lady was absent, she marched into the hospital, wanting to know how long it took to get a dozen stitches in a hand that needed to be back over at the soccer field.

Miss Irma was the grandma of Maggie's church, a thin, white-haired lady who stood as erect as a flagpole and ran the church kitchen on Wednesday nights like a drill sergeant. She barked out orders, but the results were worth it at those dinners. Maggie's favorite was Miss Irma's famous spaghetti, covered in sauce so thick you needed a fork to eat it, with homemade muffins served on the side.

Running the concession stand was nothing complicated like a church dinner. They only had hot dogs, chips, candy, and soft drinks in plastic bottles, all Pepsi products because one of the coaches worked for Pepsi. Nevertheless, the modest fare didn't diminish Miss Irma's penchant for efficiency, so Maggie steeled herself for three hours of being bossed around, while games from five different grades were played out on the stretch of three fields. The closest field was divided into pint-sized areas for the youngest players, who really didn't have a grasp of what the game was about and spent their short, thirty-minute play time just trying to get one kick at the ball.

Tony and Webb showed up in the first half hour to buy three hot dogs each. Maggie had warned Tony that they were eating at the game because there was no way she was cooking hot dogs all evening and then going home to cook something else.

"Thanks, Mags," Webb said as she handed him the stack of hot dogs and a Mountain Dew.

"Thanks, Miss Irma," Tony echoed, even though Miss Irma hadn't done a thing but hand him three packets of mustard. Maggie figured it would've killed him to actually say thank you to her.

She watched as they moved back into the crowd. She didn't see Sue anywhere, but that didn't mean much. Even without Sue there, Webb hadn't looked at her with any sort of interest except in regard to the hot dogs she was doling out. She may as well have been as white-haired and wrinkled as Miss Irma for all the attention he paid her. There had to be something she could do to get him to look at her as more than Tony's sister. She just had to figure out what.

Dixie stopped by with her little sister for a pack of Skittles and water. "She's getting ready to play," said Dixie. "I'll come back and talk later." Dixie had played soccer every year from kindergarten through eighth grade and was determined to make Cindy a top soccer player, which seemed contrary to the little girl's personality in Maggie's opinion. She expected prissy little Cindy to fall more into Sue's league, becoming a cheerleader and standing on the sidelines talking about hairstyles. She wondered why Dixie didn't see that about her.

In the distance, she saw her father and Andrea cross the parking lot and skirt around the first field to reach the second one, where Billy's game would start shortly. Billy ran ahead to join his teammates, while her father and Andrea climbed up the small set of bleachers as if they'd been coming to games together since Billy's first one five years earlier. Maggie watched them with concentration, thinking of how Andrea had joined them for church on Sunday, then spent the afternoon rearranging everything in the china hutch, removing all the school projects they'd had on display since the beginning of time and replacing them with a set of dishes she said she found on sale: bright yellow stoneware with blue flowers in the center. The entire room had looked different by the time Maggie got home from Dixie's house. On Tuesday, Andrea had gone walking with Maggie's father again and brought two new lamps with her, and a set of soft, fuzzy blue pillows for the sofa, saying the room needed a woman's touch. Maggie imagined that next she would be picking them up from school and doing the grocery shopping too. She needed to read that article in Dixie's magazine to see what other girls did in these situations.

She didn't hear Mr. Dweller approach and speak.

"Maggie," Miss Irma said, touching her shoulder to get her attention, "wake up. Clark Dweller is speaking to you."

There he was, standing at her elbow with only the counter full of assorted candies between them.

"I was asking about the washing machine," he explained. "I didn't think to ask about it the other day, what with all that happened. I hear it's a nice one."

Maggie couldn't imagine Billy starting such a topic on his own. *Hey, Mr. Dweller, you ought to see the new washer. It's a beauty.*

"It's a washing machine. That's about all I can say for it."

Mr. Dweller paid for twelve packets of candy — no doubt for his team after the game — and jogged back out to the field.

She wasn't sure which irritated her more — Mr. Dweller talking to her or Andrea stepping into another facet of their lives — but when Miss Irma saw the growl creasing her face and asked what was wrong, Maggie funneled all the emotions into her dislike for Mr. Dweller. "Why would he come ask me that?"

"Ask you what?"

"About the washing machine I bought last week."

"You bought a washer? All by yourself?"

"It really wasn't all that remarkable. I went to a store, picked it out, they delivered it. Big deal."

"An appliance like that is something you'll have around for the next fifteen or twenty years. Imagine a young girl like you taking on such a responsibility."

Fifteen or twenty years? Her entire lifetime all over again. She hadn't thought of it with such significance, such permanence.

Miss Irma continued, "Leave it to Clark Dweller to comment on it. I never did see a person for keeping tabs on the heartbeat of a congregation like he does ours. Sometimes I think he missed his calling and ought to have been a pastor, but then who would coach soccer and help with the youth program?"

Maggie wasn't to be deterred from her distaste. "I think he's nosey, always in people's business."

"Maggie, hush that talk. I never met a more godly man."

At her words, they both looked out over the fields to see him swoop Dakota Manxmen into a hug, twirl her around, and plant a kiss on her soft, sweaty cheek for making a goal.

"You see there, Maggie? He's one who celebrates life, especially where children are involved. A person could do a lot worse than to imitate him. He loves everyone, and everyone loves him right back."

Maggie sighed and decided she was the one with the problem.

Chapter
Eleven

CLEOPATRA THE CAT showed up on the doorstep again Friday afternoon. Maggie had been in the backyard with Billy, practicing soccer for an hour before cutting through the house to get a glass of water. She carried it to the front porch so she could sit in the rocker and enjoy the breeze, but when she opened the front door, there was the cat, meowing and rubbing herself up against the door as if it were Maggie's legs. The cat's coat looked even duller than the last time, as if she'd been living in ditches.

She set her glass on the railing and squatted down. "You poor thing. I think something has totally messed up your sense of direction, but your owner is going to be excited to know you're back."

She scooped Cleopatra into her arms and started up the road to Mr. Smith's house. "I can't feed you again, or you'll keep coming back expecting more." She rubbed the cat's head as they walked along. "I'm sure your owner will feed you, girl. He's been worried about you."

As she passed the Garlens' house, just before the turn to Mr. Smith's, Cleopatra arched her back, clawed her way up Maggie's shoulder, and jumped from her arms to go dashing off in the opposite direction.

Maggie grabbed her side. Pricks of pain stabbed at her where the cat's claws had torn her flesh through the T-shirt. "Crazy cat," she muttered. She stood a minute debating whether she ought to tell Mr. Smith that she'd found Cleopatra, but she thought of his stern face and imagined him accusing her of purposely not holding on tightly enough to get the cat home.

She turned and headed back home, wondering if perhaps Cleopatra had a litter of kittens somewhere, and that's what had made her run off.

On Saturday morning, knowing Andrea was sure to show up, Maggie took special care with the cleaning and scrubbed everything twice as thoroughly, just to make sure she couldn't find fault with anything about the house. Maggie wouldn't give her room to make some snide comment about her housekeeping, not that she would stick around to give her the opportunity. She avoided Andrea at every turn. Unfortunately, it also meant seeing little of her father, but in Maggie's opinion that was his fault, not hers.

Angry thoughts of Andrea and her father fed her work until she got to Billy's room to pick up the dirty clothes strewn across his floor. As soon as she entered, she gagged at the smell. Ammonia. She thrust open the bedroom window to air out the room, then flipped the blankets back on his bed to reveal the telltale patch of yellow on his sheets.

"He hasn't done that since he was five," she said to herself. She thought of calling out to him, but changed her mind. It probably had something to do with the nightmares he'd been having the past week. She'd heard him tossing and turning in bed, moaning as he dreamed, but when she asked him about it, he frowned and walked away, so she decided she would wait until he was ready to talk about it. No doubt he couldn't get the image of Smokey out of his head. She'd had a couple nightmares herself.

She peeled off the sheets and mattress cover to add to the laundry basket, and headed downstairs.

As soon as she finished the housework, she ran next door to the Grahams' house to baby-sit Kimberly for the afternoon while Mrs. Graham went shopping with a girlfriend. Maggie was glad for the distraction. Dixie had plans to go to Columbia with her mother for the day, to visit an aunt and go shopping. Meanwhile, her father was in the shower getting ready for Andrea to arrive. Maggie had to get out before she got there; she couldn't bear the idea of being home when Andrea arrived with some new piece of her long-term decorating scheme. Tony was up at Webb's house, as usual. Billy was at the Garlens' house playing with their grandson, Mark, who was visiting for the weekend. Maggie hadn't argued when he accepted the invitation; she was surprised but delighted that he wasn't going to Brad's house — to the point that she probably sounded a bit too cheery about it when Brad called looking for him, and she told him he was with another friend. Besides, she thought being at Smokey's house and especially playing with Mark, a boy who hadn't witnessed the gruesome reality that Billy had, might help him get over the dog's death.

Sunday afternoon, Maggie decided to head up to Dixie's house to see what her friend had bought in Columbia. As she stepped out onto the porch, she paused, hoping to see Cleopatra waiting for her again. The cat wasn't there, but Maggie glanced up in time to see Johnny drive by in the delivery van. She waved, but he didn't see her. He continued by her house, past Kimberly's house, and headed out a back entrance of the neighborhood that few people ever used since it meant weaving through a mishmash of roads to an apartment complex that was still under construction and then through another neighborhood before reaching a main road. She watched him until he was out of sight, wondering who else in her neighborhood might have ordered an appliance, and if they'd bought the same kind of washing machine she had, and how Johnny had managed to maneuver it himself. Or maybe he was installing something in one of the finished units and was cutting through her neighborhood to get there. Odd to think he delivered something on a Sunday.

She sighed. What other teenager thought about washing machines?

She trod up the hill toward Dixie's house, her sneakers almost silent on the pavement. A biplane droned overhead, pulling her attention upward to watch it cut across the crystal blue sky, sailing off to some distant adventure, unfettered by the world below.

The ensuing silence pricked her ears. She paused. Crickets, birds, a shrill little-girl laugh far behind her. She loved weekends and being outside.

She continued until she reached the path into the woods. One week had passed since Smokey's death. She stopped a moment, thinking of him. Leaves rustled. *Squirrels*, she thought as she moved on. Squirrels ought to make her smile. She loved watching squirrels. But something brought her up short again. Another sound she couldn't quite place. An animal? Another step and she heard it again—an unnatural rustling. She held her breath. Again it came, not quite thrashing in the leaves, but not scampering, either.

Her eyes narrowed as she peered into the thicket of brush and trees beyond. No squirrels scampering. No dog sniffing around. No friendly person.

Could it be a cat? Cleopatra, maybe?

For an instant she imagined it to be Smokey, but Smokey was dead forever.

A chill crawled over her skin.

She thought of the bearded stranger. Had he been around that week? Was he homeless and living in the woods?

Her head said, *Run!* But she didn't. She stood still and listened. Whatever it was, it was moving. Was it coming closer? How big was it?

This time the rustle of leaves mingled with a deep, guttural sound. She twisted around in place, debating what to do. No one down the road. No one up ahead. She looked up the hill and wondered if Webb and Tony might be in Webb's front yard.

She turned her eyes toward the path into the woods. A groan.

She stepped onto the path, one foot halting on the springy grass, the next in soft mud. What if it was a trap? A lure?

Smokey was mutilated.

The moan rose again. Misery. Pain.

Human.

She took a few more cautious steps. Why did she have to be the one to hear it? She glanced up the hill toward Webb's house. Five minutes to run up there and back. Another five to see if he was home and explain about a sound in the woods.

The moan fell to a whimper and pulled at her conscience, at her sense of responsibility. She had reached the point where the brush ended and the path began to weave among the trees. She tiptoed into the woods, one hesitant step at a time. As the shade of the trees enveloped her, the cries came more clearly.

She physically and mentally forced herself forward, every muscle tense, poised for escape with each footfall. Birds took flight as she moved through the woods. She knew the direction now. She knew the place — her place. Her thinking rock, where the spot of sunshine broke through the trees, where the trees thinned out and the ground was a bed of leaves as old as the trees. The spot where Smokey had been laid out like a sacrifice.

As she drew closer, she could see a dark shape, the head of a body, on the far side of the rock where the leaves were thickest. She picked up the pace, her steps less hesitant, but her heart pounded more furiously, trying to move carefully, silently, to not crunch leaves on the pathway.

It was undoubtedly a person's head. A woman's, judging from the mass of blonde locks cascading across the leaves. She couldn't see the face yet, only the shape of the head. And the hair . . . fanned out like her mother's red hair had floated across the water, glimpsed from behind her father all those years ago.

Maggie had seen death.

A few steps more, and she could see skin — flesh over nose and cheeks, dark with blood and bruising. The eyes, filled with fear, fixed themselves upon her, focused, and strained with desperation.

Still alive.

Maggie scanned the woods. Whoever did this might not be far off.

What should she do? She couldn't turn back.

A dozen more steps brought her to the rock, to the body. The mouth was sealed with duct tape. The face was swollen with bruises and striped with blood trickling from a gash—disfigured, but not beyond recognition.

It was Sue.

Maggie dropped to the ground beside her, furtively glancing around. Blood oozed from wounds in her chest and stained the torn white blouse. Her skirt was pushed up around her waist, and her panties were gone.

Maggie pulled Sue's skirt back into place and swept a strand of hair off her face, pulling it from the blood that had solidified it to her skin. She pulled at the tape on her mouth, but Sue's eyes sprang wide with pain. *What to do?*

"I have to get it off." She tugged at it, wondering if it would be better to snatch it quickly or ease it off. She held one hand against the exposed flesh, and watched tears well in Sue's eyes as she pulled at the tape. Gently, bit by bit, it finally pulled free.

Sue sucked in a mouthful of air.

"Hang on, Sue. I'll get help," she whispered.

She stood, ready to dash back down the path and up the road to Webb's house, but Sue moaned. Maggie could see the agony and fear seeping from every pore before Sue's eyes rolled back in her head.

Maggie shook her. "Don't die. Wake up. Come on, Sue, stick with me."

Health class. *What did Miss Harper teach us? Assess the victim.* Sue was still breathing, still had a heartbeat. None of the cuts were seeping blood as badly as the wound on her left shoulder, where flies hovered.

Pressure, she thought. *I have to apply pressure to the wound*. She needed something to stop up the wound. Should she pull off her own shirt? Or Sue's skirt?

There on the grass several feet away lay something brightly colored. Material? She scrabbled over the leaves and snatched it up—girl's blue underwear, wet. No good. Something farther out caught her eye—striped, round, lying on top of the leaves.

Maggie squinted at it. Sue's pocketbook. That wouldn't help. Unless there were tissues in it. But what good would that do? The blood would soak right through them.

She grabbed the side of her own T-shirt and pulled at the seam, but it wouldn't tear. Then she remembered the tiny holes that Cleopatra had made when she scrambled out of her arms a few days earlier. Thank heavens for Saturday laundry. Thank heavens she wore the same shirt.

She stuck her finger into one of the holes, pried it larger, then tore the material, splitting the shirt away at her midriff. The last bit didn't want to let go, but she yanked at it desperately until it came loose, leaving her with a long, circular strip of white cloth. She pulled the strip over her head and folded it repeatedly until it formed a thick square she could press to the wound. In seconds, it was soaked through with blood, but she kept up the pressure anyway, hoping it might help.

"Sue, are you still with me? Can you hear me?" *What should I do?* "Dear Lord God in heaven be with me. I don't know what to do. Help me save her."

She looked around again, frantically wondering if she should scream and hope someone in the neighborhood would respond, but worried that whoever did this was still nearby, close enough to hear and come back to finish the job, including killing her. "What to do? What to do?"

She kept pushing down on the rag to keep Sue from losing any more blood, and struggled to figure out a solution. If only she had a cell phone. Why didn't she have a cell phone like every other teenager?

Then it hit her. Sue had a cell phone. She was always jabbering to somebody on it.

Maggie half crawled, half ran to the striped pocketbook and threw the contents hither and yon till she found it—a small, streamlined black phone stuck in its own pocket.

She flipped open the phone and stared at it. Other kids used them every day. Other kids had theirs programmed with friends' numbers, used them for calling about parties or to tell their parents they'd be home a bit late.

She poked at the buttons: 9-1-1.

A voice came on the line. "Nine one one. What's the state of your emergency?"

Maggie's voice broke with fright as she whispered into the phone. "I'm in the woods on Hillside Road. Send an ambulance. Quickly! She's dying."

As she spoke, she rushed back to Sue's side. Her skin looked so white it was almost translucent. Maggie pushed down on the wound again with one hand, keeping the phone clasped to her ear with the other.

"To whom am I speaking?" came the female voice on the other end.

"Maggie McCarthy. The girl is Sue Roberts. She's almost dead. She's been stabbed and raped. Hurry!"

She could hear the clicking of the woman's keyboard and her muffled voice as she talked to someone else.

Every muscle in Maggie's body was taut with fear. Her head felt like it might explode. She could feel the blood rushing through her veins. "Hurry. I'm afraid he's still here. He'll come back for me. Hurry."

Something gurgled in Sue's throat.

"Oh no. I think she stopped breathing."

"Stay calm and don't hang up. Help is on the way."

"I don't know what to do. She's bleeding really badly."

"Does she have a pulse?"

She took Sue's wrist and felt for a pulse, but she couldn't focus. She laid her ear close to Sue's mouth and placed her hand on Sue's chest. If she was still breathing, Maggie couldn't detect it.

"I can't tell!" she hissed into the phone. She tried to concentrate on the wrist in her hand. *Is there a beat there? Or is it my own blood rushing through my fingers?* Then she noticed Sue's fingers. "Her fingertips are turning blue . . . Tell me what to do!"

"She's going into shock. Can you raise her feet and cover her with something?"

"I don't have anything to cover her with. Please, Sue, come on. Come on." *Oh, God, please save her. Help me out here.* "Come on, Sue. Come on!"

She set the phone down and bent her head close to Sue, trying to feel her breath on her cheek. It came, but faintly, intermittently.

"No!" Maggie moaned, afraid to speak aloud, afraid not to. "Don't give up now, Sue. Don't let him win."

She pulled the phone back to her ear. "I think she's still breathing, but just barely. Are they coming? I don't hear them coming."

"Tell me exactly where you are."

She couldn't think. Where was she? What was the main road? Why couldn't she think? She closed her eyes and took a deep breath. "In the Rockwood subdivision off Old Town Road. Hillside Drive."

She opened her eyes. "There's a path into the woods halfway down the hill on the right. They'll see it. Tell them to hurry."

How far away was the rescue squad? Would they come from the fire department out on Old Town Road, or would an ambulance come all the way from the hospital? Maggie didn't think Sue would last that long.

Finally she heard the sirens wailing in the distance, coming closer. The sound filled her with new vigor. They were coming down the road. They were stopping by the path. She could hear them climbing out, calling to her.

She screamed, "We're here! We're here in the woods! Follow the trail!"

Footsteps pounded through the woods. More sirens. More voices. Suddenly she was surrounded.

"What happened here?" asked the first rescue worker.

"I don't know. I heard her moaning and found her here. I think she's been raped."

Two rescue workers edged in front of Maggie and moved into position, one taking vitals and repeating them into a phone, the other sticking a tube down Sue's throat and attaching a bag to it, then sticking electrodes to her chest and connecting them to an instrument.

A young police officer, tall and lean, jogged up to the scene and started taking pictures as the EMTs worked, ignoring the bright flashes.

"Was she conscious when you found her?" asked the larger of the two EMTs as he scrawled down vitals on a clipboard.

"For a minute. But I pulled off the duct tape and put pressure on her wound, and she passed out. Did I kill her? I was trying to help her."

The one taking the vitals put aside his clipboard, stuck a needle into Sue's arm, and started an intravenous drip. "No, you did the right thing. She's in shock."

A second policeman hobbled toward the scene, a noticeable limp slowing him down. "Move back. We've got to get in here. This is a crime scene."

The hefty rescue worker scowled at him. "Get off your high horse, Matthews. She's gonna die if we don't get her to the hospital ASAP, and then it'd be a homicide and get turned over to Stephens. Why didn't they send him anyhow?"

"I've got seniority over Stephens."

"So does my mama, but she ain't here interfering with me saving this girl's life."

Maggie crouched a few feet away, shivering as she marveled over how the men's hands never quit working on Sue. They attached a brace around her neck and head, and on the count of three lifted her onto the gurney.

The younger officer continued taking pictures. Another cop appeared in the clearing, with another right behind. They both halted abruptly to stare at Sue.

"Don't just stand there. Get the area staked off!" Detective Matthews yelled. "Ralphie, sketch out the area and make note of where any personal belongings are."

The first rescue worker spoke into the phone again. "Stabilized and transporting."

Sue was in the ambulance by the time Tony and Webb came running into the woods, gasping when they saw Maggie covered in blood.

Tony stopped in shock, then rushed forward. "What happened? Are you all right?"

Maggie tried to stand, but couldn't. Tears flowed down her cheeks as she spoke in broken syllables. "It's Sue . . . She was raped . . . and stabbed. She's almost dead. Whoever did it is around here somewhere."

A policeman stepped forward. "You boys need to go on home. We have an investigation to conduct here, and we need to question this young lady."

"She's my sister," Tony said.

"Where's Daddy? Where's Billy? Get them, Tony. Get them now."

Webb pulled out his cell phone, dialed, spoke quickly, and snapped the phone shut.

"We're going to have to take you in to fill out some paperwork," the officer said.

She stared at him, wide-eyed and pale. "No. It wasn't me. I'm not a criminal."

"We just need a statement about what happened. The details. We have to know exactly how everything looked when you arrived, what you touched, that sort of thing. You may have disturbed evidence."

"I wasn't worried about evidence. I was trying to save her life."

"I understand that, but we still need to know all the details."

Maggie felt like a cat surrounded by growling dogs. No one was hearing her. Her voice rose a notch as she pointed. "I—I didn't move her. She was lying right there."

"Calm down, Mags," said Tony. "That's Asby Jones's uncle. He's just asking you a question."

Webb stepped in front of Tony and touched her shoulder. "Don't answer anything else till your dad gets here. You might need a lawyer."

"For saving Sue's life? That's nuts."

More people arrived on the scene: a cameraman lugging a huge camera and some other guy carrying a microphone and light. A pretty brunette woman in high heels was picking her way over tree roots.

Behind them came her father, pushing between the cameraman and the female reporter to reach her side. "Mags! Are you all right?"

She nodded. On some level, she felt like she was supposed to rush into his arms and hide her face, but, instead, she felt stronger than that. Even as he stepped toward her, pulled her up, and took her into his arms, rubbing her back and kissing the top of her head, she felt she had to remain in control of the situation so it couldn't control her and strip her down to bare nerves. She moved away from him and folded her arms across her chest as she stood tall. "It was Sue. Someone attacked her."

Other people arrived—neighbors gawking at the scene and at her. Most were stunned. But then she caught sight of Mr. Dweller, with Brad in tow, evaluating the area like he had when they found Smokey.

Policemen started shooing them away. "Folks, we have work to do here. You're going to have to leave the area."

Without warning, the television camera was aimed at Maggie, shooting her and the surroundings, and then the woman was in her face. "Are you the one who found the victim?"

Maggie nodded.

The reporter turned to Maggie's father, ignoring Webb and Tony, who were still standing there as if they didn't know what to do with themselves. "Do we have your permission to ask her a few questions?"

He looked to Maggie with raised eyebrows, then back at the lady. "Yes, if she wants to talk to you and you don't get too personal."

The reporter gave the cameraman a moment to adjust his equipment before she stepped up with the microphone. "A sixteen-year-old female was found less than an hour ago in these woods in Rockwood subdivision—raped, stabbed, and left for dead. Rescue workers say that if she lives, it's because of the efforts of this teenage girl." She turned to Maggie. "How did you know the girl was back here?"

Maggie felt like the question came from far away, and she answered it with detachment, as if she were watching a rerun in her mind and hadn't really experienced it all firsthand. "I heard her moaning."

"Tell us what happened."

Maggie thought of every hesitant footstep and every startling sound along the way. She thought of Sue's eyes, her bruises and cuts, her disheveled figure. But she wouldn't say any of that. "I was walking up the road and, like I said, heard a noise, so I came down the path and found her here."

"Did you see anyone else?"

"No."

The interview went on for several minutes, asking what measures Maggie took to save Sue.

"We're speaking to this very heroic young lady. . . ." The reporter continued recapping the situation as the camera zoomed in on her, releasing Maggie to search out her father, now fifty feet away, talking to Detective Matthews.

Webb intercepted her, his face twisted with anxiety. "Are you sure she was raped?"

Was he asking out of curiosity? Out of love for her? Or maybe because it disgusted him. It didn't matter; he had to know the truth.

Maggie wouldn't sugarcoat it, not even for Webb, whatever his reaction. She pointed to where the policemen were searching the ground. "Her underpants are over there."

The color drained from his face. He looked at Tony. "We've gotta get to the hospital."

Maggie's father approached with the detective and took Maggie's hand gently in his. "Maggie, they're going to take us with them to the hospital. You need to give them a statement."

"I want to come along," Webb said.

Detective Matthews eyed him up and down.

"I'm her boyfriend."

"We'll need to talk to you too. Let's go."

"How about her parents?" Maggie asked. "Has anyone told them?"

"A law enforcement chaplain has been dispatched to their house. They'll meet us at the hospital."

Maggie led the way down the path. Her father laid his arm across Tony's shoulders. "You go to the Garlens', get Billy, and take him home. I'll call you when we know more."

At the hospital, the detectives led her and her father to the Quiet Room, a meeting room where they could talk privately.

Maggie was barely seated when Andrea walked in. She turned to her father, but he looked just as surprised.

He stepped forward and pulled out a seat for Andrea. "How did you know?"

"They called me."

They? Who? Why would anyone have called Andrea? Who even knew she had anything to do with their family?

Maggie opened her mouth to demand an answer, but then closed it when she saw relief ease her father's frown. She couldn't let him get whacked out over this. Better to handle it herself.

Andrea reached her hand across the table. "They're going to ask you about the crime scene and exactly what all you touched and what you did when you found her. Just answer the questions with complete honesty. It will help them solve the crime and know better what happened to the victim."

Maggie sighed.

Andrea asked, "Do you know her?"

"Yes. Her name is Sue. She lives in the neighborhood."

The detective picked up from there and carried the discussion. Andrea took notes, as if she somehow had authority, writing down every detail of what Maggie said.

"She was still conscious when you found her?"

"For a few minutes, yes."

"Did she speak?"

"No. She had duct tape across her mouth. I pulled it off, and she passed out."

"Continue," he said.

When Maggie and her father returned home hours later, she had to face her brothers.

Billy jumped up from the sofa and ran to her side. "Tell us what happened."

She couldn't bear to go through it all again. "Daddy will tell you."

"Is Sue okay?" asked Tony.

Maggie started up the stairs. "She's in critical condition. She has some head injury, and she's unconscious. They'll know more tomorrow."

"How did you find her?" Billy asked.

"I heard her. Look guys, I can't do this again. I have to go to bed. I'm exhausted."

"C'mon, boys," her father said, waving them back to the sofa. "I'll tell you. Let Maggie alone."

Tony spoke again as she reached the top of the stairs. "We saw you on the news."

The news. She'd forgotten. She supposed that was a big deal, but it meant nothing right then. She just wanted to forget about all of it. She wanted to empty her brain of all the images, and sleep.

It was hours before the house settled into the quiet of slumber. Maggie lay awake in bed. She couldn't shake the feeling of being full of knots, knots tying up her veins and throbbing in her head. Every time she closed her eyes, she saw Sue again, the tears in her eyes, the gash on her face, the blood oozing from her shoulder. She kept thinking of how lifeless Sue looked when they took her away.

In the quiet of the house, Maggie heard the ping of pipes and the creak of the house settling, but they were no longer safe sounds; they were men hiding in the walls and peeking in the windows. She turned on her light and looked under her bed and in the closet, knowing there was no one there but needing to reassure herself.

Taking out her diary, she wrote down every gruesome detail, not to save it to read later, but to empty it from her mind onto the page. It didn't work.

She read a few pages of *Wuthering Heights*, but the moor winds turned into Sue's moans and kept her from concentrating on the thread of the story.

She ached to be smoothed out and made whole again, her present self washed away into nothingness, leaving her new, cleansed, free.

In the end, she closed her eyes and prayed, not just for herself or Sue, but also for every person she could call to mind, until she reached another place in her mind and fell into a fitful sleep, unaware of how much the tragedy would impact her life.

Chapter
Twelve

REALITY CAME FLOODING back with the early morning light. Dark bags hung under her eyes. She pulled her hair into a ponytail without even brushing it and put on the baggiest shirt she could find. She wanted to hide away from the world, and the best way she knew to do that was to ignore herself and hope everyone else would do the same.

Andrea was there, dressed for work and having breakfast with her brothers and father. "I brought fruit and bagels, Maggie. Would you like some?"

Maggie shook her head and headed for the cereal.

Her father reached out and caught her as she passed his seat. "Fruit would be better for you today, really."

She sighed as she dropped into her seat and pulled a clump of grapes to her place mat, trying to imagine Tony making it past first period without being hungry with only fruit in his stomach. He didn't say anything, though. He ate a bagel, drank some juice, and at the sound of a horn out front, headed out the door with Billy in tow. Their father pushed his chair back and carried their dishes to the sink.

Maggie's head was in a foggy daze. "Who's that picking up the boys?"

Her father bent down and kissed her cheek on his way by. "Webb's mother. She's taking them this morning. I'll pick all of you up this afternoon."

"Who's taking me? I'm not ready to go."

"Andrea. She's going to help you with the interview and take you to school later on."

"What interview?"

"The investigator wants to talk to you again," Andrea said. Her voice was quieter than usual, soothing. "We have to meet him down at the police station."

Her father looked unsure of himself. "Do you want me to go with you?"

Maggie pressed her lips together and envisioned a reenactment of the last round of questioning. She would have to describe it all again, as much as she could remember. She knew her father didn't want to hear it and connect it to his daughter.

She shook her head. "No, Daddy, go on to work. I can handle it."

He kissed her on the cheek again and pulled her up into a hug. "You'll be in my prayers all day, Mags. I'm sorry you have to go through this." He leaned back so he could look into her eyes. "I love you, you know."

"I know, Daddy. I love you too." She leaned into him, wanting to absorb everything she could from him, to keep him with her all day long like a shadow with protective powers.

He kissed the top of her head. "Okay, Mags, I have to go. I'll pick you up by the flagpole this afternoon. Your brothers and Webb will meet you there."

Andrea rose to escort him to the door, but she paused in the kitchen doorway. "Why don't you take a few minutes to collect yourself? Change your shirt, brush your hair, and gather your thoughts."

Maggie didn't move. Andrea had no right to barge in and tell her to change clothes again.

She had no right, either, to walk her father to the door and kiss him good-bye as he left for work. Maggie listened to them talking at the door.

"I'm taking her out for a while after the interview, Frank."

"Where?"

"Trust me on this. It's my job, you know."

"I know. I'll leave you to it."

Maggie gritted her teeth. Taking care of her was most definitely not Andrea's job. When she returned, Maggie was still seated at the table methodically shoving grapes into her mouth.

They sized each other up for a moment before Maggie spoke. "I wasn't going to start another ruckus in front of my father, but let's get one thing straight. I've said it before, and I'll say it again: You're not my mother. You will never be my mother. Taking care of me isn't and never will be your *job*."

Andrea laughed. "Let's get you changed."

"Don't tell me what to do."

Andrea stopped at the door. "Does everything have to be this difficult with you? Does that red hair go soul deep or what?"

"You said I'm your *job*. I'm not. I'm not anything to do with you. You can date my father, if that's what he wants, but you are so *not* in control of me and never will be."

Andrea slung the door open. "I didn't mean *you* were my job. I assume Frank hasn't told you what I do for a living?"

Maggie couldn't resist the chance for a stab. "He never said a word about you until you showed up with him for dinner. Not even the mention of your name."

"Well, I run the abuse center for women. I handle cases of abuse and rape every day. I know what you're going through."

"Really? And what might that be?"

"We'll talk about it later. Right now we have some shopping to do. Let's get you changed. We have to leave in a few minutes."

"Will you quit with the clothes? This is how I dress, see? How do you want me to dress? Like Sue? Put on belly shirts and hip-huggers so some weirdo can't take his eyes off me? So I'll be irresistible to some guy, and I can be raped too?"

Andrea sat down and leaned forward on the table. "Let's get something straight here. It was not Sue's fault she got raped. She didn't do anything wrong. It wouldn't matter if she were wearing a bikini while walking down the road. That man had no right to rape her, no matter what she was wearing. Do you understand that? He had no right. It's her body. No one should ever touch your body without your permission, even if you're wearing a miniskirt or have a pierced bellybutton or whatever. None of that matters." Her face was red with exertion.

Maggie stopped eating and stared at her plate. She didn't want to listen, but Andrea's words were hard to ignore.

Andrea leaned back in her chair. "Let me back up and say that I don't think the Lord wants girls prancing around half naked. I don't think it's right to flaunt yourself and give anyone the impression that you're a floozy, okay? You understand that? And I'm not saying I think you ought to dress like that. But how you dress, or how you walk, or dance, or whatever—none of that gives a man the right to molest you or rape you. He is in command of his own body, and he has to control his urges. God has given him that free will, and like all temptation, he has to resist.

"On the other hand, you can certainly dress nicely and complement your features without offending God. He made you beautiful. Your body is a temple of God, and it should be adorned as such, not dressed in nasty old T-shirts to keep anyone from noticing it."

Maggie pulled away. "I'm comfortable this way."

"You can't hide inside baggy clothes. It doesn't work. Sue's clothes are not what made that man attack her. And dressing that way won't protect you. It just makes you ugly."

Maggie trembled as the color drained from her face. She couldn't believe Andrea had called her ugly. She knew she was ugly. She felt ugly all the way to her bones, but she didn't need Andrea saying it to her.

"I didn't mean that the way it sounded. I don't mean you're ugly. It's your clothes. You'd be so pretty if you dressed better. And I understand your need to hide right now, but this isn't going to help. You need to feel good about yourself, and the right clothes always help improve your self-image."

Maggie popped a couple more grapes into her mouth.

"You don't have anything else, do you?"

"Of course I do."

"Show me."

Maggie pushed her chair back, anger building from the stress and the lecture, making her determined to prove herself equal to Andrea. She ran out the kitchen door and fled upstairs with Andrea a step behind, straight to her dresser. She pulled out the shirt Dixie had given her for her birthday and flung it on the bed. "There, see? It's not a T-shirt."

"Pretty. Try it on for me."

Maggie turned her back to Andrea, pulled the T-shirt off, and pulled the green shirt over her head. She hung her head as she turned around.

"I love it. Beautiful color on you."

"It shows too much cleavage."

Andrea laughed. "Dolly Parton has cleavage. You have a shirt with a pretty V neckline."

Maggie looked at herself in the mirror. "But it shows—"

"It shows God did a wonderful job when he made you, and it's not even flirtatious, let alone slutty-looking, if that's what you're worried about. Let's go."

Maggie pulled it off and tossed it into the wastebasket, then pulled her T-shirt back on. "No. I won't wear it."

"Maggie—"

"Sue had one just like it."

"Oh, Maggie." Andrea moved to her side and pulled her into her arms. "I promise you, it's all right. I'll take you shopping myself. We'll find something you like that isn't a T-shirt. But right now the detective is waiting. We'll worry about it afterward."

The questions were slightly different this time around, as if the police were trying to find holes in what she said the previous day. She had to go over everything that happened several times, every detail. Had she seen anyone in the woods? Seen anything unusual? Heard any strange noises? Then they wanted to know how well she knew Sue. Who she hung around with. How well she knew Webb.

She knew where they were going with that. "I've known Webb all my life. He's not responsible for what happened. He was with my brother playing video games. That's what they do every day."

"What kind of games?"

"I don't know. I don't play them. Car races I think."

Andrea mentioned the deliverymen. "They delivered a washing machine a couple weeks ago."

"And why would they be suspects?" he wanted to know.

"Because Maggie was alone at the house when they came, and they may have come back on their off-time to see if they could catch her alone again."

The detective wrote something in his notes.

Maggie thought of the way Johnny had blocked her in, of his breath hot on her face. "Johnny and Diego. Those were their names." She thought of Johnny's sister and felt a pang of guilt for mentioning him as a suspect; but if she closed her eyes, she would remember Sue's damaged body lying in the woods, and nothing mattered more than that.

"Got friendly with them, did you?"

"They had name tags on their shirts. It could be them. I saw Johnny drive by in the delivery truck right before I found Sue. He was heading out the back entrance of the neighborhood."

"We'll check their delivery schedule," he said as he scrawled notes.

"But I don't think they had anything to do with Smokey."

"Who's Smokey?"

Maggie described how they'd found Smokey in the same spot. "The two have to be connected, don't you think?"

He nodded as he wrote. "Interesting. We'll have to investigate that further. They may or may not be related."

Her mind whirled, thinking of who else might be a suspect. *The bearded man!* "There's also this other guy I've seen hanging around the neighborhood. Not young, but not really old. Middle-aged, I guess, except I've never gotten a good look at him. He has a black beard and he wears a ball cap." She told him where and when she'd seen the stranger. "He might drive an old green Cadillac, because I've seen one of those a couple times."

The detective scrawled notes another minute before he finally stopped and looked up at her. "Anything else?"

She wanted to mention Mr. Dweller. Everything in her screamed it, but they would all look at her like she was nuts. There was nothing to implicate him. *I think it was Mr. Dweller. Why? Well, because he likes my brother too much, and I think he's creepy.* They would say the whole thing had messed her up, and they'd put her in therapy for two years.

"No, that's it." She looked at her watch. "I'm late for school, you know."

Andrea patted her leg. "It's okay. Your father already called in and told them what's going on. They saw it on the news, you know."

She hadn't thought about her classmates seeing it on the news. Everyone at school would know about Sue. Everyone would know Maggie was the one who found her. Everyone . . . "The guy who did this — what if he saw me on television?"

"You didn't see him," Andrea replied. "He has nothing to gain by coming after you."

"He didn't have anything to gain by going after Sue, either."

"If it was a stranger, he probably had it planned out. He put his sights on her and worked himself up to doing this. If it was someone she knew, it's a totally different ball game, a date gone wrong, and has nothing to do with you."

Andrea's words didn't reassure her. She felt vulnerable.

"Don't worry, Maggie. We're not leaving you alone. Someone will be with you around the clock. We're not going straight to school, either." Andrea slung her pocketbook over her shoulder and turned to the officer. "If you're done, we'll be going."

He nodded.

Maggie followed her out. "Where are we going?"

"The mall."

"The mall doesn't open for another hour."

Andrea glanced at her watch. "Right you are. Well, the salon is open. We might as well start there."

"The beauty parlor?"

"Sure. Nothing like a new hairstyle and a makeover to make a shopping spree even more delightful."

She flipped open her cell phone and punched the numbers. "Sylvie? Andrea. I'm with a client. You okay with handling everything at the shelter this morning?"

A short babble ensued as Andrea unlocked the car and the two of them buckled up.

"Great. No interruptions. I'll see you after lunch." She snapped the phone shut. "That gives us plenty of time."

"I'm not the spa and clothes type. I don't want to do this."

"I know. You're thinking the last thing you want to do right now is draw attention to yourself, but the truth is you're going to be the main attraction at school right now no matter what you do, so you may as well look good."

"I don't think there's anything wrong with the way I look." It was a lie, she knew, but she didn't want Andrea insinuating she was plain, homely, ugly. She'd taken about all she could from this woman.

Andrea's voice softened. "Look, Maggie, I know what you're going through and the range of emotions you're about to experience. I know how to help you cope and how to pull you through the mire of uncertainties you're going to suffer, starting with facing yourself in the mirror without feeling guilty."

"Guilty? Why would I feel guilty?"

"Because he chose Sue instead of you. What made him attack her? Was she just in the wrong place at the wrong time, or was it something about her? Was it premeditated and planned out days, weeks, maybe months before it happened, or could it have been you? If that thought isn't there yet, it's growing somewhere inside of you, and if it doesn't hit you tonight, it will sometime this week. You'll be wondering what the chances are that it could have been you instead. You'll start wondering what would have happened if you had arrived there five minutes earlier or five minutes later. You want to know what he looks like and how he got her into the woods, and would you have been dumb enough to do the same thing and get yourself in the same fix. You're wondering if it was one of those deliverymen, or a stranger, or a boy she knows, and what led him to your neighborhood. But I'm here to tell you that it doesn't matter what his motives were. You can't spend the rest of your life, or even today, trying to hide yourself behind a mop of hair and old T-shirts. You have to live your life for each new day. Everyone is going to be talking to you about what happened, and I'm going to do my part to get you looking and feeling your best, so you can stand tall and face them with confidence."

Tears welled in Maggie's eyes. She swiped at them with her sleeve. How could Andrea know all that was in her mind? All the questions and uncertainties clashed together like cymbals, making it impossible to think straight. And now Andrea was telling her everyone at school would be asking her questions, demanding to know what happened. She hadn't thought of that. She had imagined slinking into the classroom and burying herself behind her books, whispering to Dixie in the hallway and crying on her shoulder about all the fears strangling her heart.

Andrea handed her a tissue. "It will be okay. I'll get you through this. And for the next two hours you don't have to think about anything but being pampered."

In the salon, Andrea turned her over to three women who set to work on her as if she were a movie star.

"Oh, what gorgeous red hair."

"There's so much of it."

"Don't you dare start thinking about straightening it, Clara. It's beautiful."

One started clipping, while another did her nails and the third draped colored scarves over her shoulder. "These colors, Andrea, and you can't go wrong."

Her hair was washed, then brushed, blow dried, curled, and sprayed. Makeup came next. A touch of eye shadow, mascara, a light blush—which let her freckles bleed through but brought her eyes to life—and a touch of translucent pink lip gloss. At last the women spun her around to face Andrea.

"Gorgeous. I knew she was in there somewhere."

Maggie spun back around and stared at herself. It was her, and yet not her. She looked so alive.

She was still feeling incredibly shy over it all, as Andrea dragged her back to the car to head to the mall. "One hour. How many clothes can we buy in an hour?"

"About two hundred dollars worth if Dixie was with us and she had the money in her hand."

"Works for me," Andrea said.

"What? You aren't buying me that much. The salon alone must have been a fortune."

"Don't worry about it. I consider it an investment."

Shirts were easy to find. The women had shown Andrea what colors to look for. She pulled the yellows and pinks out of Maggie's hands and shoved them back on the rack, and selected deep greens and baby blues. The jeans were a bit harder. Maggie kept tugging at the hip-huggers.

"There's nothing wrong with them if your belly isn't showing and they aren't skintight. It's just a different cut. They look good on you."

Maggie sighed. She wanted them, but it was hard to feel comfortable changing so much at once. She was going to feel like there was a sign hanging around her neck that said, *Here I am! Look at me!* She'd barely gotten a second look when she wore the Claddagh necklace, but this was altogether something—someone—new.

Andrea helped her settle on a stack of tops and three pairs of jeans; then on the way to the register, they stopped at the shoe department to pick out a pair of high heels.

"I have clogs at home I can wear."

"Not with these clothes," Andrea said. They chose a pair and added them to the stack, then hauled their purchases to the nearest register. "Ring these up first," she instructed the saleswoman. "She's going to put them on before we leave."

"I am?"

"Yes, you are."

She couldn't walk into school wearing this stuff without getting used to it. Everyone would look at her.

But isn't that what I wanted?

She lugged the clothes back to the dressing room and changed.

Maggie was quiet for the first half of the car ride. She had so many things she wanted to ask Andrea, but the biggest question was obvious. "Why are you doing this?"

"I told you. It's an investment. And it's my job. I know what you're about to experience, and I figured I would start the defensive actions before it even struck."

"Sure is strange how God works things, isn't it?"

"How's that?"

"Dad didn't have a girlfriend in all the twelve years since my mother died, and he starts dating you right before this happens."

Andrea laughed again.

"What? You don't think this was God's doing?"

"Sure it was. That's not why I'm laughing. What you don't realize is that I'm just the first date your father *told* you about."

Maggie didn't know what to make of that. How did Andrea know her father had dated other women? "Have you known him a long time?"

"Several years. He used to date a friend of mine. Well, if you could call it dating. They went out to dinner a few times. No telling how many other women he's been out with."

"I don't believe that. He would have told me."

"Why would he? He knew you'd have a hard time handling it. He figured there was no reason to cause you anguish if nothing was going to come of the relationship."

That gave Maggie something to pause over. The insinuation was pretty clear. "So something is going to come of your relationship with him?"

"We think so. Meeting all of you was the next logical step."

If they hadn't been in a car, Maggie would have run fast and hard as far as she could until her lungs labored to breathe and her legs ached with pain. Sitting still was almost impossible. "The next step toward what?"

"To whatever comes next." She craned her neck to see around Maggie to make a turn. "Don't panic. We're just testing the waters a bit deeper than dinner and a movie, okay?"

It wasn't okay. It was very *not* okay. But there was nothing she could do about it.

Andrea pulled up to the curb. "Here we are. Do you want me to walk you to the office?"

"No," Maggie said flatly. "I can take care of myself." She seemed to be repeating that mantra a lot lately. She opened the door. "You'll be back to your office earlier than you thought. It's not quite noon."

Andrea reached into the backseat and hauled Maggie's book bag up front. "Don't be naïve. I'm meeting Frank for lunch."

Maggie slammed the car door, hefted her book bag over her shoulder, and walked toward the school, bobbing her head and making a face as she mimicked Andrea. "'Don't be naïve.'" She plucked at her new shirt. "Sure, an investment. She's buying her way into the family, and I was the first to go."

Chapter
Thirteen

MRS. REDMOND HANDED her a hall pass. "I know your father called in this morning, Maggie, but I prefer to have a written note to put in your file."

"I'll get the detective to send you one. It's his fault I'm late."

"How is Sue doing?" She asked the question as she plucked a paper clip out of a plastic case and slid it over the papers in her hand, as if Sue were just home with the flu, not lying in the hospital fighting for her life.

"Okay," Maggie answered, knowing the woman didn't really care, anyway. She cared even less how Maggie was coping. She only cared whether or not her files were in order.

Maggie took a shortcut down the senior hall, through the atrium that separated the gymnasium and cafeteria, where the freshmen were lining up for lunch, their squeaky voices echoing unbearably from the high, domed ceiling and brightly painted walls. It was an impressive reception area. On clear days, the sun filled the space with brilliant light and created a sense of peace—when the room wasn't crowded with rambunctious teenagers. Maggie maneuvered between the freshmen, Tony's classmates. Few knew her by name, so she passed through unnoticed and veered off to the right, into the sophomore quadrant where the halls were silent except for the drone of teachers' voices from behind closed doors.

Mr. Baire would have waved her to her seat without even looking at the hall pass, but her classmates were on her the instant she walked through the door.

A dozen voices collided with questions.

"Maggie, what happened?"

"How is Sue?"

"I can't believe you found her."

"I saw you on the news last night."

Clarissa came out of her seat, giving Maggie's hair and makeup a second glance before rushing to her side to hug her. "Oh, Maggie, tell us what happened. Were you scared?"

Dixie was two steps behind. She looked Maggie up and down, then scowled at Clarissa, miffed that she was in the way.

Maggie smiled at Clarissa, then reached around her and hugged Dixie. "Sorry I couldn't come over last night. Daddy and Andrea—"

"I know. Mama said the same thing." She felt the silky sleeve of Maggie's new shirt.

Clarissa wouldn't be put off. "Tell us."

There was a crowd around her now; even the boys looked attentive, probably not because they were interested in what she had to say as much as they were taking advantage of the opportunity to put an end to Mr. Baire's lecture on the Middle Ages.

Sean's deep voice cut through the rest. "How is Sue?"

Maggie turned his direction. Maybe they did care. Sue wasn't just one of them, she was an idol, a symbol of what so many of the girls strived to become. Maybe their feelings went deeper than just the superficiality of looks. Maybe they really cared about her as a person. Or maybe they were dealing with some of the same thoughts she was—wondering, if this could happen to Sue, couldn't it just as easily happen to any of them? Or maybe it only happened to girls like Sue who were already in the spotlight.

Mr. Baire clapped his hands. "Back to your seats. Back to your seats. I understand you're all concerned, but we have work to do."

The students ignored him.

Maggie glanced toward Mr. Baire and back at the throng around her. "I haven't seen her today, but when they took her away to the hospital, she was in critical condition."

"We already know that from the news," someone in the back said.

"What did she look like? What did he do to her?"

She cringed, coiled inward like she used to do when a softball was pitched in her direction. The gory details. That's what they wanted. She didn't want to go there. She didn't want to recall the images, but they were there just the same, unforgettable.

"I wouldn't have recognized her if it wasn't for her hair. She was bruised and cut, and in a lot of pain. I'm sure he left her for dead. She was barely breathing when I got there."

"Was she naked?" Asby asked.

Maggie glared at him. How could he ask that? "You are a complete jerk."

Everybody snickered.

"I'm just curious," he said.

Dixie hooked arms with Maggie. "Go crawl back in your hole, Asby."

Jeanette, a quiet girl still in her seat in the front row, rose and approached. She placed a tentative hand on Maggie's forearm. "Is she going to live?"

Maggie matched her quiet reserve. "I don't know. If you'd seen her . . . She must have fought hard to live till I got there, so if she keeps fighting, maybe she'll make it. I just can't say."

Jeanette nodded. "Mama and I prayed for her all night."

"Me too."

Mr. Baire clapped his hands again. "Okay, okay, let's move to the lunch room. It's time anyway. Out you go. But plan to work when you get back in here."

The lunchroom brought more of the same. With lunchtimes staggered every ten minutes throughout the high school, the flow of students was nonstop, and kids were constantly crossing the cafeteria to hear what happened, how she found Sue, what Sue looked like, what the police said. More people talked to her in half an hour than normally would in an entire year. She answered their questions as plainly and honestly as she could, but she avoided details. The detective had told her not to give out anything that might ruin the case.

Clarissa brought her lunch to the table, followed by two of Sue's friends, so they could hear the whole thing firsthand over and over again as kids from each class passed by with more questions. Dixie took on the role of right-hand man and bodyguard, keeping people in their places and answering when Maggie became overwrought.

Even the students that didn't approach still pointed and talked about what happened. Maggie felt like a bug under a microscope.

It wasn't until the end of lunch, on their way back to class, that Dixie finally managed to lean into her privately. "By the way, you look fantastic. What happened?"

Maggie frowned. "Andrea."

"Tell me!"

"Later," Maggie replied. She needed time to think. Clothes and hair seemed so incredibly unimportant with all the discussion flying around her. Besides, no one had even noticed her make-over. She figured she'd been so invisible before that even having her hair down and styled didn't strike anyone as being different.

Sue would have noticed, though. That was the irony of the whole thing. The one girl who would have commented on Maggie's new look was lying in the hospital almost dead, the cause not only for all the attention but also the reason no one registered the great change in Maggie's appearance. How different it would have been if Andrea had come into her life two months ago and "invested" in her then. Sue would've ridiculed her, and her classmates would've followed suit. But now by God's hand, she was linked with Sue, pulled into Sue's circle by circumstance.

She wondered what Sue would think of that twist of fate.

Mr. Baire forced them all into their seats with threats of a pop quiz for anyone who didn't comply and picked up his lecture where he left off earlier.

English class went entirely differently.

Mrs. Newell perched on the edge of her desk, one leg bouncing as she waited for students to take their seats. If her leg stopped bouncing, her hand would start patting her thigh, or her index finger would play with the long lock of hair by her cheek, or her fingers would rhythmically flip a marker back and forth like a tiny baton. Maggie had tried the latter herself, but she wasn't coordinated enough to maneuver a marker through more than three fingers before it clattered to the floor.

Maggie tried to remember back to her first year in high school, the beginning of her freshman year, to recall whether Mrs. Newell had been such a case of nerves back then or had become this way only after her brother died in a car accident the previous December, but she didn't have an image of her then. She hadn't really looked at Mrs. Newell until she was absent for a short period during her brother's internment in intensive care, and an additional week after his funeral. Mrs. Newell's preoccupation with her brother's death and her obvious vulnerability attracted Maggie's sympathy, as if on some deep, unexpressed level they had something in common, their lives irrevocably changed by the death of someone else: Mrs. Newell's brother and Maggie's mother.

This day, Mrs. Newell's restlessness appeared exacerbated. She pushed herself from the edge of the desk and moved to the window to pull on the white string that released the louvered blinds and lowered them over the view of the world outside. She stepped away, then back to angle the slats so that the sunlight fell in subdued stripes across the floor. Maggie was glad for the darkness. Dimming the lights would help too. She remembered how the blackboards in elementary school toned down the rooms, absorbing some of the horrible frankness of the fluorescent lights, but the junior high and high school had been built just a few years earlier, and the design team had installed white dry-erase boards as being much cleaner. Apparently teachers preferred markers to the dusty chalk on their fingers. But the endless stretches of glossy white boards gave Maggie a headache.

Mrs. Newell's navy-clad figure stood out against the white like a woman in a low-budget photography shop standing against a cheap backdrop. She moved from the window to her desk, adjusted a stack of papers, picked up a dry-erase marker, and tapped it against the desk as the last few students found their places.

She strode across the room, closed the door, and then proceeded to front and center, where she stood with one hand tapping the marker into the palm of the other as she waited for silence. Maggie recognized this stance. There was going to be a speech.

"As you know, your classmate Sue Roberts is in the hospital, in intensive care to be exact. I don't know how many of you understand what that means. It means she's seriously bad off. It means she's sitting on the line between life and death, and her spirit and body have to make a decision which direction she's going to step. Being drawn to life can be vital to her recovery. That's where y'all come in. Today, instead of writing that essay on *The Devil and Tom Walker*, you're going to write a letter or essay to Sue. You're going to tell her at least one thing you really like about her. You're going to remind her of at least one good thing she's done here at our school. In other words, you're going to make her want to come back here.

"Mrs. Jones has plans for her students to do likewise in art class today. We'll put those pictures in with these essays to cheer her up or remind her of school."

Two rows back, Asby muttered, "Cheering up and school don't hardly go in the same picture."

Mrs. Newell cast him a look that dared him or anyone else to expand on his comment. She was in her element. She'd quit fidgeting and was standing stone-cold still with her feet planted a foot apart, her nostrils flaring. She had a cause, and she intended to do everything in her power to bring about a different result this time than the one last December.

"Maggie will take everyone's letters to the hospital this evening."

Maggie sat up straighter and blinked. *I will?*

She wasn't at all sure she could face Sue again. The vision of her in the woods was still so strong. She wanted to set it all aside, to quit thinking about it; but sitting there with thirty pairs of eyes trained on her, she knew that was impossible. They weren't going to let her forget, at least not anytime soon, until some other bit of news, some tragedy or gossip, pushed Sue's misfortune off the school radar.

Hadn't she done enough for Sue by saving her life? How could anyone expect anything else from her? She stayed after class to say so to Mrs. Newell. "Can you please get someone else to deliver the letters? I really don't want to go back to the hospital."

"Nonsense. God has appointed you to take care of her, so you must follow through." Mrs. Newell was never afraid to discuss her faith with students. Rumor had it that she'd told the principal she would quit if he had a problem with it. She never forced her faith on her students or preached Christianity, but she wouldn't omit God from her dialogue.

"I saved her life. Isn't that enough?"

"You got her to the hospital. She has a long way to go before she's well."

Frustration emanated from every pore of Maggie's body, but she didn't want to get on Mrs. Newell's bad side.

She took the stack of papers from Mrs. Newell and headed to her next class. It wouldn't be that much trouble to take the letters by the hospital. She would get Dixie to go with her.

Her father was waiting at the flagpole right on schedule, with Tony and Billy already in the backseat and Webb seated between them.

"People asked me about Sue all day long," Billy said. "They all wanted to know how you found her."

She slid into the front seat. "I know, Billy. It's been like that all day for me too."

Her father looked her up and down. "You look nice."

She'd actually put her new appearance out of her mind. "Thanks," she said. It just didn't matter as much as it once might have.

Webb didn't say much. Finally, halfway home, he leaned forward. "Did she ask for me?"

Maggie shook her head. "She didn't ask for anyone, Webb. She cried as I peeled the duct tape off her mouth, and then she passed out."

The look in his eyes told her that he hadn't imagined it that way. He sat back and stared out the side window.

Maggie's father offered to go with her to the hospital, but she preferred to go alone with Dixie. She didn't want to worry about doing and saying the right thing. She just wanted to deliver the letters and leave. Besides, going with Dixie would make up for the two of them not being able to talk the night before or all day long at school.

The ICU was eerily quiet, making the beeps and whirs of machines prick at Maggie's ears.

Dixie looped her arm through Maggie's. "It stinks like pine cleaner and alcohol in here."

Maggie didn't reply. Dixie didn't understand yet. She hadn't seen Sue. She hadn't looked her in the eye as her lifeblood seeped out onto the leaf-strewn ground. It wasn't real to Dixie. It was just a headline at school.

As they reached the door, a young nurse approaching from the opposite direction stopped them. She had the smooth skin of a model, and her sleek blonde hair was pulled away from her face to reveal wide eyes that expressed a beauty much deeper than flesh. *Jennifer*, according to her name tag. "Only family is allowed up here," she said.

"I'm Maggie, the girl who found Sue in the woods. Our teacher asked us to bring in these notes, to encourage her to get well."

"Well then, just for a moment." Jennifer waved them in. "Her mother just left. Sue isn't conscious, you know. She's in a coma from the trauma to her head."

The two girls stepped into the room with Jennifer just behind them. Sue looked like a stranger. Her face was swollen into one large purplish bruise, with white bandages slanting across one eyebrow and the opposite cheek. They barely recognized her.

Dixie stood with her back flat against the wall, her face as pale as Sue's bandages. Maggie stepped to the foot of the bed while Jennifer adjusted a pillow, inspected the intravenous drip, and checked her vitals. "Can Sue hear us if we talk to her?"

"It can't hurt. If she were my friend, I would talk to her."

Maggie laid one hand on the white covers, on the lump of Sue's feet. She really didn't have anything to say to her. She didn't even like her, as ugly-mouthed as she'd been in the past, but she felt sorry for her. What could she say? Nothing. There was nothing to fill up the silent room. She raised the papers in her hand. "These are for you, Sue, from all the kids at school. We want you to get well." It was all she could manage to say. She laid the stack of pictures and letters on the wheeled table and turned to go. "Thank you, Jennifer."

"Sure."

In bed that night, Maggie couldn't quit thinking of Sue. Not the nightmares of the attack like the night before, but seeing her lying there so still, all covered in bandages, unaware of life going on without her. She thought about what Mrs. Newell had said. Would hearing an encouraging voice help Sue recover? Seeing her that way, so still and oblivious, was like watching a kid sitting alone on a park bench while all the other kids were getting free ice cream. She needed to be shaken. She needed to fight to live.

She didn't say anything to Dixie about it the next day. By daylight, it seemed less like her problem. She'd done well by Sue twice—saving her and taking the papers to her. She'd done what she was supposed to do.

At least, it seemed like enough until Mrs. Newell's class.

"How is she?" Mrs. Newell asked.

How could she answer that? She hadn't even asked. "No change, I guess."

"Did you talk to her?"

To her? How about *at* her. "Briefly. I'm not a relative, you know. They didn't want me there."

"Nonsense. You go back."

Maggie nodded, but she didn't really mean it. Why should she go? Sue had always been miserable to her, yet she'd saved her anyway, risked her life walking into those creepy woods where that freak was probably hiding, watching. Wasn't that Christian enough? No one would expect her to stand around begging Sue to live.

Mrs. Newell saw her leaving school. Her eyes lit up. "If there's any student in the school I can depend on, it's you, Maggie McCarthy. God knows that. That's why He had you find Sue. You're the one that has to pull her through. Any other girl would've freaked out. You're stronger than that."

Am I stronger? She'd always considered herself weak. The quiet, withdrawn one at school. The one who held her tongue. The one who minded her own business. The one who did what was expected of her instead of going off on some wild tangent like her peers. How could that be stronger? She felt like she didn't even have a will of her own.

And now she was being told to do something else that she didn't want to do. She didn't want to go back to the hospital. She wanted to pretend that none of it happened, that Sue didn't exist, and that the only thing she had weighing on her mind was what time to put the Stouffer's frozen lasagna into the oven that evening.

"You don't understand, Mrs. Newell. Sue doesn't even like me. She's made fun of me for ages. She calls me names and treats me like dirt. Why should I visit her?"

"It's easy to love those who love us. Even our enemies do that. But when we show love to our enemies, then we have truly shown love." Mrs. Newell smiled and walked away.

Maggie stared into the sky. *Is this what you're asking of me, God? Was it not enough just saving my enemy? Am I supposed to show her love too?*

How hard is it to show love? The thought came like a clear reply in her head. *It feels like a punishment, doesn't it? But I'm not asking you to die on a cross. I'm only asking you to show compassion.*

Maggie stood shaken by the revelation. Love your enemies. It had always seemed like some abstract idea that had to do with war and politics, not the school's hottest blonde cheerleader.

As she contemplated this new perspective, she knew she would go. She realized that she needed to go back. Alone, so she could stare at Sue without Dixie thinking she was weird, and so she could think out what to say without the nurse judging her words. What could she say to Sue? Why would Sue even want to speak to her?

At the hospital, all the way up in the elevator, Maggie had to keep convincing herself she needed to be there. *It's no big deal. Ten minutes, then go home.*

Her resolve weakened as she approached the room and pushed the door open.

She stood inside the door for a minute, just staring at the unmoving body on the bed. Intravenous tubes were strung to her arms. Another tube ran down her throat. The machines were beeping, little electronic charts running jagged lines across screens, so Maggie knew Sue was alive, but it was disconcerting to see her so still and almost lifeless. The entire episode in the woods came back full force, flooding her senses and overwhelming her.

She sank into the chair beside the bed and gathered her wits, at first unable to speak, but as the beeps and blips ticked away time, Maggie's heart rate slowed. She bowed her head and prayed a moment, as much for courage for herself as recovery for Sue. When she raised her head, she took it all in again, allowing her gaze to move from the top of Sue's head to her feet, under the blankets at the bottom of the bed.

"You have so much to live for. Mrs. Newell is really worried about you. You can't let her go through all that sadness again. It's about to kill her. She can't quit pacing around the classroom. You can't do that to your mother and brothers." She bit her lip, then continued. "You can't do that to Webb and Tony. You've got to get better." She picked up the stack of papers and flipped through them. "Everybody at school made these for you. You've got to wake up and check them out. Even Sean Black drew you a picture. It's of Becca of course, but hey, he's never, ever shown his artwork to anyone else before this. To tell you the truth, I don't think he intended to turn it in, but Mrs. Newell didn't give him a chance to get out the door with it. She didn't even fuss that he'd drawn a picture instead of writing a letter. I can see why. It's really good. He's talented."

She looked more closely at Sean's sketch, a modern mosaic with all sorts of images woven in. The longer she looked, the more she saw. And then her eyes found it, a Claddagh worked into the picture like a belt around Becca's waist.

"It must be nice to have someone love you so sincerely," she said aloud, but not really to Sue. Sue was still lying there, not listening, breathing to the rhythm of the beeps and whooshes of machinery. "Of course, you're loved too. You've got Webb. If that's not worth pulling through for, I don't know what is."

Chapter
Fourteen

THE NEXT DAY, after spending the afternoon together, Dixie sat on her front steps and watched Maggie until she hooked up with Tony at Webb's house, and the two of them progressed on to Brad's house to get Billy. None of them were to venture down the road alone anymore. The cops felt the rapist wasn't likely to strike again so soon—it had only been a couple days—or so close, because guys like that often packed up and moved on to a new town after making a strike, but no one in the neighborhood was taking any chances, despite the deputy car that seemed to have taken up a schedule of patrolling the area.

Maggie hurried Tony down the road to the Dwellers', anxious to see how Billy had fared, since he hadn't played with Brad in a while.

Mr. Dweller met them at the door. "The boys are in the basement playing Ping-Pong, Tony. How about you run down and get them. You know the way."

"Sure thing," Tony replied and headed down the stairs.

"Hey, y'all help yourselves to an ice cream while you're down there. They're in the refrigerator at the bar," Mr. Dweller called after him. He gave Maggie a lopsided smile. "He'll find 'em. He's helped himself often enough."

Mrs. Dweller bustled into the room with an old-fashioned white apron tied around her bulging waistline. Maggie didn't know women wore aprons anymore, but it struck her as a smart thing, really, saving clothes from being splattered with oil or covered with flour or whatever. Cooking could get messy.

"Maggie McCarthy," she said, "you sweet thing. I haven't seen you in ages, darling. Can I get you some lemonade and cookies?"

Maggie felt like God was going to strike her down for thinking ill of anyone in this household; they were all so generous. "No, thank you, Mrs. Dweller. I've only stopped in to take Billy home."

"You're such a good sister to that boy. Just like a mama to him, I'm always saying. Let me wrap you up some cake to take home with you. I know those boys are always hungry. Bless their hearts."

She walked off, leaving Maggie alone in the hallway with Mr. Dweller, whose shirt was stretched around his gut like a pregnant woman's. She chided herself for thinking ugly thoughts about him, but everything about him rubbed her the wrong way. Like his ears. They poked out. Couldn't a doctor tack them closer to his head? And his feet. She'd never noticed them before, but there he stood on the tile, legs splayed apart, bare feet flattened under his weight so that they looked like the flippers Billy used at the city pool the summer he spent retrieving pennies from the bottom of the deep end. Billy had walked funny with the flippers on. He lifted his knees higher than normal and flopped each foot down with a whacking sound. As Mr. Dweller crossed to a seat in the living room, he walked that same way, feet slapping on the floor, but without such an exaggerated bend of his knees.

"Come join me, Maggie," he said. "You know how the boys are. They'll be a while."

What choice did she have? He hadn't invited her to follow Tony, and she couldn't head home alone. She took a chair near the door, an ornate piece with intricately carved wood around the high back and down the legs. The cushions looked like they would be hard, so she wouldn't get too comfortable, but surprisingly, the firm-looking square gave way under her as she sank into the chair. She felt like it swallowed her.

"That chair is a mite worn out," Mr. Dweller said with a laugh. "A family antique better for looking at than sitting in. Why don't you come join me over here?" He patted a fat red rose woven into the tapestry of the couch.

She adjusted herself so the springs wouldn't poke into her tailbone. "I'm fine."

To compensate, he shuffled down to the end of the couch closest to her. "I've been wanting to talk to you. . . ."

She tried to fix a smile on her face to cover whatever reaction she might have in the course of a discussion with him, but her face seemed to have gone numb. She couldn't say whether she was smiling or frowning.

"You know," he continued, "about finding Sue. That was so brave of you. Tell me, how did you have the guts to go in there? Into the woods?"

Guts. Guts made her think of Smokey and how his torn body had been laid out on the stone, as if the stone were an altar and he some horrid offering. How *had* she gone back there again? "I heard a noise."

"But after seeing what happened to . . . what was that dog's name?"

"Smokey."

"Yes, that's it. Smokey. Weren't you scared of what it might be?"

The hair on the back of her neck rose. Or that's the image that pervaded her brain. She really didn't know if she had hair on her neck. It was more of a prickly sensation all over her head, like her brain was a soda that had just been opened and all the fizz was bubbling out of her hair follicles. Even her father hadn't asked her how she felt or what led up to the rescue. "I thought at first it was Cleopatra."

"Cleopatra?"

"Mr. Smith's cat. She went missing, you know, about the same time Smokey —" She wasn't sure how to end the sentence. When Smokey was murdered? Mutilated? Butchered?

Mr. Dweller didn't care to hear the ending. "So you thought it was the cat? Why?"

"I heard a scratching noise and a cry. Cats cry sometimes."

He started biting his thumbnail, beginning on one side and gradually twisting his hand around to get at the whole nail, his lips curled up, peeled back to reveal a set of teeth that would have been perfect except for a chip out of one in the front. "So," he said, "you ran into the woods expecting to save a kitty and instead you found Sue."

She nodded.

"Did you see anyone? Do you know who did it?"

"No."

"Not even a hint or a trace?"

"No."

"Come on. You must have seen something. He must have been close by watching you."

Why won't he stop?

"What did she look like?"

The gleam in his eyes disturbed her. His whole demeanor relayed excitement, as if the horrible event were some movie and not something that happened to a girl in their neighborhood. Maggie sat motionless, blinking her eyes to ensure that she could still move something on her face.

"When you found her," he said more specifically, as if she may not have understood the first time, "what did she look like?"

Everything about that day flooded back, filling every cavern of her mind. The blood, the torn flesh, the scattered clothes, and the waiting through each beat of her heart for the rescue team to arrive.

She wouldn't tell him a word of it.

The sound of the boys in the hall saved her.

Mr. Dweller leaped from the couch. "Did you boys get that ice cream like I told you?"

"Yes sir. Thank you, Mr. Dweller," Tony replied, waving his ice cream bar. Billy nodded, traces of chocolate around his mouth.

Mr. Dweller reached for Maggie's arm before she could escape him. "Let me help you. It's tough to get up from that chair."

Maybe if I were ninety, she thought, hating the feel of his hand on her arm.

He patted her back. "We'll have to talk again soon," he said. "I sure am proud of you. Such a bright, brave girl. I want to hear all the details real soon."

Tony had heard enough about Maggie being brave—she saw it cross his face and quicken his steps to the door.

"Tell me," Mr. Dweller said, not ready to let her go, "has she woken up and described him yet?"

Maggie had managed to push past Tony to get to the door, so she tugged it open and ran down the steps without giving him an answer. Billy was hard on her heels.

Tony, halfway down the porch steps, answered over his shoulder as he ran toward Maggie and Billy. "No. She's still out, and they don't know if she'll ever be right again."

Mr. Dweller followed them out the door. "What a shame. Such a lovely girl."

His wife joined him on the porch, her arms outstretched with a cellophane package. "Darlings, come back. You forgot your cake."

Chapter Fifteen

THE ATTENTION DIDN'T let up all week. Every morning was the same. Everyone wanted to know how Sue was faring. Maggie visited her in the hospital most evenings, sitting by her bed for an hour, sometimes reading, sometimes praying, sometimes just letting her mind wander over life, but there was never anything new to tell the kids at school. By the middle of the second week, interest started waning. Oddly, though, one change had developed and remained steadfast: Sue's two buddies, Tammy and Heather, gathered at Maggie's locker every morning and sat with her every day at lunch. They didn't have any classes with her. They took classes like chorus and current events instead of honors biology and advanced programming.

Maggie wasn't excited by their presence. At first it just felt weird having them there. Heather would stand there with her long legs going on forever and her thick blonde hair hanging down her back, in clothes meant more for a modeling runway than a high school hall. Tammy, with dark hair, huge brown eyes, and tanned skin, knew she was gorgeous and evaluated every other girl by how they measured up against her. Neither of them had ever shown anything but total disinterest in Maggie and Dixie. Maggie attributed their sudden attention to shock over what happened to Sue, but she couldn't understand why it extended to sitting with them at lunch. After a few days, their presence became somewhat annoying. She couldn't have a conversation with anyone, not even with Dixie, without the two of them chiming in.

Is this another test, Lord? Or the answer to my prayer? Is this the equivalent of being popular? She would greet them with a smile and tolerate their presence. She considered it an extension of helping Sue heal, helping herself heal, by allowing them that same courtesy, that same time of adjustment to accept what had happened and find a new path through their changed lives, but the more they hung around, the more she reevaluated what it meant to be popular. *Is this what I wanted? To be associated with them? Has it improved my life or changed who I am?*

Dixie was eating it up. She couldn't believe Tammy and Heather considered her a friend now, or that they were interested in what she had to say. She convinced her mother to take her out to the same store Andrea had taken Maggie to, bought a new wardrobe, and began flat-ironing her hair like Heather's and putting on airs like Tammy. On the second Friday after Sue's attack, she tested the waters a step farther and invited them to join her and Maggie at the movies that night.

Maggie didn't say anything until they were waiting at the flagpole for Dixie's mother to pick them up. "I can't believe you did that."

"Did what?"

"Invited those two . . ." She would have called them snobs, but that wasn't the right word, and she was doing her best to be a good person. You never knew when some man might jump out of thin air and kill you, and there you'd be, dead in the woods with no chance to seek forgiveness for all the bad things you said about people.

"Tammy and Heather? Like, I can't even believe they said yes. Two weeks ago they wouldn't even talk to us."

"Exactly."

"But it's great, Mags. We're *in* now. They like us."

Maggie shook her head. "You don't get it, do you? Sue was *raped.* A man tied her up, taped her mouth closed, and held a knife to her throat. He cut up her face. He stabbed her. He did things to her body that make me sick to imagine. And somehow the end result of that is us getting attention from kids at school, and you think that's all right?"

Dixie jutted out her jaw in her most stubborn stance. "Sue's not even conscious. How can it possibly hurt her if we're hanging out with Tammy and Heather?"

Maggie sighed.

"In fact, I think it makes them feel better to hang around with us, like it helps them connect to what happened to Sue."

"I realize that. That's why I haven't said anything until now. Still, I don't want you thinking I'm hanging out with them permanently, because I'm not."

"I thought this is what we wanted—to be popular."

"Being popular for who I am is different from being popular because I found Sue almost dead in the woods."

Dixie pursed her lips and folded her arms across her chest. "So what're you going to tell them? 'Go away, because I don't want to be your friend'?"

"I didn't say that. Just don't get so hyped up about hanging out with them."

"I'm not. I only invited them to a movie. Maybe they need to see a movie, have fun, go out, and think about something else besides Sue wrapped in bandages in the hospital."

"Maybe so. Too bad Sue can't."

"You're right. Sue can't. But you can, Maggie. It's not you that was raped."

Maggie sighed again.

Later that night, Andrea echoed Dixie's observation when Maggie was telling her father that she had to go by the hospital early that evening in order to make it to the movie.

"You're spending too much time pining over her, Maggie," Andrea said. "It's very kind of you to sit with her, but you have your own life, and I'm afraid if you keep tying yourself to her this way you're never going to recover from the shock of what happened. I think it's time we started some therapy sessions."

Maggie glared at her. She wasn't about to succumb to therapy with some psychiatrist. "I guess I'll recover easier than Sue will," she replied as she headed out the door with the keys to her father's car.

Maggie and her family made new driving arrangements over the weekend. Andrea would pick their father up in the morning and take him home after work so Maggie could have the car. It was less disruptive to everyone's day, and the only reason her father left the office was to have lunch with Andrea anyway, so it just made more sense.

Something about driving into the school lot and parking her car, instead of being dropped off by the flagpole, boosted her confidence. She felt stronger, more empowered, and ready to handle the lingering madness at school. So she invited Clarissa to join them for lunch.

Clarissa had never hung out with Sue's crowd. She was more down-to-earth than that, pretty in a girl-next-door way, with eyes that sparkled with inner charm. She laughed at Maggie's lunch suggestion. "Are you crazy? I've noticed Heather and Tammy sitting with you every day."

Maggie shrugged. She knew what Clarissa was thinking because she felt the same way, but Heather and Tammy had been tolerable at the movie. They weren't bad girls, really. A bit snooty for Maggie's taste, but not bad, except for the way they gossiped about everyone. Every time they made a snide remark about some loser wandering into the theater, Maggie had cut them short. After the third comment, they got the message and started telling jokes instead. She never felt like she would be a bosom buddy with them like she was with Dixie, but she decided that they really weren't much different from other girls; they just had more clothes and bigger earrings.

"They aren't so horrible after all. Just come for today. I want to talk to you."

When Clarissa gave her a hug, Maggie knew she understood without an explanation, making Maggie wonder why they hadn't been closer all the way through school, instead of just crossing paths once in a while.

She felt better with Clarissa joining them. It felt more normal, more wholesome. Clarissa wasn't impressed by Heather and Tammy like Dixie was, and Maggie felt grounded again, back to being herself, not stepping out on some precipice where she was vulnerable to falling off the edge, even with Dixie giving her somewhat of a cold shoulder and hanging on Heather's every word.

The feeling of normalcy didn't last long. On Thursday, Kelvin Myers and Elliott Bailey approached her and Dixie at their lockers after English class.

Kelvin stood out like a teen catalog model: trim, fit, clean cut. His parents made him keep his hair short. He had long eyelashes, clear skin, and blue eyes that spoke a language all their own. Maggie considered their last real conversation to have been in fifth grade when they had to race frogs for a science experiment. Since then, they'd been in many classes together but had never really spoken. She had figured out a logical explanation for Heather and Tammy hanging around—she now had a tie to their best friend—but when she saw Kelvin heading toward her, she shook her head and laughed, sure he couldn't suddenly be tuned in to her existence.

"What are you laughing at, Maggie McCarthy?"

"You, Kelvin Myers. You have a frog to race, or what?"

It took him a minute, but he remembered. "Maybe. My frog would win this time."

She slammed her locker door. "Don't count on it."

He leaned on the lockers. "How about you and Dixie going out with me and Elliott on Friday?"

She winked at Dixie, who gaped, speechless, at hearing the exchange, and grinned at Kelvin as she replied, "To race frogs?"

"No frogs. Pizza and a movie."

"I don't know. Let me think about it."

His pretty blues widened in surprise. "You have to think about it?"

His assumption that she would automatically jump at the chance to date him made her laugh again. "Yes, I have to think about it."

A voice rang out down the hall. "Hey, Kelvin! Coach wants you!"

"Well, there you go. Time to think about it. I'll be back in a minute."

Elliott left with him.

Dixie grabbed her arm. "I can't believe you! How many years have we waited for this? You and me, asked out by guys like Kelvin and Elliott?"

Dixie was right. It was a dream come true, but it didn't sit well with Maggie. If they hadn't liked her before, then why now? The only difference a few weeks had made was her new celebrity status, and that was at Sue's expense, gained from Sue's wreckage. "It doesn't feel right, Dixie."

"Get over it, Maggie. These guys just didn't notice us before. This is exactly what we wanted!"

The boys were heading back toward them.

"Say yes, Mags. What's there to lose? Maybe we'll actually end up with dates for the prom. And not just any dates—dates with Kelvin and Elliott."

Dixie pleaded with her eyes like a pet-store puppy. Maggie thought of all the things they'd stood through together and considered that perhaps she owed it to Dixie. Hadn't she prayed for popularity? Kelvin wasn't the hottest boy in school or anything, but she'd hardly ever seen him without a girl on his arm.

He headed toward her, his steps long and confident, so typical of him, breathtaking in his loose jeans, a navy T-shirt tight enough to show off his chest muscles, and his hair looking as if some girl had just mussed it with her fingertips. He never doubted his place in the halls of his school. He paused to make a comment to a passing buddy, a smirk twisting his smile before he reached Maggie's side and leaned on the lockers again. "So how 'bout it, Maggie? We got a date?"

She looked at her feet, then pulled her gaze upward to meet his eyes. A new realization welled in her—she could be in control.

This wasn't something she had to do. She wasn't begging him to take her out. He was the one asking. If it fell through, it was no loss. She could do it on her terms. "Sure, but I have to pass it by my daddy. Call me at six."

He nodded, a short bouncing nod with eyes laughing at a private joke and a crooked grin full of beautiful teeth. "Six. Got it."

He slapped Elliott on the back, and the two headed to their next class without Elliott saying a word to Dixie. Maggie supposed they must be a package deal.

Dixie poked Maggie. "'Check with your daddy?' Oh, please. Now he thinks we're dorks."

Heat rushed over Maggie's body as she blushed. "And how has that changed in the past three years? If he can't handle me checking with my daddy, he's not the type of guy I want to go out with."

"Like you've got a string of them waiting."

That stung, especially coming from her best friend. "Doesn't matter. If I have to stoop to dating jerks, I won't date at all."

Dixie glared at her. "Not me. I'm going even if I have to sneak out of the house to do it."

"You are not. We're going home and telling your mother all about it."

Dixie frowned a minute, looking like she might say something that might never be mended between them, but suddenly, as if a new thought occurred to her, she hooked her arm around Maggie's and pulled her across the hall to their English class. "If you weren't my best friend, I wouldn't put up with you, you know."

"I know."

Maggie had to force herself to concentrate in Mrs. Newell's class. Mrs. Newell was telling them about a presentation they would have to give. An oral presentation. While everyone moaned over the assignment, Maggie sat dazed, wondering what to do about Kelvin. Should she go out with him?

Word spread during the day. During biology, Clarissa leaned across the aisle. "I heard you're going out with Kelvin."

Maggie blushed. Had she become a school headline? *Freaky Girl Finally Gets Date.* "Maybe," she said and turned to listen to Mr. Brampton's discourse on the temporary pseudopodia of an amoeba.

Clarissa wasn't about to be put off so easily. She waited until Mr. Brampton turned back to the board. "Kelvin asks you out, and you say *maybe*? Are you crazy?"

Maybe she was.

After supper was over and she'd washed the dishes and finished helping Billy with his homework, she found her father stretched out on the sofa reading the paper. She debated how to bring up the subject of the date while she moved in and out of the room like a shadow, fiddling with things, straightening books, picking up the boys' socks, and watering the spider plant that Mrs. Graham had helped her grow from a sprout off the one on her porch. She picked up a DVD, put it back in its case, and placed the remote back on the television. Her father didn't even look up. Finally, she fixed him a cup of coffee and carried it to him. It couldn't hurt to put him in the right frame of mind.

When he sat up, she plunged in and spilled out the words she had rehearsed. "A boy at school asked me out on a date. Kelvin Myers. Everybody knows him. And Dixie is going too, with his friend Elliott."

He didn't react quite the way she expected. "Well, it's about time my beautiful Maggie had a date. Where is he taking you?"

No twenty questions? "I don't know. Pizza and a movie."

"Sounds like fun. Friday? Do you need money?" he asked, fishing his wallet out of his pants pocket and pulling out a desperately thin stack of ones.

"No, Dad, but thanks," Maggie replied, relieved that she had recently baby-sat Kimberly. "I have some money saved up. I'll take that."

She ran upstairs and phoned Dixie to tell her the news. "I can't believe it. Daddy said yes."

On Friday, Kelvin had already picked up Elliott and Dixie before arriving at Maggie's house. She had changed outfits three times, and she would've changed again, except time was drawing short. She decided to wear one of the new outfits Andrea had helped her buy: a pair of hip-hugger jeans, a deep green blouse with a ruffle down the front, and her new high heels, which she'd only worn that one day to school. Her hair was making her crazy, so she topped it with a blue-jean cap that calmed her mass of curls and complemented the outfit. She felt great.

She tried to slip out the front door when she heard the car, but her father stopped her. "Not till I meet him, Mags." He stepped into the doorway and shook the boy's hand. "Hello there. Calvin, is it?"

"Kelvin Myers, sir."

"Have her home by 11:30."

"Yes sir."

As her father gave her a kiss on the forehead and stepped back, Tony and Webb sauntered down the stairs to the family room.

Kelvin raised his hand. "Hey, Webb. Y'all going to the game tomorrow?"

Webb's glance moved from Kelvin to Maggie and back again. "Sure. See you there."

Maggie could see Webb puzzling over the scene. What did he think about Kelvin taking her out?

Dinner at Antonio's Pizzeria turned out better than she expected. They all talked and laughed over stuff at school and things they remembered about their frogs, and then some other kids from school joined them at the table and Maggie relaxed, feeling less need to talk with so much chatter going on around them. She sat back, content to listen and be part of the group, and watch Dixie come to life with all the attention. She hoped Dixie's and her friendship went too deep to break just because Dixie was having fun with a few new friends. She wondered where it would leave her if she stepped back and declined to join future outings. Would she lose Dixie forever? Was she crazy not to want to keep up with the rest of the crowd?

It turned out everyone was going to the movie. They moved en masse from one parking lot to the other, the cool evening air whipping around their legs and flushing their faces. Maggie walked carefully, thinking she wouldn't have worn her awkward new heels if she had remembered she would have to strut across two parking lots and the road in between, but there was nothing to do but concentrate on each footstep.

As they stepped off the curb onto the street, the wind shifted and whipped around her, sending her hat flying across the road. She dashed after it, stepping clumsily in her heels as she grabbed at the hat, twisted her ankle, and fell to the ground.

Kelvin loped up to her side. "Are you all right?"

Maggie blushed all over as the kids stared down at her. "Sure. I'm fine." The hat was gone. "My hat . . ."

Kelvin pointed ahead of them. "Greg is getting it." He offered a hand and helped her to her feet, but one sandal had lost its heel. He laughed at her. "I guess you'll have to go barefoot."

She felt as dumb as a rock. She wanted him to reach down and pull the other heel off like some hero in a movie, but he didn't. He stood and watched as she peeled the shoes from her feet, then led her across the parking lot by the hand like a disobedient toddler.

Everyone had a good laugh over it as they stood in line. Greg reenacted Maggie's lurching scramble three times for good measure, making her feel even more stupid, as though she was being put back in her place. But her awkward feeling faded when they got inside. Kelvin concentrated on the movie and his popcorn, hissing to Elliott at various points, and other than draping his arm across the back of her seat occasionally, he ignored her. By the end of the movie, she was okay, only blushing when she thought of everyone mentioning her folly again at school. Maybe she would be able to laugh about it by then, but she doubted it.

She was relieved when the chitchat outside the theater was over and they headed home, her with hat and sandals both in hand. Elliott got out at Dixie's house to say good night while Kelvin took Maggie down the road to her house. As Kelvin stretched his arm across the back of the seat behind her, she wondered if Dixie and Elliott were standing under the porch light kissing, where Mrs. Chambers could see them from the window, or if they'd walked down the road a piece in the dark. She heard a couple of dogs yapping into the quiet of the night, and imagined them announcing Dixie and Elliott's progression toward the empty lot midway down that road.

Kelvin touched her shoulder with his fingertips. "So you wanna hang out at the football game together tomorrow?"

She tingled all over at his words. She'd rarely even gone to a football game with Dixie, let alone with a boy. She had to admit it was nice being escorted around, feeling like a normal teenager. She decided that going out with Kelvin really wasn't any reflection on what happened to Sue. Sitting home and continuing her dateless life wasn't going to help anyone. She didn't ask for Sue to be raped. She didn't ask the news to draw attention to her. So if she ended up having a date, it wasn't as if she'd planned it this way, benefiting from Sue's misfortune.

She told herself that as she agreed to go out with Kelvin again, but deep inside she felt like scum.

The sounds of furniture being dragged around woke Maggie on Saturday morning. Downstairs, Andrea had two men rearranging the family room furniture.

Maggie strode across the family room and through the kitchen door to where her father was sitting at the table drinking a cup of coffee and reading the paper as if their whole lives weren't being redone by his girlfriend. "Is there no limit to what you'll let her do?"

He turned a page of the paper without comment.

Maggie grabbed a banana and continued out the back door. She was glad she'd agreed to baby-sit Kimberly for the day. When she returned to get ready for her date that afternoon, she barely recognized the place. The family room was totally rearranged, and the kitchen had been painted a blinding white.

She was beginning to understand why so many teens stayed away from home as much as possible. Her date with Kelvin would be a welcome escape. Even if she didn't really like him or feel completely comfortable with him and his friends, being at a football game with him would be better than being at home with Andrea, or traces of Andrea, staring her in the face.

The game was different from the movies. Kelvin slung his arm over her shoulder on their way in. The weight of it felt peculiar to her, but glancing behind her, she saw Elliott's arm around Dixie too, until they all reached the bleachers and had to ascend single file. The boys led the way, stopping to talk to a group of their school buddies.

Greg asked to see what shoes she was wearing.

She made light of it. "Gym shoes today, Greg, in case I have to run again."

He laughed and moved up two more rows.

After that, her nerves calmed down. She quit feeling like the odd one out and began to enjoy herself. Kelvin talked with everyone else, but he included her. They laughed and cheered when their team scored, and roared with the rest of the crowd in the final countdown when their wide receiver made the winning touchdown.

Back in the car, Kelvin drummed his fingers on the steering wheel waiting for traffic to clear, then turned his attention to her. "We still have half an hour. Want to ride around awhile?"

She nodded, even though she felt uneasy. At least he didn't want to dump her off as fast as he could—that was a good sign—but it all felt so strange. She knew so little about him, even after their being in school together for years. She knew how he acted at school. He was one of the guys, accepted, joking with other boys in the hall, hanging out after school, shooting baskets, going to parties, the whole routine. He belonged to the Spanish club just to get out of class, and to the debate team because his mom made him, but he was also the top debater, and he drank chocolate milk every day at lunch. Last year his hair had been spiky just to be weird, but this year he'd gone for a more classic look, and he talked more about sports and less about video games. He was in all her classes, except he had drafting when she had art appreciation. Nevertheless, she still didn't know *him*. She didn't know what made him tick, what he valued, where he was headed . . . or what he really thought of her.

She shivered. In some odd way it was exciting to be sitting next to a virtual stranger, out on a date, trying to get to know him. It amazed her that life had been run this way forever—boy and girl going off together to test things out. That they could go from being complete strangers to getting married. For some people, it happened in a matter of weeks. How could anyone get to know someone else in a few weeks? Was it all emotions with no real knowledge of each other behind it? Could two people be so trusting of each other that they would take such a risk? Life and love lived through gut reaction? *Maybe that's how it was with my parents,* she thought, but knew it couldn't be that way with her. She was too cautious. She was still searching for who she was. How could she possibly be ready to join her heart and soul to someone else?

Kelvin had one hand draped casually over the steering wheel and the other stretched across the seat behind her, but as he steered the car down a dark road and parked under a huge oak tree, he pulled his free hand back to shove the gearshift into park and turned off the ignition. He unsnapped his seat belt and turned to face Maggie, one arm resting across the steering wheel, the other now in his lap, so he was facing her straight on, assessing her with his sweet blue eyes.

"Did you enjoy the game?" he asked.

"Sure. Your friends really get into it, don't they?"

"We've got a good team this year."

He unlocked her seat belt, then touched her face. "Come here."

Every nerve in her body felt electrified. He was going to kiss her, and not just a good night kiss. A real kiss.

She almost needed to pinch herself to believe it. She was out on a date with a popular boy, sitting in his car getting ready to be kissed.

She moved toward him, lifted her chin, and let him push back her mass of curls. His breath was soft on her face. He smelled of grass and dirt—outdoorsy boy smells—mixed with a musky aftershave that tickled her nose.

He leaned forward and pressed his lips to hers. His mouth was wet, his lips soft.

His hand flirted across her stomach, touching her skin where her top had inched upward. She jerked away from him.

"It's okay." He eased his hand around her back and pulled her toward him. "I just want you closer."

The moonlight drew her attention. Clouds had cleared just enough that the moon looked like a white eye keeping watch over the world. "Look how pretty the moon is tonight."

He used her comment as an excuse to slide even closer to her, to put his head next to hers and peruse the sky from her vantage point. "Just needs a cow jumping over it and it could be from a picture book," he said as he turned back to her.

As her own gaze slid from the moon to Kelvin's face, a movement down the road caught her eye. Was it the bearded man? Was he watching them? She blinked and looked again. There was nothing there but the shadows cast by moonlight against the trees.

Kelvin touched her cheek. "I like the way it shines on your hair."

She had to laugh. There was no way Kelvin could possibly have meant that with any seriousness.

"Don't laugh. It's true." He swept his hand through her locks, or tried to. His fingers tangled in them, but he pulled free and ran his hand over the top to gather the full mop in both hands at the nape of her neck. "You wouldn't look the same without your halo of red curls."

My halo of red curls? Was he for real?

He leaned into her and took her into his arms. She resisted for a minute, then gave into him. He made her feel normal, wanted, pretty. He was kissing her, Maggie with the wild hair, Maggie the dork. Maggie with the halo of red curls.

He eased one hand under her shirt and rubbed small circles on the bare flesh of her back. The other was lost in the curls on the back of her head. Her heart palpitated while her head screamed, *It's no big deal!*

As his hand moved up her back, she pulled back, so he stopped and smiled at her, whispered in her ear, and continued kissing her.

She felt the moon-eye watching her, and then she felt his hand slip forward, underneath her bra.

It stunned her for a moment, so smooth was the transition. He was touching her! She jerked back and slapped him.

She hadn't meant to slap him. He held his cheek and cussed. "What's wrong with you?"

"You don't even know me."

"Huh? We've been in school together for ten years."

"This is our second date. You think you can touch me like that on our second date?"

"You're crazy," he said, and started the car.

Crazy? What happened to Maggie with the halo of red curls? Maybe he didn't understand the significance of a halo.

As he pulled the car back onto the road, headlights approached, slowed down beside them, then kept going. It was the deputy who had been patrolling the neighborhood. Maggie recognized his car. She wondered what he would've done if they'd still been parked.

She didn't wait for Kelvin to open her door. She pushed it open and ran up the front steps, into the house, and straight to her bedroom. She had to know how Dixie was faring. Was she still out with Elliott? She dialed her number, but Dixie didn't answer the phone; her mother did.

"I thought she was with you," said Mrs. Chambers.

Oh no, she'd gotten Dixie in trouble. "We were together at the game, but we rode home separately. I just walked in the door. I have to talk to her. Can you have her call me? Can she come spend the night here?"

Mrs. Chambers chuckled. "In desperate need of girl talk, eh? I remember those days. Tell you what, why don't you come up here and spend the night? I'm sure she'll be home any minute. I'll have a cup of hot tea waiting for you."

Mrs. Chambers thought a cup of hot tea fixed everything, but that was okay with Maggie. With Maggie's Irish heritage, hot tea was a common thing in her house too.

She could tell by her father's expression that he wasn't too happy with the idea. He kept fiddling with the remote—a sure sign that something was eating at him.

"What?"

"You go out on two dates and I don't hear a word about either one?"

He didn't understand. She'd had to act as her own mother all these years; he couldn't suddenly step into that role. She couldn't tell him what had happened. Or could she?

She twisted a lock of hair, thinking.

He stood up and walked toward her. "Okay, so you need to talk to Dixie. Take the car, but be back in plenty of time for church in the morning," he said. He wrapped his arms around her in a tender hug. "We'll talk tomorrow."

She grabbed the keys and left him with a kiss on the cheek—and a noticeable tear in the corner of his eye.

Dixie arrived two minutes behind her. They dashed upstairs together, pulled on pajamas, and reconvened in the kitchen to lean on the table with hot cups of tea clasped between their hands.

They didn't even have to discuss the details. Maggie could tell from the flush of Dixie's cheeks that she'd had a great time.

"We made out down by the pond," Dixie whispered when her mom left the room. Maggie gulped her tea, now not so sure if she was ready to share the details. Dixie would think she was lame for not giving in to Kelvin.

Chapter
Sixteen

"WHERE'S BILLY?" MAGGIE asked her father as she walked into the family room Sunday afternoon.

He looked up from his paper. "I sent him off with Brad. He and his dad came to the door asking Billy to go to the Columbia zoo with them."

"And Billy wanted to go?"

"Not really. I made him go. He's been spending too much time stuck in his room lately."

She cringed at the thought of him being forced to go somewhere with Mr. Dweller. All the angst she'd held toward him returned as his face rose before her.

She didn't say so to her father. He wouldn't understand.

"So much for taking him shopping for new tennis shoes," she said instead. At least it was one less thing on her to-do list. "In that case, I'm going up to Dixie's house, and then I'll run errands. Can I use the car?"

He glanced at his watch. "Well, I was supposed to pick up Andrea in an hour, but I'll tell her to come get me instead. Go ahead."

On the way back from the store she stopped at Webb's house to give Tony a ride home. "You know Daddy doesn't want us walking home alone. Come on home now so I don't have to come back up here for you."

Webb's attention didn't leave Tony's progress as his fingers flickered across the game controls. Tony was so deep in concentration his tongue stuck out the corner of his mouth.

"In a minute."

"Come on, Tony. You can pause the game and play later tonight. I've got to get supper started before Daddy gets back with Andrea."

"Hang on. I've got to finish this race."

She sighed and sat down at Webb's desk. She would give him ten minutes, no more. The milk would spoil.

She didn't say anything for a while. Boys seemed to live on a different plane. How could they care so much about a video game and winning a silly car race? Just like the date and Kelvin. Were all boys like him? Was getting to the next base all Webb and Tony thought of too? Was sex just another game to them? How could they think about girls that way? How could they be so different, so uncaring? Didn't they want to be friends with the girls they hung out with? Didn't they want to do fun things together, get to know them, and go out with them just because they wanted to be together? Or maybe it was just her. Maybe most girls only thought about sex too, and that's why they showed off their boobs and bellies all the time. Maggie had thought it was just to get boys' attention, but maybe the girls wanted sex as much as the guys. She couldn't believe it. She wanted so much more from a relationship.

"Boys are so stupid. They think they can do anything. I can't believe Kelvin touched my boob."

Her face went beet red. She hadn't intended to say that out loud, and now it was too late. She wished the floor would open up and swallow her. Her body became enveloped in a heat wave, a full-body blush. She had talked about her *boobs* in front of Webb and her brother! She thought she might vomit.

Tony's fingers stopped midmove. His mouth hung open. His eyes flared wide.

Webb leaned forward, his brow furrowed seriously. "So what'd you do?"

"I slapped him."

Tony snickered. "I'm sure he can't wait to ask you out again."

"Not a problem since I wouldn't say yes anyway. Why do guys just want to have sex? Why don't they want to go out to have fun? To do things together?"

"Sex *is* fun, you idiot," said Tony.

Maggie glared at him. Tony hadn't ever been with a girl. He was all talk. "It's supposed to be meaningful. How can it be meaningful if you've only been together for the duration of a two-hour date?"

Webb leaned back against his orange pillows. "Meaningful?"

"You've been reading too many sappy romances," said Tony. He turned back to his game. "Snap! You made me miss that turn. Man!"

"I don't read romances. I read classics." She was disgusted by their reaction. Had Webb actually been with a girl? Had sex with a girl? She shuddered to consider what he may have done with Sue before the rape. They probably didn't even know each other's middle names. They probably didn't know what made each other cry, or what their most precious memory was, or who most influenced their lives, or where they wanted their lives to go, but they would've shared the most intimate act possible.

It took a moment to think of how to put words to all those thoughts and emotions coursing through her. "You mean you really don't want more than a body in the backseat of a car? That's so desperate."

Tony shrugged.

"If that were true, if that's all guys really wanted, there wouldn't be divorce because husbands wouldn't care what their wives were actually like as people."

"Of course we care what the girls are like. I wouldn't date just anyone," Webb explained.

"Then what? What are the criteria? She has to be pretty? She has to have a nice voice? Her hair has to be shiny and blonde? Is that all it takes?"

"Well . . ."

"So you ask this girl out because she's hot, and that's it, you think you've got a claim over her?" She clenched her fists. "What makes you think that just because a girl goes out with you, you have the right to expect her to take her clothes off?"

"It's what they expect."

"No, it's not. Girls want guys to care about them, to be interested in them for who they are. It's not about sex at all. Sex is supposed to be an expression of love after you've committed to each other."

Tony harrumphed. "It's bad enough that Dad makes me go to church on Sunday. I don't need you up here preaching quotes from youth group. You're such a dork."

"What? You're too cool to believe in God? You don't think we ought to obey what He says? You think sex is okay anytime you feel like it, with whoever you want?"

"I would hardly call a guy touching your boob the same thing as having sex."

"You wouldn't, huh? I've kept my"—could she say *boobs* again in front of Webb?—"breasts covered up for sixteen years, and you think a guy has a right to undo that just because he took me out for pizza? No way. Not this girl."

"Maybe some girls like it," Webb said.

He was looking at her so intently it was hard to face him with an answer. "I didn't say they shouldn't like it. It just shouldn't be done with just any guy. In fact, a guy shouldn't want it from just any girl! It ought to be like a well-kept secret. You don't share a secret with just anyone, do you? You would be afraid they'd tell someone else. It would be gossip and everyone would think differently about you. That's what touching is all about; it's sharing the most personal secrets of your body with someone else. That's how God planned it."

The boys both stared at her without comment. Tony poked Webb. "Just call her Sister Margaret Ann. She'll be an old hag of a nun someday, never even kissed."

"No." Maggie stood up. "I'll be happily married to a man who really cares about me. I'll have waited for someone who is my best friend and ready to share my secrets. You'll marry some ditsy girl with pretty hair and wonder why she's staring at you with a blank expression when you're trying to tell her about work, or whatever. And then when she quits putting on her makeup one day, you'll wonder why you married her."

"Just shut up, will ya?" Tony shot back at her. "I'm not married to anybody, and I don't plan to be for a long time. Your problem is you already act like a wife and mother. You're old and you're not even out of school."

He had her there. It deflated her to hear him say it too. He'd never said anything like that before. But then again, she'd never been so outspoken before either, and right here in front of Webb.

She felt sick. There was nothing else to say. He was right. She was old before her time, but it wasn't by choice; it was just how life worked out. *Maybe it'll keep me from making the stupid mistakes I would've made if I hadn't thought about all this. Maybe I wouldn't be me.* The realization came like an exclamation mark at the end of their tirade.

She crossed her arms. "If you want a ride home, come now. Otherwise you can walk on your own."

Tony threw her a glance that answered her plainly: he would walk home later.

As she left, she heard him mutter, "Ignore her. She's just freaked over what happened to Sue."

"It's all good, man. We're *all* freaked by what happened."

She figured that was the end of it, all her thoughts and words hitting a dead end. They would probably bury their heads in the game and forget everything she'd said. It was probably a mistake to say anything to them at all. One way or another, it was sure to come back to haunt her.

Chapter Seventeen

MAGGIE WOKE IN a sweat in the wee hours Monday morning and stared into the dark. She couldn't sleep without images of Kelvin in the car turning into the rapist, his face twisting into an obscene mask of evil, glowing eyes and scarred flesh coming at her with a knife, chasing her out of the car and into the woods.

She must have cried out in her sleep because she could hear Billy stirring in his room. She must have awoken him. Tears rolled down her cheeks. She wanted desperately to get over it all, to wash the image of what happened to Sue from her mind and get on with her life.

She tried to look at it analytically. Was it Sue's rape that made her push Kelvin away? No, she decided. She wanted to wait for marriage; that was God's plan, even if other teens thought it sounded stupid. Maybe the rape was coloring her perceptions and making her overreact to everything around her, but it didn't change how she felt. She wasn't going to let any boy take advantage of her, or convince her to do something that went against her beliefs.

Billy moaned.

Was he having nightmares like she was? She got up and went to his room. "Are you okay, Billy?"

"I can't sleep," he said.

"Do you want me to lie down with you, tell you a story or something?"

"No!" He said it so abruptly, so emphatically, that it stabbed at her. She stumbled back to her room, tears flowing again.

She needed help. She needed someone to empty it all from her head and leave her back where she'd been such a short time ago—without all the ugly images and emotions crowding her brain.

After a few more fitful hours of sleep, she got up and got ready for school. She knew where she had to go. She thought about it all day. After school, after she'd dropped off the other kids, she headed downtown.

She checked the address again. It didn't look like she expected. It wasn't an office building. It was an old house and not in very good condition. The grass reminded her of Tony's hair—just a little too long and unkempt. Blue paint was peeling from the clapboards, a few of which were loose and bowed, needing to be nailed back into place. The white trim definitely needed to be redone, but there was a sign swinging from a post by the red front door: *The Crisis Center.*

Maggie stepped inside, tentative, not sure what to expect.

The lobby area was obviously a converted living room. A counter ran the length of it to separate it from the work area. Two women bustled around behind the counter. Another, on a stool, bent over paperwork while talking on the phone.

The woman closest to the door was acting as receptionist. Only her brunette bun was visible to Maggie at first, but when she looked up, a shuttered expression fell away and her blue eyes sparkled with friendliness. "May I help you?"

Maggie felt small, out of place. This lady was expecting a beat-up woman dragging a string of starved children behind her, or a pregnant girl looking for options. Maggie felt like an imposter. She drew herself up to look businesslike instead of desperate. "Is Andrea here?"

The woman grinned. "Oh, you must be Maggie McCarthy. I should have known by your hair." She punched a button on her phone. "Andrea, you have a visitor. Maggie." She hung up. "I meant that as a compliment. It's gorgeous. Your hair, I mean. All my life with this wimpy brown mop."

Maggie warmed all over. Imagine anyone thinking of her hair as being gorgeous.

Andrea appeared between double doors at the opposite end of the room and beckoned Maggie to come in. Maggie walked underneath the archway into what must've been the dining room. Stacks of files gave the office a feeling of being in transition and disorganized, not what she expected of Andrea, despite the fact that a bay window overlooking a tiny backyard made it seem less cramped.

Andrea had already gone back to her chair behind a battered desk. The desk, at least, was neat, even with the files lying open across it with an array of papers she must've been working on before the interruption.

"This is a pleasant surprise. Take a seat."

The seat held a phone book and a stack of papers, so she leaned on the desk. "I want to know why."

"I can't talk with you towering over me like that, Maggie. Sit down."

Maggie wondered how Andrea managed to always stay so in control of the space and people around her. It was more than being demanding. Maggie could be demanding, but she didn't evoke the authority Andrea did.

Maggie sighed and placed the junk on the floor before sitting on the edge of the seat and leaning toward the desk. "Why?"

"Why what?"

"Why did he rape her? Why her? Why there?"

Andrea crossed her arms and leaned back in her chair. "There are so many possibilities, it's hard to say. All I can do is speculate."

"So speculate."

"Some perpetrators are seeking to exert power over women. These men have frustrations that escalate into vendettas against women, and from there they develop a need to overpower women as a form of revenge. Other perpetrators feel that no woman would willingly have sex with them, so they choose a victim and force themselves on her. Then you have some men who stalk women, psychologically thinking they've developed a relationship even if they've remained virtual strangers. They often misinterpret the smallest social signal, such as a smile or nod, as meaning much more than just casual manners. But the truth is that stranger rape applies to only a very small percentage of cases. Date rape, or acquaintance rape as we like to term it, is much more common, where the rapist is a neighbor, relative, or some other casual acquaintance."

"Raped by a neighbor?"

"Sure. Or molested."

"Molested?"

Andrea stared off a moment and twirled a pen in her hands. Maggie wondered why this question seemed more difficult, but she waited patiently.

"Molestation means inappropriate touching of any kind. Molesters are often people we know and trust, like teachers or coaches or friends."

"Okay, so back to Sue. Why?"

"Let's assume it was someone she knew. He lured her into the woods and then forced himself on her. Obviously, given Sue's condition, she didn't consent. But Maggie" — her expression softened — "why he did it is impossible to say until we know more."

The picture building in Maggie's mind was not something she wanted to face, but she suspected she had to if she was ever going to get beyond it, a problem that had to be examined and cried over before healing could take place. She wanted to shut the whole thing out, not hear another word, and yet she also wanted to face it straight on.

"Do you think whoever did it is still here waiting to attack someone else?"

"You're afraid he's going to come after you. I understand that fear, but it's not likely. Sometimes perpetrators will return to the scene of their crime, even during the investigation, because they want to see if they're getting credit for the deed. But some realize they've committed a crime and take off. Again, there are a lot of psychological factors to figure in."

"You mean he might've come back and watched the police investigation?"

"Maybe."

Maggie tried to remember if there had been a stranger among all the faces. She couldn't remember. That part of the day had become a blur.

She stood to go.

"Look, Maggie, before we end this, I want you to understand something. As hard as Sue's rape is to understand, it's an example of the exception instead of the rule."

"What do you mean?"

"Girls are much more likely to be date-raped. Boys make them feel like they have to comply, and the girls aren't strong enough, physically or mentally, to stop them. Boys often tell girls they know that they really want sex even if they say no, and that it's the girl's fault for leading them on to the point they can't stop. That's bull, Maggie. Don't ever let a boy use you that way."

She thought of her slap to Kelvin's face. A boy wasn't likely to have his way with her. In fact, she figured that once the word spread she probably wouldn't ever be asked out again. She would become an old maid and live forever in her father's house.

Compared to what happened to Sue, she decided that might not be such a bad thing.

Chapter Eighteen

AS MAGGIE MADE her way through the school halls and out to the car that Tuesday, she realized how much she loved the freedom of driving herself to school, parking in the student lot, and wandering out at the end of the day at her own pace. It empowered her. Better yet, it made Tony rely on her to get home, which meant Webb rode with them too, and that gave her a sense of superiority over them for a change. They always made her feel like such an imbecile, but driving them around reversed the roles. It renewed her authority over Tony and made her less embarrassed about the whole sex discussion.

The parking lot was clearing out as she sat tapping the wheel, waiting for them to show up. Dixie jumped into the car and started chattering about Max Carter's upcoming party, while Maggie searched the thinning crowd for signs of Tony's round head and floppy hair.

"We've got to go, Mags. Everyone will be there."

"I'm not going to his party."

Despite their efforts to keep their friendship on the same plane, it kept shifting. Their paths were diverging, and they both knew it.

Dixie snapped at her. "Come on. So you don't want to go out with Kelvin again. I can live with that. I still plan to date Elliott. But you have to go to this party. We'll be social outcasts again if we don't."

Maggie sighed. She was more concerned with finding Tony than making party plans. She couldn't see him anywhere.

Billy stepped up to the car. "Wuz up, Mags? Let's go." He'd come from the middle school, but the two schools shared joint playing fields, so it was almost like one huge campus and not that much of a walk.

Maggie hadn't been expecting him. He usually rode home with Brad on soccer practice days. "What are you doing here? What happened to soccer practice?"

"I don't need to go today."

"Really? Why?"

"I don't know."

"So where's Brad?"

"With his dad."

"And you didn't want to ride home with him?"

"No."

Whatever had happened between Billy and Brad still wasn't resolved, but she wasn't going to push him about it. He would tell her eventually. "What if I'd left you because I didn't know you were riding with me?"

"I get out ten minutes before you do. I'd have to be a snail not to get over here before you left."

She dismissed it and went back to scanning the area for Tony and Webb.

Billy snapped his seat belt into place. "So, let's go."

"Haven't you noticed that we seem to be missing Tony and Webb?"

"I talked to them in the parking lot a few minutes ago. They got a ride home with somebody. Long hair, ripped jeans, had a cigarette stuck over one ear. Introduced himself as something Jones."

"I bet it was Asby Jones," Dixie said.

"Weird name," Billy commented.

Maggie thought of Asby's pretend joints in history class and wondered what on earth he might lead her brother to do.

Dixie snapped her seat belt. "Those boys are so stupid. Let's go."

"Where do you suppose they went?"

"I have no idea, but I have to get home. I've got piano this afternoon, and then I'm picking out what I'm wearing to the party on Friday. We're color coordinating so we'll look good."

By "we" she meant Tammy and Heather. Maggie ignored the comment. She was more irked by Tony's behavior. She dropped Dixie off at home and swung by Webb's house. The back door was locked, and no one answered when Billy pounded against it.

"I suppose you want me to drop you off at Brad's house?"

"No. I told you I didn't want to ride home with him, and I don't want to go over to his house, either."

"Why not?"

He didn't reply.

Maggie wished he wouldn't shut her out. She remembered back when Billy and Tony told her everything that happened in their lives. Billy was only twelve now and already putting up a wall. There was something bothering him. This was the third time he'd turned down a chance to play with Brad, and she had never known him to turn down a chance to play soccer. All he wanted to do was sit in his room by himself.

Maybe it was just his age. Tony was fifteen now, so maybe twelve was when he had quit confiding in her too.

It made her feel lonely for the old days.

She laid into Tony when he wandered in the door at five o'clock. "What do you think you're doing riding home with Asby Jones?"

Tony shrugged. "What's it to you?"

"Are you kidding? Everyone knows Asby is a dopehead."

"Right. We left school to smoke a couple joints. That's why I'm flying high now. What do you take me for?"

"Sometimes I don't know what to think of you, to be perfectly honest."

"You're so stupid. He got a new Xbox game Webb wanted to see."

That sounded more like Tony than smoking marijuana, and he didn't have that clingy sweet smell she often detected in the high school bathrooms, but how much was there that he didn't tell her anymore? How did she know he wouldn't start hanging out with someone like Asby because of his Xbox and end up joining him to get high or drunk? "You could have told me you had a ride with him and not left us waiting there forever."

"Billy told you, didn't he? I gave the message to him."

He had done that, she had to admit, but that wasn't the same as telling her.

"Besides, you're not my mother. I don't have to report to you at all."

"No, I'm not your mother, but if we don't watch out, Andrea might be."

"I can't see where that would be so bad. She got us a new TV, didn't she? And she bought me a couple games last week.

Now with the old TV in my room, I can play without anybody bugging me. That's all right with me."

Maggie turned and ran upstairs. She couldn't say anything to the rest of them. She'd been the first to sell out to her father's girlfriend.

Two down and one to go: Billy.

At supper, Andrea picked at her salad, watching the rest of them eat as if she were a talk show host evaluating her guest stars. She chatted amicably for a while, but when she sat back in her chair, Maggie knew it was a sign of some proclamation or other; the gesture had that largeness to it.

She let silence build a moment before she made her announcement. "Billy needs a dog."

Maggie gripped the napkin in her lap. *A dog?* "I don't think so."

Andrea had been concentrating on Billy, waiting for a clap of his hands or a silly grin or something, and totally ignored Maggie's reply. In fact, she acted like she had the authority to make such a decision all on her own, an outsider who had stepped through a magical door that placed her at the head of the clan.

Their father shook his head. "A dog is a lot of work."

Billy looked from one person to the next as if he hadn't even grasped the notion of what was being discussed.

"What do you say, Billy?" Andrea persisted. "Would you like a dog?"

Maggie churned up a noise of disgust in the back of her throat. "I don't think we need a dog."

"Why, Maggie, you're such an animal lover, I'm surprised you would object."

Maggie bit back what she wanted to say and turned to her father. She could say as much with her eyes and body as she could with words.

Her father was caught between them. "Let's talk about this later," he said.

"Good idea," Andrea replied as if it were her idea.

"Later" turned out to be while Maggie was stuck in the kitchen washing dishes. Andrea seemed to have taken control of their house, but only the areas she wanted, not doing mundane chores like cleaning up after supper.

Maggie pushed the swinging door open intending to ask her father if he wanted any more coffee before she dumped out the pot, but stopped herself when she caught the conversation.

"I'm sure all this new behavior Billy's been exhibiting is because of what happened to that dog. I see this kind of reaction in my clients all the time. It's a form of shock, of shutting down from reality, and I think the best way to get him beyond it is to give him a new puppy to focus on. It will help get the image of Smokey out of his mind."

What about the images in my mind? Maggie thought, but her concern for Billy won out over worries about herself. Billy never wanted to play with Brad anymore, or play soccer, or do anything else he used to be crazy about doing. All he wanted nowadays was to sit upstairs alone in his room or play video games with Tony, which he had rarely done before. She'd been hoping it was just his age, that he'd reached the point of being more interested in video games than sports. She'd also been thinking he and Brad would patch things up and be off playing again, but that hadn't happened.

She knew the real reason she hadn't worried too much before, though. She was relieved he wasn't at the Dwellers' house all the time. So much so that a part of her admitted she was jealous of Mr. Dweller's relationship with Billy, and it made her happy that he didn't want to play there anymore. Billy was home with her now, where he belonged, which greatly lessened the ill feelings she harbored toward Mr. Dweller.

Now, here was Andrea saying she had noticed a change in Billy, even though she barely knew him. Not only that, she was saying it was a reaction to seeing Smokey mutilated in the woods.

The thought stabbed at Maggie. She should have realized it sooner. She should have known to look for aftereffects. Not just his avoidance of playing outside, but that he'd been having night-mares and wetting the bed. She had cared for him all his life yet missed diagnosing the effects of a major trauma. He relied on *her* to take care of him, not this woman who had invaded their house, and she had let him down.

"I can see your point," came her father's reply. "It must've been horrible, seeing Smokey cut up like that. A hard image to get out of your head. But it can't be worse than Maggie finding Sue."

"People react differently. Billy is younger. Maggie is more analytical. She's working things out mentally, but I don't think Billy is. It's eating at him."

"But a dog? There's no way you tell all your clients to go out and get dogs."

"No, but they aren't little boys. Billy needs to replace the bad memories of Smokey with earlier, happier memories. He didn't see Sue, but all this talk about her keeps reviving the memory of how he found Smokey. A puppy is a small price to pay to see a smile back on his face, to see him laughing and playing again, isn't it?"

Maggie's father looked resigned, the way he did more and more around Andrea. He wasn't used to holding his own against a woman who put herself in charge. Maggie never challenged his decisions, and he never challenged hers, so there were no heated discussions or debates about major changes in their lives. They simply kept things on an even keel, him making the money and handling the more important financial decisions, and Maggie taking care of their everyday lives. All three kids had come to expect that life in their house would forever remain as it was. They didn't bother asking for things that other families had. Even getting a DVD player had been a complete surprise to them since the VHS player was still working.

Andrea had brought some great imbalance into this setup, though, making Maggie wonder if perhaps her father lacked backbone, and maybe if she'd pushed for things she'd wanted, he would have granted her every wish. If she hadn't been the one watching every penny, life may have been completely different.

"Really, Andrea, the expense . . . ," he said as if reading Maggie's mind.

"My treat," Andrea replied. "I bought presents for Maggie and Tony, so it's Billy's turn."

Maggie sighed. Buying Billy; that's what this was about. She wondered what her father was thinking as he gave in. "Okay, we'll visit the animal shelter and pick one out."

Andrea's whole body smiled with triumphant superiority. "Good. We'll go this weekend, at eleven on Saturday."

Maggie mentally reassembled her life around the idea that her father had actually caved into the idea of getting a dog just as easily as he caved into changing the lamps, the television, and the paintings and curtains.

She desperately wanted to march into the room and tell Andrea what she thought of her lame-brain idea. The last thing Maggie wanted was more responsibility. It was laughable to think that Billy might actually take care of the dog himself. He couldn't even remember to put his cereal bowl in the sink. The problem was that Andrea's theory made sense. Maggie wished she could erase the image of Sue from her mind, to stop the dreams and terrors she kept reliving. Likewise, maybe Billy was agonizing over what happened to Smokey. Maybe getting a dog would put him back in better spirits.

So she dumped the coffee down the sink and said nothing. On the chance it would bring Billy around, they would get him a dog.

Chapter Nineteen

WEDNESDAY EVENING, MAGGIE kept vigil at Sue's side while Mr. and Mrs. Roberts went to church. Maggie sat staring at Sue's unconscious body, her chest rising and falling in steady breaths, and thought about the oral presentation Mrs. Newell had assigned. A speech about a current issue wouldn't be hard. The choice of subjects was a no-brainer, too obvious to even leave her an option.

Public speaking had never been her forte. She didn't like the eyes of all the students on her, staring at her hair, judging how she looked, how she stood, how she spoke. This time, though, she was going to set all that aside. The topic was important. She was going to talk about rape. Violent rape by strangers like what happened to Sue, and date rape.

After school the next day, she headed to the Crisis Center again, this time to do research.

"I'm glad you're tackling this," Andrea said as she handed her pamphlets with statistics, advice, and action plans. "It'll be tough to stand in front of your classmates and talk about it, but the timing is perfect."

The prospect of standing in front of everyone, having them all watch her while she talked about rape and intimate relationships, hadn't really manifested itself. Fear gripped her heart. How could she look Kelvin or Asby or Sean in the face and talk about what jerks boys and men could be? She set the pamphlets down. "Maybe this isn't such a good idea. I'm not the right person. I'm the least likely candidate. What do I know about any of it? Finding Sue in the woods doesn't give me the right to assume that I can understand even an inkling of what she suffered."

"You're right. You'll never know what she suffered. But you can raise awareness to prevent it from happening to other girls, and to keep your friends from succumbing to date rape, and to seek help if they are molested."

"How can I talk about date rape? I freak out if a guy even touches me."

Andrea leaned back in her chair, her mouth a grim line of consideration. "You don't have to experience date rape to abhor it. Your feelings about your body should encourage you even more to talk about this issue, to make it plain to other girls your age how you cherish your body, and that to violate a body is to violate God Himself."

Maggie couldn't speak. Just thinking about the subject in front of Andrea was embarrassing. How did she ever think she could talk to a classroom full of peers?

She had to admit, though, that Andrea knew what was in her heart. The way Andrea had stated it was exactly what she had tried to express to Webb and Tony. "You ought to do the speech, Andrea. You know how to say it without blushing."

She shook her head. "I do make rounds to schools on occasion, but I think God put you in Sue's path for a greater purpose. There is someone else out there besides Sue that you're meant to help. You have an urging to do this as your speech, and I think that's exactly what you need to do. Don't be surprised if it leads you further into the issue."

How much further could she go than taking it from a personal conversation among friends to a public speech to her class?

Andrea answered the question without her even asking it aloud. "Never underestimate how God uses us to benefit others. There may be some girl in your class just waiting to hear this message from you."

Maggie gathered up the pamphlets. "It's going to take a lot of guts to do this."

"Very few things worth doing are easy."

Maggie sighed and turned to go.

"I'll get everyone here to pray for you at our afternoon meeting, Maggie. You're fulfilling an important mission."

Maggie closed the double doors behind her and hoped that the prayers would take away the feeling that she'd just swallowed a stomach full of lead.

Doing the research wasn't fun. Some of the pamphlets Andrea gave her only provided tidbits, and she had to dig deeper, going to the library to look at online Web sites that revealed information she would rather have not seen.

Andrea stopped by the house that evening to see Frank and check on Maggie's progress. It struck Maggie as odd that at this one juncture where Andrea ought to have taken the high hand and come across as an authority, she seemed to bend her persona to become a friend and confident. She joined Maggie, sitting on the end of her bed as if she were a teenage girl stopping by for a chat. "How's it going?"

"Some of this stuff is hard to handle."

"You've got that right."

"It says a lot more kids are molested than raped, so I'm thinking I ought to include a portion of that in my speech."

"Many more. In fact, one in four girls are molested by people they know and trust—often people at church because children are taught to trust them as people of God. When an adult that a child is supposed to respect slowly starts petting her, caressing her, and gradually touching her in more and more inappropriate ways, the girl often feels unable to stop it."

"Why don't they just tell their parents?"

"Good question. Sometimes they do, and their parents ignore them. After all, this adult is a wonderful person they have entrusted with her care, whether it's for religious education, choir, or some other function. Sometimes the child is just too embarrassed to tell her parents. She's afraid it will reflect badly on her. She begins to think it's something she's doing, or something that's normal, that she's supposed to tolerate."

"I can't imagine tolerating that."

"You would be surprised how bad it gets for some of them." She yawned and stretched. "Well, I'm going down to watch a movie with Frank. Holler if you need me."

"I think I'm done with it for today. I have a few weeks to finish it. I'm going to go see Dixie for a while."

They walked down the staircase together and parted ways at the bottom. It still didn't feel right to leave the house knowing her father was about to settle on the couch with Andrea beside him. He would put his arm around her and probably kiss her or worse. She couldn't think of her father as a man. She couldn't even think of Tony and Billy as being guys with girlfriends some day.

Maybe that's why Tony ignored her comments. Maybe knowing what went through other boys' heads when they looked at her made it impossible for him to think of her as a girl.

She shook the thoughts away. She'd been so wrapped up in the research that it was coloring everything. That's why she needed to go visit Dixie, so she could feel grounded again. Even if Dixie was putting on airs and had more interest in Heather and Tammy than her, she was still an old friend and they could laugh together for an evening.

Still, thoughts of Webb returned as she got in the car. She couldn't help wondering what he thought when he looked at her, especially after the whole sex conversation. Maybe he thought she was even weirder now than he had thought before.

Chapter Twenty

ON FRIDAY EVENING, Dixie called Maggie and begged her again to go to Max's party. She wouldn't let up. "Come on, Mags. What're you going to do? Sit in that house and watch your dad make out with Andrea?"

That was the exact button it took. Maggie changed and brushed her hair, and headed out the door to pick up Dixie.

Tony joined her. "Give me a lift."

"You're going to this party?"

"Duh. We have to pick up Webb. His mom's car is in the shop."

Maggie frowned.

"It's either you take me, or Asby picks me up."

That left her with no choice. She couldn't believe she was even contemplating a party that included Asby Jones.

Almost everyone from school was there, all crammed into the main living area of the house. Guys lounged against the kitchen counter, swigging ice-cold beers they'd pulled from the three coolers stacked across the kitchen table. Girls leaned against the guys, listening, or chatting among themselves. Conversations wrapped around one another as people mingled.

Maggie stood in the living room doorway, taking it all in. Her classmates all looked so different away from school, their personalities heightened in the freedom of a party. Asby Jones waved a real joint in the air and disappeared outside with a buddy from some other school. Tammy and Heather were in the living room, but when Maggie joined them, they were comparing new sandals, so she turned away.

Sean Black wandered in from the back porch and collapsed on the sofa with a beer in his hand. He took a swig and laid his head back. Maggie had heard from Heather that morning that his lifelong girlfriend had broken up with him. One look and Maggie knew he was devastated. He had obviously really been in love with Becca. She wished she knew what it was like to have a guy feel like that about her.

She crossed the room and sat beside him. He was a fellow a girl could have a chat with like a best friend and not be worried about his hands seeking all the wrong places on her body. Besides, they were both Irish, which gave them a bond on some ancestral level. It probably didn't mean a thing to anyone else in the room, where they came from and who else might have such origins, but it seemed to be the kind of thing Sean would care about. Any boy who cared to ask about the Claddagh ring had to be the type to care about family history.

One of the surround-sound speakers was mounted on the wall behind them and pounded out a beat that got a few kids dancing in place while they talked and drank.

"Sorry to hear about you and Becca," Maggie said. The music was so loud that she had to move closer to him than she had intended just so he could hear her. She found herself leaning on his shoulder in order to get her voice to his ear.

He pulled his arm from under her and stretched it across the sofa so he could halfway face her. He didn't reply except for a slow nod, as if he was too overwhelmed with emotions to get words out of his mouth.

Before approaching him, she was sure they would have a lot to say to each other, but now she couldn't think of a thing to talk to him about. It wasn't like they could get into a deep discussion when they could barely hear themselves.

Sean continued to nod. It was like a perpetual motion she had started but didn't know how to end.

Dixie walked up with two beers and held one out to Maggie. "Here, this one's for you."

She couldn't imagine what Dixie was thinking. She was driving, and even if she wasn't, it wouldn't have mattered. "I don't drink."

Dixie took on an air of exasperation that seemed to come more easily of late, as if she were ahead of Maggie on some great board game of life and couldn't stand it that Maggie wouldn't catch up. She thrust one hip out and cocked her head just so. "Will you lighten up? One beer is not going to kill you."

"Unless I drive us straight into a tree on the way home."

Dixie thrust the beer at Maggie, tossed her hair around in some fashion of dismissal, and turned to Sean. "Tough luck about Becca," she said. "Don't let it get you down. The world is full of girls."

Heather sauntered up and grabbed Dixie away. "C'mon. I'm going to introduce you to the guy I was telling you about." They went off arm in arm without so much as a *"Come join us."*

At least Dixie's comment had stopped Sean's steady nod. He was back to zombie state, his focus on some distant point across the room. "I shoulda seen it coming. Always busy lately."

Maggie wondered what she'd gotten herself into. There was no one else in the room she could talk to. Even Tammy had disappeared, probably following the tracks of Dixie and Heather, and she hadn't seen Clarissa at all. Sam, the quiet boy from English class, leaned against the opposite wall, drinking a Coke, but he never had anything to say to anyone. She was surprised he was even at the party.

The beer hung in her hand cold, heavy, and wet like a snowball melting in her palm. She'd never actually tasted beer. For lack of anything else to say to Sean, she ran her fingers up and down the bottle, playing with the rivulets of condensation streaming down the sides.

Sean came back to earth and noticed she was still sitting there. He raised his beer. "Here's to new starts."

She raised her bottle up so that they clinked together, like she'd seen on television. "Cheers," she said. She wondered if that was appropriate, given that he wasn't cheerful at all and certainly wasn't celebrating.

The bottle following the path from there to her mouth seemed like the most natural thing in the world. It may have hesitated halfway for a slight second, but she couldn't toast and not take a sip, could she?

It foamed into her mouth. The bitterness of it surprised her, almost making her spit it out. The taste of it filled her mouth and nose and contorted her face. She held it up to look at the label.

Sean touched her fingers. "You're wearing it."

Wearing the beer? What was he talking about? "Wearing what?"

"The Claddagh."

She swapped the beer to her left hand and held her right hand out so they could both admire the ring. "I never take it off. It's the only thing I have of my mother's. This and the choker, but I don't wear the choker very often."

He went back into nodding mode for a minute before taking another swig of his beer. Maggie felt like a marionette parroting the motion with her own beer, cringing again when it hit her taste buds.

"My mother loved that story. Maybe you could come over and show her the ring sometime."

Sure, that seemed likely. About as likely as Asby Jones showing up at her house for supper. She would just knock on Sean's door and say, *"Hi, I'm here to show you my ring."* As she thought about it, the beer found its way to her mouth again, this time with less reaction. Her taste buds were getting used to it. She was relaxing a bit too. The party didn't seem as strained as it had a short bit ago. She chugged a couple of mouthfuls down.

"I thought of getting one for Becca. I looked on the Internet, but they were too expensive. You know what that thing is worth, being an antique? A couple grand, easy."

She brought the ring, hand and all, up to the light. How could she have something worth that much hung on one finger?

The music switched to a softer song.

"I knew someone would play that. I've been sitting here waiting for it." He cussed. "That was our song."

She still had half the beer left. It still tasted bad, but she was tired of holding it. She tilted it upward and drained the bottle. The beer seemed to swish around in her head, and then the room swished around to the same rhythm, making her imagine what a fish must feel like when it's caught in the churning tide of the ocean, unable to get away from the waves crashing repeatedly over its head.

She put her ringed hand on Sean's shoulder, something she never would've done before, but she needed to steady herself, to make the spinning stop. She felt so relaxed now. Besides, her hand was wealthy. It was worthy of being on a boy's shoulder. "I really am sorry, Sean. I hope someone else will come along for you."

She pushed herself up, putting her weight into his shoulder without meaning to, and he responded by steadying her, pushing up on her arm, helping her stand, but instead of letting her go, he followed suit and stood. Before she knew how it had happened, they were dancing, her in his arms, moving around in tiny steps in a tiny circle. Other couples joined them in the small open area of the living room, all of them staying in place like the wooden couples that danced in circles on her grandmother's cuckoo clock every time it chimed the hour.

She marveled at how natural it all seemed, her small sandaled feet settling within the border set by his large tennis shoes. His hand, still clasping his beer, rested over her shoulder, while the other wrapped around her back. It was like she imagined dancing with a boy was supposed to be. They moved together like they'd been dancing for ages, but without the complications she would've run into with another guy. Sean wasn't trying to touch her skin or slip his hand into her pants or up her shirt.

She hadn't noticed how tall he was. The top of her head only came to his chin. She had to look up to see what kind of effect the dance was having on him. He leaned closer, not to kiss her, but to whisper in her ear. "Thanks. You don't know how much easier it is to listen to this song with you helping me through it."

That's what she was doing—helping him through a song.

He didn't move his head away. His breath flowed warm and moist into her ear through a few beats, a few measures of them shuffling their feet around, and then his lips found their way to her earlobe and neck, a soft nuzzling not much different than the whisper of his voice in her ear, like Smokey's nose against her hand when she had offered him some tidbit she saved for him from lunch. She almost wasn't sure that Sean was nuzzling her neck, thought maybe it was some type of whispering that just wasn't reaching her ear, until a voice cracked through the air.

"Way to go, Sean!" It was Kelvin, rising from where he'd been lounging in the corner where the dining room met the living room, hidden from view in the midst of his buddies. "Dump Becca one day and get into Maggie McCarthy's pants the next. Way to play the game, dude. That's what I'm talking about." He started a slow, loud clapping that some of the other boys joined in.

The realization of what he said didn't sink in to Maggie right away, but as all eyes turned to them, she came to a standstill, feeling her face turn as red as her hair.

Kelvin wasn't done. He had the kids' attention, and Maggie knew there was nothing Kelvin enjoyed more than playing a room. "You know that hot Irish blood. What did I tell y'all? She was a real surprise. So quiet all these years. And now look. The Irish blood in those two can't even wait till they're alone."

He pointed toward his victims, but his gaze was taking in the whole room, measuring the effectiveness of his speech. "Just wait till you see how deep that red hair goes, Sean."

Maggie pushed way from Sean, knocking his beer so that it sloshed across her shoulder and down her arm. "How would you know, Kelvin?"

"Everybody knows we went parking."

The memory of it, of his hands touching her flesh, sent a chill over her. "Nothing happened, and you know it."

"She didn't want anything to happen, is what she means. But she didn't know she was dealing with Kelvin the master. No one can resist the master."

"Stand up for her, man." The hissed words came from behind her, and she recognized the voice immediately, bringing a greater shock than seeing Kelvin in front of her. It was Webb talking to Tony. "It's your sister, man. Do something."

She turned around and saw the shaking of Tony's head. Webb crossed the room and, with one hand landing squarely in the middle of Kelvin's chest, pushed him backward. "Leave the girl alone. There's no way she did it with someone like you."

Kelvin caught himself against the wall and sprang back into Webb's face. "Like how would you know?"

"Because she told me."

"So what are you now, her kid sister?"

Webb reeled back and punched Kelvin in the chin, knocking him to the ground, and in a single motion turned around, caught Maggie by the arm, and whisked her from the room, through the kitchen, and out the back door.

He had her leaning against the car, catching her breath, when Tony caught up to them.

Webb shook the pain of the punch out of his fist. "You knew he was lying, man."

"He's a foot taller than me."

"Eight inches, max. You're a wimp."

"And you're an idiot. What's my sister to you?"

"Your sister, man. Ain't that enough? We've all been friends since forever. I don't owe Kelvin nothin'. He's a jerk."

A cool wind whipped across the ground, tickling Maggie's neck and chin, bringing her out of shock enough to realize she was still holding a beer bottle. She tossed it to the ground and slid into the front passenger seat.

Webb got into the driver's seat and held out his hand for the keys as Tony crawled in the back and slammed the door.

Maggie still had enough mind about her to remember where she was. "Go find Dixie. We can't leave her behind. I'm responsible for her."

"You go find her. She's your friend," Tony said.

"Go find her, man. Mags can't go back in there."

Tony cussed, pushed the door open, and disappeared back into the house.

Maggie closed her eyes for a moment, but it made her feel worse, so she fixed her gaze on a tree in the yard. It was an ancient oak with branches sprouting all the way down its trunk like a natural ladder. She couldn't help thinking it would be a great climbing tree. They didn't have any trees like that in the woods around her, and the yards had all been stripped bare before the houses were built, so the trees were all young; not huge, grand things like this oak. If she wasn't feeling incapable of walking, she might've slipped off her sandals and climbed to the top, but there was something more pressing she was supposed to be dealing with.

She needed to process everything that had happened, but it seemed to be ten frames ahead of her, and she had to rewind it all in her mind to figure out exactly what played out. She couldn't remember much more than the end, hearing the smack of Webb's fist against Kelvin's chin. "I can't believe you did that for me."

"Shut up. I've been looking for a reason to kick his butt ever since he beat me out of a place on the baseball team in seventh grade."

"You couldn't find a good reason before now?"

"Sure. I've found about ten of them, but I never delivered it hard enough to satisfy myself."

She thought about that a few moments. "Think it satisfied you this time?"

He was still rubbing his fist. "Guess it depends what else comes out of his fat mouth."

Her mind kept skipping around. The taste of the beer rose in her throat and reminded her of why she felt so disjointed. She shouldn't have had a beer. "I guess I didn't choose the right path tonight, drinking a beer and all."

"It was a surprise, anyway."

Maggie, through her fuzzy drunkenness, realized she'd always suspected that Webb drank like all the other boys, but maybe he didn't. His father was an alcoholic who'd gone on drinking binges years earlier, before he sobered up. Webb never talked about it. Maybe he was afraid of becoming what his father had been.

Dixie and Tony were almost back to the car. She didn't have much time left to talk to him.

Webb reached over her and buckled her seat belt. "It's kind of a relief to know you're not perfect."

Her head had flopped back against the seat. It felt so heavy she was sure she would never be able to lift it upright to get out of the car. "I could have ended up in a bad situation."

"Maybe. Probably not with Sean. He's a decent guy."

"I guess," she said. She was getting very sleepy.

"Anyway, you're all right."

"I'm all right," she echoed and, as her eyes drifted shut, wondered if he could ever mean that in a more meaningful way, the way he did in her dreams.

When they got home, she was lucky her father was still out with Andrea. A note on the table said Billy had gone to spend the night with Brad, probably because she and Tony were both out at the party and her father hadn't wanted to leave him alone. Maggie was too out of it to think it through, to wonder how Billy could've gone from not wanting to play after school with Billy to actually spending the night at his house.

She stumbled up to bed.

Chapter
Twenty-One

MAGGIE WAS LYING on the couch, still suffering the aftereffects of the party when Andrea arrived at their house at eleven o'clock sharp on Saturday.

"Is everyone ready?" Andrea asked after entering with little more than a cursory tap on the door. Before long, Maggie expected even the single knock to be gone, and then Andrea would progress to having her own key to come and go as she pleased.

The pounding in Maggie's head obliterated any kindness she'd felt toward Andrea earlier in the week when she was helping with her research. At the moment she felt only resentment over Andrea's invasion into their home, resentment toward this know-it-all ingratiating herself into their lives and gradually exerting her authority over them. Is this what other kids at school lived through? All those kids with stepmothers and stepfathers? What made her father bring Andrea home after years of barely even dating? She couldn't begin to fathom it.

She tried to consider Andrea objectively — her modest makeup, her camisole top with the silk blouse hanging open over it like a jacket that somehow managed to emphasize her cleavage rather than cover it, the form-fitting jeans, the two inch heels. Okay, so maybe there was a logical reason why her father was attracted to her, but why now? What would it take to make her go away and leave them as they'd been before? If she could erase everything that had happened in her life over the past weeks and go back to being who she used to be, then she could look at Webb without being embarrassed by her comments on sex or her drunken escapade. Then she could still look at Tony with some kind of authority, instead of begging him with a glance not to tell their father what she'd done the night before.

While Maggie tried to undo the knots in her brain, Billy lay stretched out on the carpet, propped up on his elbows, with *Ed, Edd n Eddy* on television, not bothering even to acknowledge Andrea's arrival. Maggie assumed he'd arrived home that morning while she was still asleep. He didn't speak to her when she came downstairs and seemed to take Andrea's presence in stride, as if it had no bearing on his existence.

His innocent freckled face reminded her that he had spent the night at the Dwellers'. Mr. Dweller's face rose up before her, observing Billy with the same weird expression he'd had when he examined Smokey's remains. Her stomach turned as she made the connection. Mr. Dweller had been in the crowd when she found Sue.

Mr. Dweller.

She glanced from Billy to Andrea, who had come to stand over them. She thought of her father. Would they believe her if she told them she thought Mr. Dweller might be a suspect?

Andrea poked Billy with the toe of her right sandal. "I thought you would be ready and waiting."

"For what?" he asked without taking his eyes off the screen.

"To go get your puppy."

That brought him to his feet. "Really?"

"Yes. Get your shoes on. Where's Frank?"

Frank. It irked Maggie every time Andrea used his given name.

"Here I am," he said, coming down the steps in a T-shirt, shorts, a beat-up ball cap, and white athletic socks that stretched up to his knees, which meant he was headed outside to mow the grass.

Andrea looked him over from head to toe, eyebrows raised. "I thought we were going to the animal shelter."

"Well, I've been thinking. . . ."

"What do you mean? We had it all settled."

"Sure, but who will take care of a dog during the day? We can't just let it wander the neighborhood. We wouldn't want the same . . . Well, you know, we just can't let it wander around."

"So put up a fence."

"I never really pictured our yard with a fence."

Exasperation edged up Andrea's neck and face in red blotches. "You didn't picture your house with any decent kind of furniture, either. What's wrong with a fence?"

"It's so confining."

"Confining?"

"Yes. The neighbors might see it as a blockade to keep them out. We're not like that. We love having them wander into our yard for a chat. Why, what if Mr. Childers thought he couldn't walk over and join us for a burger on Sunday afternoon because the fence was keeping him out?"

One look at Andrea's face proved she had no idea who Mr. Childers was, or that he came by every time they put anything on the old grill out back—ever since Mrs. Childers passed away and he was left alone with no one to talk to during his evening meal.

"He could go through the gate like any normal person, couldn't he?"

"It wouldn't be the same. He would have to make a point of coming into the yard instead of feeling like he was just stopping by. It's like seeing someone in the yard and stopping to talk instead of knocking on the front door to bring them outside."

Maggie's father had sent Andrea into a daze that took her a moment to shake off, but she wasn't about to be defeated in her new quest. "Well, we'll put one of those square kennels in the back corner. You can shut him in during the day, and Billy can let him out when he gets home from school."

"A kennel?"

"Yes, you've seen them. Four pieces you assemble. They're ten by ten or something. That will be perfect. Now come on; it'll be lunchtime soon if we don't get a move on."

Maggie looked from one to the other, waiting for the outcome, pulling for her father to find another comeback.

"I don't know, Andrea."

That was all the uncertainty Andrea needed. She moved to his side and placed her hand on his arm. "How are we going to get anywhere if you don't respect my professional opinion as a counselor and let me have some say in the family's future? This is important to me because it's important to Billy."

Maggie felt like gagging. "Give me a break," she muttered under her breath. She could see her father turning to mush under Andrea's touch and catalogued it: *How to manipulate a guy to get what you want.*

His reply was no surprise. "Okay, we'll go look, but I'm not promising anything."

Tony stumbled down the stairs in his usual Saturday morning stupor. His hair was plastered to one side of his head. "What's up?"

"We're going to get a puppy." Andrea was beaming. "Get your shoes on."

"No, thanks."

"Don't be a wet blanket, Tony. I just convinced Frank that this is a great idea, and we're all going together."

"Not me. I have better things to do on a Saturday than look at a bunch of yapping mutts."

In her mind, Maggie was jumping in the air giving him a high-five for not going along with Andrea's plans, but in reality she stayed frozen on the couch like a meek five-year-old.

That's when she realized it was a competition. It was her against Andrea. For what, she wasn't sure. But the larger part of her was coming undone, losing the grip on who she was, like a soldier being demoted, his stripes stripped from his uniform, or a deputy whose star was being ripped from his chest. She was no longer the mother. She was no longer her father's right hand. Every time Andrea exerted control, she lost ground in maintaining her place as a pillar of decision. If Andrea weaseled her way any further into the household, Maggie would lose her place in the world. This house, this family, was all she had, and she couldn't let Andrea steal it from her.

She had so many words building up inside of her that she wanted to spit out. She wanted to say she didn't have time to pick up dog poop, or make sure a puppy was fed, or brushed, or had its shots and whatever medicine puppies needed, but then there was Billy with his big blue eyes now filled with dreams of a furry friend, and if she stood in his way, she would come off looking like the bad guy. It wasn't fair. No matter how she reacted, Andrea would win this round.

Suddenly Billy was at her side, hugging her, not Andrea. "We're getting a dog, Mags. Can you believe it? A dog."

How long had it been since he hugged her like that? She put her arm around him. Mr. Dweller hadn't hurt him. He was right here with her. She was letting her imagination and her dislike of the man get to her.

She gave Billy's shoulders a squeeze. This clinched it. She couldn't rebel against a dog now, not with Billy at her side. She had to put on a happy face and share his enthusiasm and hope all would go well.

Then genius struck. If there were problems, they would fall on Andrea, not her. That brought a smile to her face.

She grabbed Billy's hand, feeling the warmth of the blood flowing through him, the same blood that flowed through her, and she realized that she had one advantage that Andrea could never top—Andrea would never really be one of them.

"C'mon, bro. Let's go get a dog."

Two hours later they returned with a German shepherd mix about eight months old, not at all what Maggie had envisioned, but Billy insisted he wanted a dog instead of a puppy, and a breed that no one could attack like they had Smokey. That was understandable. At least the shepherd was a better option than the Doberman pinscher he first pointed out. The shepherd had a lolling tongue when he was playing, but eyes that sparked with intelligence when Billy whistled to him. His ears flopped, but Maggie rather liked him that way; it made him less imposing than a full-blooded shepherd, though an inkling of trivia tickling her memory made her think the ears might stand straighter as he matured.

Tony showed up looking for lunch and ended up helping assemble the pen in the lower corner of the backyard. He showed a bit more enthusiasm toward the dog when he saw him frolicking around the yard, leaving his scent on every bush. "We ought to call him Whizzer."

"Wizard. That's an excellent name," Andrea said.

"I was thinking of calling him Gollum," Billy said.

"Ah, from *Lord of the Rings*. Literary. Very cool," their father said as he fit a nut onto a bolt. "But don't you think Gollum was a bit ugly? This fella is much more handsome than that."

"Wizard is much better," Andrea said.

Maggie smirked, sure that Andrea was either too stupid to know what Tony said and had the audacity to think she'd won him over with the dog ploy as easily as she had Billy, or she intentionally pretended to misunderstand what he'd said.

"Sure," Tony said. "Whizzer it is." He actually grinned at Maggie, and for a minute they connected.

Kimberly heard the commotion in the yard and left her mother's side to run over to meet the dog. "Oh, Maggie, you got a dog. I've always wanted a dog," she exclaimed in her sweet five-year-old voice.

Mr. Childers wandered into the yard next to have a look himself, making Maggie glad her father had at least stuck to his guns about not putting up a fence that would make the old man feel less than welcome to join their festivities. "Reminds me of a pup I had in my day," he said, rubbing the floppy ears and grinning as Whizzer licked his old wrinkled hands.

Andrea looked disconcerted with the neighbors gathering around, but she quickly pulled herself together and introduced herself as if they ought to have known her already.

Maggie sighed and concentrated on the dog. He was, after all, a loveable fellow whether he was Andrea's doing or not.

After supper, she gathered her pocketbook and keys to head out to the hospital.

"Do you want me to go with you?" her father asked.

She wouldn't mind the company in the car and crossing the parking lot, but she wanted to be alone with Sue. It helped to talk to her, whether or not Sue could hear what she said. She was working things out in her head just by listening to herself talk, and she had a lot on her mind — Billy and the dog, Kelvin and their date gone wrong, everything she'd said to Webb and Tony, and getting drunk. Nothing seemed to be going right lately.

She kissed her father on the cheek. "No, I'll be okay, thanks Daddy."

Dusk had settled over the town. A few people were in the parking lot heading back to their cars. Evening created a sense of quiet around the area belying the anxiety of so many hearts inside the white walls of the hospital.

She moved through the halls, familiar now with the layout, wondering who was behind each door. Who was recovering? Who was battling death? Were they frightened, or did they welcome the relief of drawing their last breaths?

She slipped into Sue's room and took her seat by the window. Twice she'd run into Mrs. Roberts keeping vigil at Sue's side, but she'd learned Sue was usually alone at suppertime when her mother went home to fix supper.

"Here it is mid-October, four weeks since you were attacked. Do you ever hear anything I say to you?" Maggie asked Sue's still body. Nothing indicated that she was ever going to come out of the coma. The nurses constantly shifted her body to keep her from getting bedsores, and her wounds were slowly healing, but she still had tubes running into her arms, and she was still unconscious. Jennifer had told her that a coma rarely lasted as long as four weeks, but Sue hadn't developed pneumonia, so her chances of surviving were still good.

All the pictures and notes from kids at school had been taped to the walls, making the room look somewhat like a kindergarten class. Some were in color and some were just black and white sketches, some were modern art in swirls of odd shapes with indecipherable meanings, and others were attempts at realistic portrayals of life at school—a picture of the school itself, including the flagpole, was in the middle of the wall directly in front of Sue, if she would just open her eyes to look at it. Another was a closeup depiction of cafeteria food on a notorious orange plastic school tray. Maggie wasn't sure if that was something meant to pull someone back to school or not. Maybe it would remind her that school food was bad, but not as bad as hospital food. One drawing showed a stack of books spilling out of a book bag. Some were portraits of other students, or groups of kids at games, pep rallies, or just standing in the parking lot.

Maggie didn't say anything for a while. She looked at the pictures for a few minutes, then bowed her head and prayed for a bit, asking the Lord to be with Sue, to help her heal. When she opened her eyes again, she looked at Sue, hoping this would be the day she would look back, but she didn't.

Maggie's gaze went back to the walls and fell on her favorite picture. She hadn't known what it was at first. In fact, she'd passed over it time and again until her last visit when it finally sorted itself into something recognizable—a closeup of a cheerleading pom-pom. Initially she dismissed it as frivolous, but as she sat there in thought, it began speaking to her about perspective, that maybe cheerleaders got so wrapped up in what they were that they couldn't see the truth for all the trappings. Pom-poms were nothing but plastic streamers stuck to a handle that cheerleaders waved around to get attention. Sure, cheerleaders brought enthusiasm to the game, revved up the audience, rousted the players into the spirit of things, but was that really how the cheerleaders viewed themselves? Or as status symbols?

She knew the answer in Sue's case. Sue didn't care a whit about cheering anybody on, unless it was a boy that had the hots for her. Or at least that's how she used to be. Maggie wondered if that would change now, if this event would color the rest of Sue's life.

"What are you thinking in there, Sue? Do you hear me when I come here and talk to you?"

Her body lay motionless, without reaction to Maggie's questions. The monitors kept bleeping and blinking.

"I keep wondering if you know who did this to you. Could you have done something to make it all end differently?"

She stared again at the pom-pom, thinking back to her birthday, to getting the new shirt from Dixie, to seeing Sue snuggled up next to Webb, to the wish she had made over her birthday candles that sixteen would be a great year, and to the prayer in her heart that she would be as popular as Sue. How could that have been such a short time ago? She no longer envied Sue. Maggie's life wasn't perfect—in fact, it was pretty messed up right now—but she wouldn't trade it for anyone's. All the resentment she'd felt toward Sue had evaporated. She felt sorry for her now.

She took Sue's hand in her own and held it lightly. "You know what, Sue? I can finally say, totally honestly, I'm glad I'm not you. Not just because of what's happened to you, the rape and all this, but everything. I have your friends now, not because I want them, but because they want me. I have guys asking me out, and I don't care about that either. They're jerks. Or maybe I'm just different from most girls and I'm not ready for a relationship like boys expect nowadays. Everyone at school talks to me, including the teachers and the principal, the quarterback and the hottest boys going. I've been the center of it all. And you know what? None of it matters. None of it makes me a better person. In fact, I went to a party last night and got drunk, and felt the stupidest I've ever felt in my life. If anything, living in your circle has put me in jeopardy of thinking of myself too much, of putting importance on the wrong aspects of life. I've learned I like myself more than that. I like my life and my family. I am who I am. All these years I've wanted to be more like my mother because I thought she was beautiful and popular, but where did that get her? Pregnant with me and then miserable enough to commit suicide. I guess we have to find happiness in who we are without seeking gratification from other people. I have to be happy with myself, not put on an act to impress anyone. I don't want to be fake or draw attention to myself. I am glad I'm me, the me I was before all this happened.

Your world seems superficial to me. I don't want that anymore. I don't ever want to be you."

As she finished her speech, she realized it was probably the wrong thing to say to someone lying at death's door on life support systems. It was a selfish admission that didn't help anyone but her. She placed Sue's hand gently back on the bed, closed her eyes, and sighed, feeling bad that she had dumped all her thoughts on Sue, even if she couldn't hear her.

When she opened her eyes, the room was still the same. The machines were still beeping. Sue was still breathing steadily.

She sat for a while longer, just looking at Sue, thinking about what this new revelation about life meant, where it would lead her, what direction her life would go now that she was ready to walk her own path without feeling beaten down about it.

She didn't want to leave yet, so she picked up the book Mrs. Roberts had left on the side table and began reading. *Everlasting Love.* A romance, and not her usual reading fare. When she reached the third page, the door swung open. It was Webb.

"Oh," he said, "I didn't know you'd be here this late."

She shrugged and stared down at the book in her lap, embarrassed to see him face to face after having to be rescued at the party. Between that and her admission of what happened with her and Kelvin, she couldn't imagine what he thought of her now.

"Feeling better today?"

She blushed. "Yes. Thanks for . . ."

"Sure, no problem." He stepped in and closed the door.

She kept her eyes on the book.

"Why do you come here to visit her?" he asked. "She was always so mean to you. I know you don't like her."

Maggie flipped the page even though she hadn't finished reading it. She couldn't have said what she'd read in the first three pages. Her eyes moved down the page, but didn't really read the words. Her mind was busy with its own business.

"I come because I have to."

"No, you don't. No one is making you sit here day after day."

She turned another page, and then another. By this method she could finish the book in ten minutes.

Webb was waiting for her answer. She couldn't tell him what started her coming there—Mrs. Newell telling her to love her enemy—not with Sue being Webb's girlfriend. Besides, her reason had slowly changed from doing what she thought God wanted her to do, to doing what she thought she needed to do. She decided she could admit that; maybe it would ease the tension in her heart. "Because I feel responsible."

"Huh? It wasn't your fault. You saved her. How could you be responsible?"

She slowly turned four more pages. "I saved her from dying, and now here she is still alive with no one around her. I have her real life. I have her friends. I have guys asking me out. I have everything she had. I wished for it so hard. I wanted it so much. Now I just want to give it all back to her."

"I don't believe that."

"Believe what? That I wanted her life?"

"That, or that you've taken it over." He glanced at Sue, then leaned against the wall and studied Maggie. "I lay in bed thinking about all of it last night after I took you home. Not just about the party, but watching Kelvin take you out, and Heather and Tammy sitting with you at lunch, with Dixie and Clarissa riding on your coattails. Don't you see? You haven't changed. The people around you have. You're still plodding through school being exactly who you've always been, so sure of yourself, so grounded in your beliefs. It's just that they all suddenly woke up and noticed you were there."

"Because of Sue."

"That's not your fault, Maggie. You can't help that she was attacked."

"Yes, it is my fault. I asked God to make me popular, and then this happened." It was a relief to finally admit it.

Webb cussed. "That's the dumbest thing I've ever heard. I may not be a big churchgoer like you, Maggie, but I know God didn't have Sue raped to make you popular. How could you even think that?"

Maggie shrugged and fought back tears.

"Maybe that day was planned out long before your dumb prayer. Maybe God knew Sue was going to need help, and maybe everything that's happened in your life—taking care of Billy and Tony and all the other junk—was to make sure you'd be there to save her. Who else would have stomped into the woods to see if someone needed help? You couldn't *not* do it. You would've rushed in to save Smokey if you could have. Did you think of that? That God used you to save Sue because He has some other plan for her, and none of it has anything to do with you at all or your stupid wish to date Kelvin?"

She glanced up at him, then back to the book. She was having a hard time holding the tears back. A couple dribbled down her cheek, and she swatted them away. He had no clue she was crazy about him, not Kelvin. "I didn't care about dating Kelvin. That's not what I prayed for."

Something registered on his face for a split second before he responded. "You're missing the point. Things happen for a reason."

Hadn't Andrea tried to tell her the same thing? She had prayed for God to lead her down His path and to give her purpose in life. Maybe God was setting her down a path that had nothing to do with popularity. Maybe popularity was just something that temporarily blocked her sights from what she was supposed to be doing.

"You did the right thing," Webb said. "God just put you in the right place at the right time."

The sound of his voice drew her eyes up again to see how the fluorescent lights glared across his face, making his forehead shine. It was almost too much to take in, him thinking such deep thoughts, especially about her. He was still Webb with the black hair brushing his collar, his shirttails hanging out, his tennis shoes tied so loosely they may as well not have been, yet it didn't seem like him at all.

Something had shifted between them. They were seeing themselves and each other with new eyes.

Chapter
Twenty-Two

ON SUNDAY NIGHT, Webb showed up at seven to take her to the hospital. "I figured if we were both going, we may as well go together."

As she walked out to his car, it struck her how odd they must look, the two of them spending a night at the hospital, sitting with a girl who didn't even know they were there. It felt like a date in some alternate world where teenagers didn't do normal things like go to parties and movies, and dates were for talking instead of making out.

Unlike most guys, Webb was usually content to let her and Tony drive him to school and such, only driving when there was no alternative. Tony said it was because his mother gave him such a hard time about using the car; she always needed it for something. So, riding with him driving was a new experience.

He drove much more cautiously than Maggie expected, with his eyes steady on the road. She thought he would be sloppy, like the way he slumped on his bed playing games with Tony and piled up dirty dishes on his desk until milk curdled in the bottoms of cereal bowls and dribbles of iced tea turned hard in the bottoms of glasses. His driving wasn't like that, though. He paused a good ten seconds at every stop sign, arching his neck out to look both ways. He was overly deliberate in the way he turned on the blinker—using his whole hand instead of clicking it with one finger. Maggie smiled to think of him listening to lectures from his mother about safe driving.

When they arrived at ICU, Jennifer was at the nurses' station. Maggie leaned on the counter. "Any change?"

Jennifer shook her head. "She's still out. Her body has mended, but . . ."

She didn't finish the sentence. She didn't have to. Maggie knew how dire the situation had become. Mrs. Roberts rarely left Sue's side for anything anymore, but she and her husband attended the Sunday evening service at their church and stayed for the fellowship dinner afterward, knowing either Maggie or Webb would show up to sit with Sue.

This time, Sue had them both. Maggie and Webb entered the room quietly and stared at Sue a moment. Over the passing weeks, the bandages had been removed from her wounds, and the bruises had faded. The puffy red slashes across her face had calmed to pink lines. Her eyes were surrounded by pale dark circles.

As Maggie gazed at the wreckage, she wondered what Webb saw. Whatever beauty there had been would take some time to rejuvenate.

Webb dropped into a chair. "She was so beautiful. I always wondered why she wanted to hang out with a guy like me."

"She's still the same person."

"Is she?"

Maggie couldn't answer that, but probably for different reasons than Webb. "She looks much better. You saw her at her worst."

"My mom says that with what she's been through . . ."

Did he picture what Sue had been through? Did he lie in bed at night and envision what the attacker must have done, how Sue must have screamed? How the blood must have run cold in her veins as she understood his intent? Had Webb put his mind through those steps and tried to put himself in Sue's place?

Maggie had. She had gone through it so many times that it played in her head like a movie rerun. "She's right. . . . It's bound to have an effect on her."

"I doubt she's going to want a guy around."

Maggie hadn't thought about it that way. Would Sue equate all men with what this one creep had done? "It could be she'll need you even more. You know, as support, as proof that all men aren't jerks. Someone to protect her."

"Maybe."

As they thought about Sue, there was silence between them, not empty, but filled with all the possibilities of how this one event might shape her future.

Maybe it was the concentrated power of their thoughts — of their eyes blazing into her face, trying to reach what could possibly be going on in her mind — and the power of all the prayers bestowed on her, but whatever the reason, as they studied her face, her eyelids fluttered.

Webb leaned forward. "Did you see that?"

"My gosh, yes."

She opened one eye, as if it was too painfully bright to expose both her pupils to light, then abruptly closed it.

Webb stood and moved to the side of the bed, crouching down to touch her arm and examine the movement of her eyes up close. "Sue!"

Sue blinked.

Maggie headed to the door. "Stay with her. I'm getting Jennifer."

Jennifer was nowhere in sight. There was a different nurse at the station, a thin, wiry girl that Maggie judged to be not much older than she. "Where's Jennifer?"

The girl blinked her big browns at Maggie like a doe in the woods. "Who's asking?" She had absolutely no look of authority, except in the point of her chin, which was sure to be her worst feature when she got as old as Andrea and all the freshness had been worn off by years of taking care of people dying in ICU.

Jennifer appeared around the corner, her soft white tennis shoes moving silently on the linoleum floors.

"Jennifer!" Maggie shouted, not caring that she was in the ICU where people were meant to use quiet voices. "She's awake."

Jennifer grabbed a clipboard from the nurses' station and headed to the room.

Maggie followed, but Jennifer stopped her. "You're going to have to wait out here. In fact, why don't you call her mother? That would be a great help."

Maggie stepped in just far enough to confirm that Sue's eyes were still open, that she was still conscious, then backed up as Webb came to the door, the two of them moving into the hall.

Webb called Mrs. Roberts, knowing that when her cell phone interrupted the church service, everyone in the congregation would know it was either really bad news, or something fantastic. After giving Mrs. Roberts the news, he held the phone away from him as she squealed before hanging up. "I'd say she's a bit excited."

Maggie had her ear to the door.

"Is she speaking?" he asked.

"I can't tell."

"Do you think she knows who raped her?"

Maggie paled at his directness. What had the rape done to Webb's image of Sue? Did it make her less appealing to him? Or was he full of anger and ready to avenge her? "She just opened her eyes. I don't think that's going to be the first thing she's going to say."

What would she say? Would she even remember what happened? Had she heard Maggie talking all these times she had visited? Did she know Webb was here, in the hallway? "I'm thinking she might want to see you, considering . . ."

Webb turned away and leaned on the wall. Maybe he was trying to fill in the blank—considering *what*? Considering he was Sue's boyfriend? Considering this man had violated her in the most personal way, in ways Webb may or may not have attempted himself, even if under totally different circumstances and with Sue's permission? It was still a huge issue that only Webb and Sue could confront.

"Will they let us back in tonight?" he asked.

"I don't know. But being her boyfriend and all . . ." There, she'd said it out loud. She'd said Webb was Sue's boyfriend. But it didn't feel cleansing like the rest of her admissions. She'd gotten over everything else about Sue—the looks, the popularity and what-not—but Sue's relationship with Webb still struck her in the gut. She was full of jealousy. She had been nothing more than friends with Webb since elementary school, and it was obvious that's all he considered her. She wished she could dismiss her thoughts about him, but she was drawn to him like a moth to a porch light.

Mrs. Roberts showed up minutes later, rushing past them both, into the room, with Mr. Roberts hurrying behind her. With a glance of mutual consent, Webb and Maggie turned and left. Sue didn't need anyone but her parents for the moment, and neither of them knew what to say to her anyway.

The next night, Maggie was sitting on her bed studying Spanish when Webb and Tony clomped up the stairs. She had taken to hiding in her room more and more. It was a sanctuary, the only place Andrea hadn't touched.

She looked up at her door, slightly ajar, wondering whether the boys would stop to say hello, but they didn't. She sighed as they continued down the hall to Tony's bedroom. She had enjoyed talking with Webb at the hospital. She felt like they had connected on some new level, but she decided it must've been one-sided. He only went to see Sue; it had nothing to do with something between the two of them.

Still, she thought he would stop and tell her if there were any updates. Maggie had struggled all day with the idea of going back to the hospital to see Sue, but seeing her unconscious and just sitting there looking at her was different than facing Sue awake. What would she say to her? Would Sue still look at her with disdain and say something mean? Would she even know that Maggie had kept vigil at her side for weeks?

Seconds later, she heard muffled voices and a light tap on her door. Webb poked his head inside. "Got a minute?"

Strands of music from Tony playing his guitar entered with him, floating from Tony's room like the tail of a kite tied to Webb, fluttering behind him. She put down her textbook. "Sure. Did you go see Sue?"

"Yeah, just a while ago. That's what I wanted to tell you."

"How was she? What did she say?"

"We didn't talk much. My mom was with me."

"Oh."

"She didn't want to talk much anyway."

Maggie felt the big question standing there between them, knew they were both thinking it without it being said. Maggie couldn't bring herself to ask. To ask would be to face the reality of it all over again, to face the question: Could it have been her instead of Sue?

Webb joined her on the bed, sitting at the corner away from her. "She doesn't remember."

Maggie absorbed the words. "None of it?"

"Bits, I guess. But not who or how it happened. Her mom said they think she'll remember more as time goes on."

Maggie nodded. All the waiting and still no end to it. A part of her was relieved, not wanting a final answer, but she was also frustrated, wondering how long it would drag out before they knew who the police needed to hunt down. Would he attack again before they knew who he was? She shivered.

Webb was watching her changing expressions. "Don't think so much about it. Let it go. We can't do anything about it."

"Is that what your mother told you?"

"It's what I figured out on my own."

They sat in silence, visions of that day filling Maggie's head despite Webb's words of wisdom. She couldn't shake the memories away.

Webb nodded toward the stack of novels on the floor by her bed. "I was thinking about those books you read. Got any recommendations? We've got to do a report for Mrs. Major's class. . . ."

It took Maggie a minute to catch up with his words, to rise from the horror of her vision to hear his ordinary request, something real and solid in the here and now. He was asking her for a book? Had he actually listened to her that day she'd mentioned reading classics?

She forced her body to move, to pull a couple choices off her bookshelf. "Here, try these."

He settled on her bed to look through them, then flopped on his belly beside her and began to read.

Afraid to break the moment, she bent back over her Spanish book and pretended to study, but she hardly absorbed a word.

He stayed fifteen minutes, then sprang to his feet. "This one's good. Can I keep it awhile?"

"Sure."

"Well, I better get back to Tony. See ya."

With that, he was gone, and she was left staring blindly at her Spanish work.

Tony barged into her room after Webb left. "Stay away from my friends, dork."

It was silly, but his reaction brought tears to her eyes. She had so many emotions coursing through her that she didn't know how to deal with any of it. She didn't need more friction between her and Tony. He barely listened to her as it was, especially with Andrea spreading herself all over the house and all over their lives. And Billy talked to her less and less. She didn't belong anywhere anymore. Not at home, not at school. Not even with Dixie; the two of them hadn't even spoken since the party.

Life had left her in no-man's-land.

Chapter Twenty-Three

ON TUESDAY SHE got up the nerve to visit Sue, to look her in the eyes and hear what happened. She had to face the demons roaring in her head.

Sue was propped up in bed when Maggie got there. The intravenous tubes were gone. She didn't look surprised to see Maggie. "You found me in the woods, didn't you?"

"Do you remember?"

"No. My mother told me. She says you saved my life."

"I just did what I would do for anyone."

"Then why do you keep coming here? The nurse keeps asking me where my friend is. I thought she meant Heather or Tammy, but she meant you, didn't she?"

"She could have meant them."

"No, she didn't. They only came once. They sent flowers. I think they're afraid to be around me now, like being raped will rub off on them."

Maggie hesitated. Could she say what she was really thinking? "I don't think it's fear. It's selfishness. You don't meet their agenda anymore."

Sue sighed and closed her eyes. "I suppose you think I deserve that."

"No. No one deserves that."

"So why do you keep coming here? You don't owe me anything. You already saved my life. Are you waiting for me to thank you or what? 'Cause I'm not thanking you. I have to lie here in this bed and relive that horror over and over again—what I can remember of it. I'd rather be dead. Do you hear me? Dead. You didn't do me any favor."

Maggie stepped back a couple paces, ready to leave. "I didn't ask you to thank me. I don't know why I keep coming. I came because I had to. I came because Mrs. Newell asked me to. I came because I've been reliving it every blasted night too. Not like you, I know, but imagining what you're reliving because I was that close to it and can't get it out of my mind. I keep praying, and I thought when you woke up it would make everything better and make the thoughts go away."

"Too bad."

Maggie picked up her pocketbook. "Yes, too bad."

A few nights later, Mrs. Chambers offered her tea in the kitchen while she waited for Dixie to get out of the shower. "You seem troubled. Come sit and chat."

Maggie settled at the table, ready to spill her story. Mrs. Chambers was something glorious between a mom and best friend, better than either one because she offered sage advice without exerting judgment or authority. Why hadn't she thought of talking with her sooner?

Where should she start? With Sue's reaction to her visits? She couldn't talk about that because it made her think of all the horrible alternate endings to the rape — to her being the victim instead of Sue.

What did that leave to divulge? How Dixie wanted to hang out with new friends? That would be too close to home to discuss with Mrs. Chambers. She would defend Dixie, and that's not what Maggie needed right now.

So she thought of her other problems. Her feelings of resentment for Andrea. What could Mrs. Chambers say about that? How could Maggie express her shifting roles, her feeling of being cast afloat on an enormous sea?

She decided to start with one small segment of it. "It's Tony. He doesn't listen to a thing I say anymore, and he stays sullen all the time."

"He's fifteen now," said Mrs. Chambers.

"Well, not for two months."

"Have you looked at him lately?"

What a silly question. She looked at him every day of his life, from his unbrushed hair to his untied shoes. "Sure, I've looked at him."

"He's growing up. He's almost a man."

Tony, a man. That was funny. He couldn't even make a sandwich without someone getting the mayonnaise out for him. "He's a long way from being a man, believe me. He still relies on me for everything."

Mrs. Chambers was rolling up a napkin, spreading it flat, then rolling it up again. "Siblings need to be able to rely on one another. I hope Cindy and Dixie always look to each other for support. But Maggie, you're not his mother."

"I may as well be for all I do in that house."

"Maybe so, but you're not his mother, and even if you were, he's reaching the age where he doesn't want one anymore."

"How do you know that? You don't have any boys."

"I have a brother. And the only difference between boys and girls at this age is that girls reach that point at thirteen instead of fifteen." She flattened the napkin again and smiled. "And girls smell better. Boys get all hairy and never use enough deodorant."

Maggie laughed. She had that right. That was Tony last year. She'd nagged at him every morning to wash his hair.

"What he needs right now is a sister."

Mrs. Chambers had progressed to folding the napkin into a series of triangles. Maggie watched as she matched the corners precisely before setting the crease and folding again.

"What is that supposed to mean? I am his sister."

"No, you've spent your whole life being his mother. Now he needs a sister."

"What's the difference?"

She got a thoughtful look on her face, the pixie part of her evaporating to a more serious, deeper self that Maggie'd decided was her business persona. "Quit telling him what to do. Quit nagging. Give him space to be a man around the house. Ask his opinion on stuff."

"I do that."

The pixie came back and laughed with eyes that twinkled. "I doubt that, Maggie McCarthy with the red hair and more Irish backbone than her daddy."

Mrs. Chambers had never mentioned Maggie's father before. "How do you know I have more Irish backbone than my daddy?"

"Ah, Frank McCarthy. I dated him once."

Dixie entered the kitchen just in time to catch the admission. "You dated Maggie's dad?"

The pixie in Mrs. Chambers was now sparkling all over her face. "Don't look so shocked. There are many things you don't know about me, you silly girls. I wasn't born married to your dad, Dixie. Yes, I dated Frank McCarthy. One time. But then"—her smile faded—"that was it. Just the once."

"Tell us more," Maggie pleaded. "What was he like?"

"A perfect gentleman," she said.

Dixie slid into a seat at the table, accidentally shuffling the chair cushion sideways to the floor. Absently, she collected it underneath her as she spoke. "Come on, Mama. You can do better than that. How did you meet him? Where did you go?"

"Nope. We all have secrets of youth. That one is mine."

"That is so weird. You two never even talk now!" Maggie exclaimed.

"We used to when you were little. We'd chat now and then. But we'd both found different people. We were both happy."

"That's lame."

"No, it's not." She looked at Dixie, that serious look falling over the pixie blush again. "He came to your dad's funeral, as you'll recall."

"I figured that was just because of Maggie."

"Not at all," Mrs. Chambers said. "He knew your daddy well too. They played on the basketball team together in high school."

"Wow. This totally blows my mind," Maggie said.

"Mine too," Dixie said, but her gaze had gone off to the picture of her dad hanging on the refrigerator by an apple magnet—as if he were only gone to work and not dead for the past two years. Maggie knew she was thinking more about her dead father than about her mother's teenage love life.

She decided to put Mrs. Chambers's plan into action first thing that weekend. She rose early, ate, and dressed. She knew better than to rouse Tony from bed if they were going to have anything close to a civil conversation, but when she passed his bedroom, the door stood open and his bed lay empty. She found him in the kitchen slumped so low over the table that his chin hung even with his cereal bowl, making it possible to slurp the cereal directly from the bowl. Maggie wondered why he even bothered with a spoon, but she wasn't interested in his manners today.

She took a seat across from him. "What do you think of her changes?"

"Whose changes?"

"Andrea's. What do you think of all the stuff she's done to the house?"

He shrugged. "The new TV is pretty cool."

Of course he would like the television. It was wide-screen and flat and cost a fortune, a luxury they never would've imagined owning. She wondered where Andrea got the money, but that wasn't something you asked a person, especially not a girlfriend you were trying to pry loose from your father. Still, if she had to admit liking anything, it would be the lamps in the family room, but that wouldn't help her argument. "I hate it all. You would think it was her house instead of ours."

He shrugged again.

"Look at this kitchen. She painted it white. Do you really like it white? It's boring. It's so plain."

He looked around the kitchen as if he hadn't really noticed it before.

"If you were going to paint it, what color would you do it?"

He took a bit more interest, looked around again. She could tell by the way his eyes paused on spots and by the way his mouth made that slight frown that he was really thinking hard, weighing the counter and the appliances into the mix. "Green. Bright green."

Maggie clapped her hands together, and he looked at her in surprise.

"That is so perfect," she said.

"It is?"

"Sure. Irish like Mom. You want to do it?"

"Do what?"

"Paint it lime green."

"Me?"

"All of us. You, me, and Billy."

"I don't know."

"Seriously. I have the fifty dollars Meemaw sent. I can buy the paint and brushes and we'll do it this afternoon. Daddy and Andrea are going to be gone all day. Want to?"

He still looked startled. She figured it was because she'd picked up on his opinion so quickly. "You have as much right to decide what this house should look like as she does."

"Okay . . ."

"So, let's go get paint. C'mon. I'll get Billy up while you get your shoes on."

She stood, and he followed, somewhat bewildered, but ready for action.

As they drove out of the neighborhood, they saw Webb was on his way down to their house. Maggie pulled up and opened her window. "Do you know anything about painting?" Maggie said.

"I helped my uncle paint a fence one time."

"Great. You're hired," Billy said, and opened his door. "Get in."

By the time they picked out the paint color, they were laughing about it together. She was careful to leave most of the decisions to Tony, and let him carry the cans of paint to the car and then into the house, to give him the position of being the leader in the escapade instead of her. Billy was so into picking out paint chips and brushes, Maggie doubted he even noticed a shift in their roles.

The work proved harder than any of them expected, but they kept at it without stopping. Maggie edged the lower areas along the baseboards and around the doors and window trim while Webb worked around her to edge along the ceiling and in the corners.

"You're dripping on me," she fussed at him.

"Better you than the floor," he said, and dripped some more on purpose.

Tony and Billy, rolling paint on the wide expanses, went at each other as if their rollers were lances, dripping paint across the drop cloths.

"Hey, st—" Maggie stifled her command and traded it for more sisterly words. "Thank goodness for drop cloths. Just don't step in the drips or we'll be painting the carpets too. I'm not sure Dad would go for that."

Billy stopped jabbing at Tony and dipped his roller into the paint again. "He's probably not going to go for this, either. Quit poking at me, Tony. I'm doing a good job here."

Maggie stood back to admire their work. "You really are, Billy. Stop and look."

"Awesome!" Billy said.

"You're right. It looks great," Webb said.

Tony grinned. "A lot different. It matches your stupid monkey place mats."

"So? You made a good choice, Tony. I love it green. The whole kitchen is full of spirit now."

She meant it. The white appliances and the white cabinets, painted during Andrea's makeover, popped with new brightness against the lime green, and the yellow countertops that had looked dated even with the white walls now looked cheery, as if an intentional part of the scheme. She would get the yellow vase from the family room and put it on the table, and bring in the two enlarged photographs her father had taken just days before her mother's death, her mother posed in a field of daisies and buttercups, holding her and her brothers. The flowers would pull out the yellow even more.

Webb laughed. "The green looks pretty good in your hair too."

Tony batted at her with a paint brush. "Maybe you should dye your whole head that color."

A day earlier, even five hours earlier, she would've taken offense, but instead she laughed. They were laughing with her, not at her. "It couldn't be worse than this red. But look at you. You're wearing half the paint on your clothes."

Even though she'd grinned at him, his smile melted away. She realized he was probably waiting for her to add scathing words about ruining a pair of jeans.

"Don't sweat it," she said. "They were old anyway. Let's finish up this last little bit and take showers, and then I have something else in mind."

"What?" asked Billy.

"Rearranging the furniture however you like it."

"Seriously?" asked Tony, making his final sweeping rolls across the wall.

"Yes. Why not? It's our house."

"Can we put it back the way we had it?" asked Billy.

She nodded as she gathered up the brushes and drop cloths. "Sounds good to me. Whatever y'all want. How about you guys shower first while I clean this stuff up, and then I'll go? One of you can use Dad's shower."

She didn't realize how much the painting had tired them all out until they started shifting furniture around.

"I don't think we can move the television ourselves," Tony said. "It weighs a ton."

Andrea had placed the new television in a cabinet at an angle adjacent to the fireplace, a bookshelf in the opposite corner, with the sofa perpendicular to the fireplace, facing the television, and their father's recliner beside the television facing the sofa. No one could watch television without sitting on the sofa.

"So, we leave the television there," Maggie said, "and move the lighter things. Daddy needs to be able to sit in his recliner."

"She did that so he would sit with her, you know, on the sofa."

Maggie grinned. "So we give him back his recliner."

Webb grinned back as he took one end of the recliner. "You guys are evil."

"We're just protecting our poor, innocent father," Maggie said.

First they tried moving the recliner directly in front of the fireplace, but it took up too much room. Then they moved the sofa so that it sat parallel to the fireplace, facing both it and the angled television cabinet, and placed the recliner where the sofa had been. Next, they took the old set of bookshelves from beside the fireplace and carted them upstairs to organize the mess off their father's desk neatly onto the shelves. "You finish this up, Billy. You're good at arranging things," Tony said, and Billy beamed with pride. So did Maggie, but she didn't let Tony see it; he had actually stepped up to the challenge, just like Mrs. Chambers had predicted.

Back downstairs, Tony, Webb, and Maggie hauled the china cabinet from the kitchen, emptied earlier when they moved it to paint the kitchen walls, and placed it in the family room against the wall behind the recliner, then carefully refilled the shelves with things they loved instead of Andrea's trinkets. Webb stretched out on the sofa while Tony added their father's favorite books. Maggie added family photos that had been crowded on the mantel, along with a ceramic teapot from Meemaw, then a soccer trophy, a signed baseball, a pretty vase Maggie had bought at a school auction, and a china doll that had been her mother's.

The shelves became a showcase of their lives instead of a showcase of decorative china.

"Not bad," Webb said.

Billy joined them, all of them smiling at each other as they collapsed on the sofa and floor to veg out in front of a movie, exhausted.

By the time their father and Andrea returned, they had lapsed into a television stupor, to the point Maggie had all but forgotten to be wary of Andrea's return. She remembered when she saw Andrea's face. "What have you done?"

Webb leaped to his feet. "See you guys," he said and fled out the front door.

Their father sniffed the air. "Goodness, that paint smell just won't fade. Every time I walk in the front door, it hits me again."

Andrea said, "Look what they've done, Frank. Look!"

Maggie sat up and grinned. "We rearranged. What do you think?"

Her father sank into the recliner. "Good job."

"Frank! How can you say that? All my hard work. How dare they just disregard it? I put a lot of time and thought into redecorating this room. And it ruins all the plans I have for it, the other things I have in mind."

He looked around. "Well, it's not as drastic as all that, Andrea. Nothing permanent. They can help you rearrange it again, can't you kids?"

Maggie glared at him. "We like it this way."

"My china cabinet! You brought it out of the kitchen! Where are all the beautiful vases and plates I had displayed?"

Andrea stomped off toward the kitchen. Maggie and Tony

exchanged glances. Billy crept over to the stairs, out of the line of fire.

As Andrea swung the kitchen door open, Maggie smirked.

"Oh, no! The kitchen! They've painted the kitchen!"

Maggie's father hadn't moved. "That explains the smell."

"Lime green. Look at this. They've ruined it!"

Their father heaved himself from the recliner to take a closer look. "Wow. That'll wake you up in the morning."

"Is that all you have to say to them? They have totally disrespected my work. They ought to be reprimanded."

He weighed it a moment, then turned to Maggie and her brothers. "She's right. Andrea really worked hard on redecorating our home, to make it nicer for all of us, and you bulldozed that effort."

"But Dad," Maggie started.

"No. Don't even start, Maggie. You know it was wrong of you. What on earth possessed you to paint it lime green when she just painted it white?"

"They're trying to undermine my plans, is what. Don't you see that, Frank? It's a plot against me. You ought to be furious with them."

"Now, Andrea, you don't know that."

"Come on! It's been untouched forever, and now, just after I paint it, they get the urge to paint it too? That makes no sense. They're deliberately trying to challenge my authority. This is a crossing point, Frank."

She took the pose of a female warrior ready to defend her post—set chin, narrowed eyes, feet planted a pace apart, and arms firmly crossed.

Maggie's father withered. "You kids really shouldn't have done this. Andrea worked very hard."

"What about our work?" Tony said. "We worked all day to get this done."

"I'm sure you did, so you can appreciate the effort she made."

"Sure. She hired people. We did it ourselves."

Andrea stepped forward. Everything in her body language challenged their father to take a stand alongside her as she leveled her own decision. "Well you can double your efforts and fix it all back."

"Yeah, right!" Tony said. "In your dreams."

"Don't you speak back to Andrea, young man. Apologize this instant."

"I would rather go to my room," he said and ran up the steps.

Billy shook his head and started after Tony. "You just don't get it, do you Dad?"

Maggie stood. "It's our house, not hers. Why shouldn't we have a say in how it's decorated? Maybe we didn't like any of her crummy ideas." She detoured around Andrea and fled up the steps behind the other two, stopping where a wall hid the upper half of the steps.

Andrea held up the bag she'd been carrying. "So much for the takeout. I say we let them stew in their rooms until they're ready to apologize, and we eat this alone."

Maggie's father was still staring at the staircase. "Whatever," he said with a shrug that very much mimicked Tony's. "You go ahead. I'm not hungry. I think I'll see if the game is on." He sank back into the recliner, turned on the television, and stared out the window.

Maggie crept up the remaining steps and joined Tony in his bedroom, flopping on his beanbag chair to listen as he strummed his guitar.

He purposely hit a bad chord. "Thanks for getting me in trouble."

"We're not in trouble. We just woke Dad up."

"Right. I should have known you had some reason why you were being so nice to me; it was just so you could point the blame at me even though it was all your idea."

"No, I'll take the fall for it. You're off the hook, you and Billy both. I just want her out of our lives, and I knew this would open Dad's eyes to the idea that he doesn't have to sit back and let her walk all over us."

"He wants her here, don't you see that? He's a guy. He needs a woman. Mom's been dead for twelve years. Besides, Andrea is all right."

"Sure. You're just saying that because she bought you stuff."

"What's wrong with that?"

"Wait till she makes you cut your hair, tuck in your shirt, and put a belt on."

"No way. She won't do that."

Maggie laid her head back and closed her eyes. "Okay. We'll see." There was no use trying to explain it to Tony. He hadn't had enough experience with girls, but Maggie knew. She knew how a girl wheedled her way into what she wanted inch by inch, step by step.

This had become war.

Chapter
Twenty-Four

ANDREA ARRIVED AT their house every evening that week with meals planned and groceries in hand. She didn't redo the kitchen or rearrange the family room, which kept Maggie suspicious, wondering what havoc was going to fall in its place. The reason came to light one evening after supper while they were all watching television.

When an ad came on, Andrea placed a paper on her father's lap. "What do you think?"

He shifted in his seat and examined the picture, his body language clearly saying this was one of those questions that didn't have a correct answer. After turning the paper in several directions, he gave up. "Maybe you better explain it to me."

"It's the layout for the renovations. Here's the rearrangement in the bathroom. See how much more efficient it is? You won't be stepping out of the tub into the toilet anymore. We expand the bathroom into what is currently the closet, and then make a new closet over here."

"That cuts three feet off Billy's room."

"So? He's a kid. How much room does he need? He plays outside. All he does in his room is sleep."

"He spends more time in his bedroom than I do in my bathroom."

She swatted his arm. "Quit being difficult. I know you like it. I'll check out the measurements of the vanity and toilet before I call a contractor, though. We want the pricing to be on the exact changes."

She turned the page around. "Now look at the kitchen. We'll take out that wall and open the family room to the kitchen. It will make the area seem much bigger, and much more modern. You're going to love it. Just think of the light that will pour in from the kitchen window."

As he slowly nodded, Maggie wondered if he really agreed or was trying to keep peace. Was he envisioning it all as one room with no division to prevent the kitchen noises and smells from permeating the family room? Was he thinking of the times she would be in the kitchen with Dixie while he was watching football or baseball, and realizing their chatter would drive him crazy, or was he thinking of some happy, bright area presided over by Andrea, scowling at them but smiling sweetly at him with promises of where all this would lead?

"It would look different, that's for sure. Let's think about it awhile."

"Men. You always want to think things out."

He laughed. "Have you redecorated houses for that many men?"

She put on a fake sweet look that turned Maggie's stomach. "Of course not. None of them were special like you." Then she leaned forward and kissed him. It was more than Maggie could take. She jumped to her feet and fled out the front door.

She couldn't go anywhere. None of them wandered the neighborhood alone anymore, especially not so late in the day, with the sun setting behind the trees and darkness slowly closing over the neighborhood. But she could wander around the yard. She rubbed the sleeves of her shirt to warm her arms as she walked, wishing she had grabbed her jacket. The days were still warm, but the evenings were getting a bit nippy. She wasn't about to go back into the house, though. She would rather freeze.

She walked around the front yard, pausing to make sure there was water in the birdbath and sunflower seeds in the birdfeeder, then looped around the house to examine the tomato plant in the corner of the backyard, to see if there might be a late tomato or two left to pick. She could hardly see it in the dark, but she dropped to her knees and peered at the vine. It was empty.

She let Whizzer out of his pen, but as he bounced along beside her, all she could think of was Andrea's part in getting him, and it ruined his company. Still, she patted her leg so he would follow her around the yard in two full circles.

At the bottom of the driveway, she noticed the pansies that Andrea had planted by the mailbox were drying up, so she back-tracked to the garage for a watering can. Billy was supposed to be taking care of them. Andrea had posted a list of chores for each of them on the refrigerator as if they hadn't been running the household fine for twelve years without her help. Just the thought of Andrea raising her voice, asking Billy whether or not he'd done his chores, spurred Maggie's steps to fill the watering can and haul it back down the driveway to the flowers. As the water sprinkled out of the can, Whizzer lapped it up. She rubbed his head, then found a heavy stick and taught him to fetch.

When they were both worn out, they circled around to the back-yard to where the grass was thick and lush. She lay down on her back, and he fell on top of her and licked her face. "Silly dog. You're the best change she's made around here, I know that." She wrestled with him, rolling him onto his back to rub his belly until he quieted beside her.

She smoothed his fur with long sweeping strokes and thought about what all had transpired in their house. "Maybe she isn't that bad. She's not being mean to us. She's trying to make our house more livable, prettier. I just wish she would ask our opinion so I could talk to her openly and she would understand how I feel."

Whizzer licked her face some more, as if in sympathy. "Thanks, but I can do without the kisses," she said, wiping off her face. She pushed him back a ways and scratched his ears. "I would talk to Daddy, but he wouldn't understand. He would think I'm just saying I don't like her, which is partially true. She's just too bossy."

Whizzer's tail thumped rhythmically beside her.

"I'm not even sure I know what's bothering me. I just feel like I'm caged in nowadays."

She stared at the clouds crossing the moon and thought about where this future with Andrea was taking them, about how Andrea had reacted to the furniture being moved and the kitchen being painted. "She's right. I was trying to get back at her. I treated her the same way Sue has always treated me." She thought back over the weeks. "How can I make Andrea understand how I feel?"

She tried to be positive about it, to think of the good things, but anger rose in her and her stomach felt sick. Finally, she closed her eyes and prayed. *God, if this is what Daddy needs and wants, and if this is Your will, please give me the strength to accept it. Amen.*

Whizzer interpreted closed eyes as permission to kiss Sleeping Beauty, and he went at it with fervor. She laughed and wrestled him some more, then led him back to his pen. As he settled in his doghouse to sleep, she felt a bit more at peace. She resolved to persevere and come to terms with Andrea in their lives.

The question was still how. And where that would ultimately lead.

Chapter
Twenty~Five

SPEECH DAY. THE class was half-asleep before she even started. Asby was rolling his play joints. Sam was doing his math homework, risking the chance of getting a zero by both teachers if he was caught. Sean was sketching a picture of Becca. She had dropped the college boy and run back to Sean on Sunday, and now they were engaged. Engaged at sixteen. Maggie felt like telling him about her parents and warning him to watch out about having babies anytime soon.

Clarissa was writing a letter to some guy she'd met at the beach a few weekends back and couldn't quit talking about. Having a long-distance boyfriend was so much easier than having one at school. No one could look him in the face to pass judgment, and there were no arguments over whether she should go out with him versus going out with her girlfriends, since he lived two hundred miles away. They could talk on the phone for hours and act all in love without either one really being committed to anything all week long or risking anything in the backseat on Friday nights.

Max was almost asleep on his desk, his head pillowed on a stack of books. The way his mouth was hanging open, he might start snoring anytime now.

Mrs. Newell wasn't likely to say anything. She probably wouldn't even notice. She was as bored as the rest of them. They'd listened to speeches about pollution, war, and the decline of education in America, delivered as lists of facts and figures that even Mr. Baire in his constant quest for new information wouldn't have found interesting. And then there was Ian's speech on the need for a citywide leash law. It was so obviously delivered off the top of his head and not researched that it made the previous speeches deserve automatic A's.

Mrs. Newell had hung her head in exasperation, but she said nothing. She slipped her nail file out of her drawer and drew it slowly across her nails, with her hands down low behind the desk in an attempt to keep her students from noticing.

Maggie was glad they were all distracted. Giving her speech would be easier if no one was paying attention. She walked to the front, took a deep breath, and began by describing what happened to Sue.

The kids looked up. Mrs. Newell set her nail file on her desk and leaned forward.

She told them about each frightened step she'd taken into the woods, how she found Sue, what she guessed the attacker did to her, and what she suffered. And then she told them the difference between that and date rape, explaining that both were equally wrong violations of a person's body—doing things to them against their will. As she described what separated rape from molestation, she became aware of their stares and worried about what they might be thinking of her. She pushed onward anyway.

"One out of every four girls and one in six boys are molested," she said, and as she did she thought of how boring the statistics had been in the previous speeches, but as her gaze moved across her audience and met each face one by one, the reality of the statistic dawned on her. One boy and one girl in every row in front of her had been touched inappropriately by some creep, a trusted family friend or person in authority, who fooled everyone, and chances were that the victims probably kept the knowledge to themselves. They probably felt ashamed and held their secrets in the silence of their hearts.

Who was it in the front row? Quiet Jeanette? That was one of the signs—an overly quiet person who feared interaction with others. Or maybe Asby Jones with his fixation on marijuana. He could be in such pain that he was using drugs to escape reality. In the third row, it could be Clarissa. A major change in behavior was a sign that a kid had been molested, and she had gone from being so vivacious and eager to join everything people were doing to suddenly hiding away, not attending anything, acting totally involved in this long-distance boyfriend. Or maybe Sam in the back row. He rarely commented on anything unless something really riled him. Maggie couldn't tell anything from the expressions on their faces. She didn't want to look at any one of them long enough to imply that she might be considering one as victim versus another.

The bell was about to ring. A couple girls in the back row were putting their hair brushes back in their pocketbooks, checking their faces in makeup mirrors, and smearing lip gloss across their lips.

Maggie brought her speech to a quick conclusion. "If this has happened to you in the past, or it's happening right now, the Crisis Center can help. They have counselors on hand to help you deal with the situation and its aftereffects, and it's confidential. No one else will ever know."

She shuffled the last index card to the back of the stack in her hand and headed to her seat. Asby Jones started clapping. "Way to go Maggie McCarthy. I actually stayed awake for that one."

Other kids laughed as they gathered their stuff to the peal of the bell ending class.

Clarissa stopped at Maggie's desk. "Can Sue have visitors now?"

"Sure. She's not in ICU anymore. She'll be going home soon."

Mrs. Newell hollered over the noise of the students leaving. "Maggie, I need you to stay after class, please."

Clarissa squeezed her arm. "You're probably in trouble for talking about sex. We were all found in cabbage patches, you know." She winked, and left.

Maggie approached Mrs. Newell's desk, not sure what to expect.

"Have you collected all your things?" she asked, as if Maggie were in the habit of leaving bits of herself behind — a scrunchy or a pen or some secret letter to a boy full of inappropriate notions. Of course, Webb was the only boy she would consider writing, and she knew she hadn't, but the mere thought of it stabbed her with worry about leaving something like that around her seat, and made her turn around to look. There was nothing but paper shreds someone had pulled out of the spirals of a notebook under a desk two back from hers. They looked like curls of paper spaghetti.

"I have everything."

"Good. Follow me, then."

Mrs. Newell strode down the hall, weaving between students like a guided missile. Students stepped aside for her, but closed in behind her, making Maggie struggle to keep up, bumping into people's elbows and book bags as she made her way down the hall.

When they arrived at the principal's office, her knuckles went white around her books. Had Clarissa been right? Miss Reno, the secretary, turned her chubby face to Mrs. Newell to inquire what she needed. That's how she put it to everyone — "Might I inquire as to what you need?" — as if she ran an information booth at a convention.

Mrs. Newell wasn't the type to put up with borders or people posted around them. She walked past Miss Reno's desk, rapped once on Mr. Pompey's door, and let herself in.

Maggie hung back by Miss Reno, waiting for permission to pass. Miss Reno had her hands on her hips and was staring at Mrs. Newell's back. From the look on her face, Maggie thought she was probably thinking about kicking Mrs. Newell's can. Maggie backed up to the wall. It was like a den of vipers with no safe place to stand. Mrs. Newell leaned on the principal's desk, her face only a foot from his.

Maggie wished the floor would open up and swallow her. She could just imagine the tirade to come. How had she been crazy enough to talk about sex in front of the class? And now she would have to discuss it with Mr. Pompey, which was a thousand times worse.

She bit her bottom lip, closed her eyes, and waited for the fallout.

"Bryan," came Mrs. Newell's voice, stern, hurried, and as usual, to the point, "this young lady just gave a speech to my class that must be presented to the entire student body."

Hearing the principal's first name distracted Maggie. She hadn't known Mr. Pompey's name was Bryan. Her mind played with it a minute. It made him seem more human, reminding her that he must have been a kid once, a boy who kicked rocks down the road on his way to school and stuck bubble gum to the underside of his desk, never realizing he would give lectures on that very subject into a loudspeaker years later. The age and weight fell off him momentarily as she pictured him in his sandy-haired youth, with round cheeks that prompted his grandmother to pinch him and tell him he was adorable.

"What young lady?" he asked.

Mrs. Newell's words swam in Maggie's head. She swallowed. A speech to the whole school?

Mrs. Newell turned, presumably looking to see if Maggie was hiding, or if she'd left her somewhere back in the halls like a puppy dog she should have hooked to a leash. With an aggravated motion of one arm, she waved Maggie into the room. "Maggie McCarthy. It's a speech about Sue Roberts and date rape and molestation." She glanced at her watch. "I've got to go. Those seniors will have my room torn to pieces if I leave them alone. What is it about seniors? They think they own the school."

She strode back out, not even pausing as she tossed an order at the secretary. "Make sure Maggie gets a pass to her next class." Then she was gone, leaving Maggie standing alone in front of Mr. Bryan Pompey. Her books felt like a shield, so she clasped them tighter to her chest. She didn't know whether to be relieved that she wasn't in trouble or terrified that she might actually have to do as Mrs. Newell suggested and talk to the whole student body.

"So," he said, looking up at her from his seat, "a presentation to the student body." He flipped through the pages of a large black appointment book until he came to the November spread and ran his finger along each day, reading notes in each square that no one else could possibly decipher. He stopped on a square halfway down the page and squinted at the words, then pressed his intercom machine as if Miss Reno couldn't hear him if he just raised his voice slightly. "Have you got anythin' scheduled for the fourteenth, Miss Reno? No pep rallies or such?"

Miss Reno began turning pages in her calendar. Maggie could hear the rustle of them, each one with a slight pause, and she imagined the secretary licking her finger between the turning of each page. "Not a thing scheduled, Mr. Pompey." She said his name regally, as if elevating him to something beyond a high school principal and thereby pulling herself up the ladder with him. "We do have an assembly earlier that week, on Monday, but we scheduled it for second period. I would suggest an afternoon assembly to avoid causing two interruptions during the same class time that week."

Maggie wondered how Mr. Pompey kept from rolling his eyes at being reminded of something so obvious. She bet that when he was a kid, and just called Bryan, he would have told Miss Reno he wasn't an idiot who had to be told everything. Of course, Miss Reno would only have been a baby and not able to talk, so he wouldn't have even noticed her, let alone paid her any mind.

"Does the fourteenth work for you?" he asked Maggie.

Maggie didn't have a calendar to check. She didn't participate in the many activities her peers had laid out in a week: dance, cheerleading practice, piano lessons, and sports. She had laundry, housework, supper, and school assignments. But just to seem in the thick of things, she leaned forward and craned her neck to look at the calendar, as if she had to examine the days to make sure the speech wouldn't interfere with something pressing in her life.

"The fourteenth," she said aloud, feeling very professional as she did so, equal to the principal, and as she thought about it, she realized that in many ways she was his equal. Didn't she run a household, keeping track of everything for two boys and a man? While Mr. Pompey had to rely on his secretary to track his schedule at school, and probably his wife to do the same at home, she kept track of everything at home and school. In fact, she was responsible for so much in her family's life that maybe she ought to carry a calendar around to start plotting out what the various days would bring. But that would be stupid. She didn't need a calendar to remember to do the laundry or clean the house. And as for her brothers, she couldn't think of anything they had to do other than Tony walking down the street to his guitar lesson once a week, and Billy's soccer games on Thursday evenings. He'd skipped the last two of the season, so even Thursdays had become open. The fourteenth fell on a Wednesday, which was the day she washed the dark load, but what did that have to do with anything? She put the clothes in the machine when she got home from school, added a scoop of detergent, and pushed the start button. It didn't take time away from anything going on at school. If she did have something, a test that period or whatever, wouldn't the assembly cancel it out anyway?

She couldn't think of anything blocking that date. "I think that would be fine."

"Does it give you enough time to plan?"

Her stomach contracted. Plan what? Would she be expected to do more than she just did in class? Then it occurred to her that they wouldn't bother calling a full school assembly for her to talk for five minutes. She would have to expand the entire thing. Make some kind of posters or something to put on stage with her. Her mind whirled back through time as she tried to remember the last assembly they'd had and what it entailed. A speaker had come in to talk about recycling, but she couldn't remember any details. It was so boring that she had pulled a novel from her book bag and read. Then there had been a couple pep rallies, and visiting musicians. None of those were any help at all and only made her more nervous about the whole thing.

How had she gotten herself into doing even more research when all she wanted to do was put Sue's attack behind her?

Talking about Sue during a five-minute speech in English class was one thing, but Maggie decided she couldn't talk about Sue to the entire school without getting clearance from her.

Sue was munching a McDonald's cheeseburger when Maggie got there. Mrs. Roberts rose from her seat in the corner. "Ah, Maggie. I'm so glad you're here. I have errands to run and I'd hate to leave Sue by herself all evening."

Maggie took Mrs. Robert's place, unsure what to say. Tension rose between the two girls, the same sense of antagonism and discomfort as always, but more intense now that she had seen Sue at her worst and Sue had seen Maggie at her best. It put them on new ground. Maggie no longer felt beneath Sue.

"So what are you here for this time?" Sue asked.

Maggie shrugged.

The television was tuned into a talk show about movie stars. Maggie wished Sue would turn it off so they wouldn't have to talk over it, but Tom Cruise walked onto the set and captured Sue's full attention.

Maggie frowned. "I can't believe Nicole Kidman was ever married to him."

Sue swallowed the bite she'd been chewing. "He should've stayed with her. She's so beautiful." She looked Maggie up and down, appraising her outfit. "I love that shirt. Where did you get it?"

Maggie smoothed the front of it. Maybe nothing had changed about Sue. "The mall. That little store at the far end. Hasty's? Something like that."

"G. P. Hastings. Who'd have thought you would shop there? What happened to all your T-shirts? Did you find a fairy godmother or something?"

Maggie pictured Andrea in a puffy pink ball gown with a wand in her hand and a tiara of diamonds stuck into her short, dark hair—not a likely sight. "A stepmother, more like, though they haven't officially taken it that far."

Sue licked mayonnaise off her fingers one at a time, then lifted the bun and inspected the burger. "That's what I get for asking for mayo; they put too much on this thing." The criticism didn't slow her down; she replaced the bun and took another huge bite, as if she hadn't eaten in days. "Looks like a good deal for you, anyway."

"I guess it could be worse." Was that how she was thinking about the situation now? She could end up with a worse stepmother than Andrea? She wasn't sure when she'd actually admitted that it might go that far. Maybe she had just come to that conclusion as the words escaped her lips, but it sounded like a conclusion she'd reached in her sleep weeks ago. She was flooded with images of future events playing themselves out: Andrea in a wedding dress, something short and contemporary for sure. Andrea's clothes in the laundry hamper. Her dishes in the sink. Her shoes and coats finding places to live in the mudroom. Whizzer trotting beside her during her morning runs, eventually with Maggie's father and Billy following along with them, like she had the dog, husband, and stepson all strung along on a great, long leash. Andrea with all her money taking them on a summer vacation, taking a separate room with their father and closing the door with a smile that said Do Not Disturb. Maggie couldn't go past that one.

"I had to give a speech in English class today."

Sue was licking the mayonnaise from the edge of the bun. She wrinkled her nose, but Maggie wasn't sure if it was on behalf of the mayo or the thought of giving a speech.

"It was about you."

That caught her attention. She put the burger down. "Me? What did you say?"

Maggie wondered what went through Sue's head. Did Sue imagine she had talked about her wardrobe, or maybe her shoe styles, or her cheerleading prowess? Maggie wished she hadn't mentioned it now. Here Sue was, trying to recover from it all, and Maggie was about to sum her up by one bad episode in her life. "Well, it wasn't really about you. I guess it would be more appropriate to say that it concerned you."

The scars on Sue's face burned redder for a moment. "Oh."

"They want me to make a presentation to the whole school."

The cheeseburger had lost its appeal. She rolled it up in its paper wrapper and squeezed it. "What did you tell them? All the details of what he did to me? How I looked when you found me? What he's done to my face and my life?"

"I'm not telling them anything at all if you don't want me to. That's why I'm asking."

"I guess it's a free world. You can say whatever you want." She poked at the lump, making holes in the wrapper with her finger-nails, which reminded Maggie of what she'd brought for her. She pulled an Eckerd's bag out of her pocketbook and laid it on the rolling tray. "Here. This is for you."

One peek in the bag got Sue smiling. She picked up the burger remains and pitched the wad across the room. Amazingly, it struck the side of the trash can by the door and fell into its depths.

She pulled out a blue nail file. "I guess it's not a secret, is it? Who doesn't know what happened?"

"That's not the same as me talking about it."

Next came purple nail polish, and then bright red. Maggie never really noticed what color Sue wore, but she'd figured some-thing flashy.

"No base coat?" She shook up the purple.

Maggie shrugged.

"I guess you wouldn't know about that kind of thing. Ask your stepmom. You've got to have a base coat to protect your nails."

"I don't want to stand up and talk about your private life without your permission."

"Private life? I don't have a private life anymore." She filed one thumbnail with a vengeance. "And you know what? It's not my fault. It's his. Talk about him. Talk about what a sleaze he is. I hope they fry his carcass when they catch him."

Maggie was taken aback. "Have you remembered who it was?"

"No. But they'll figure it out."

Maggie felt all hope whoosh out like an untied balloon released to fly around the room until deflated, leaving her disoriented. It took her several seconds to gather her wits again. "Everyone will be talking about it."

"They already are, aren't they? Is anybody in this town ever going to look at me again without talking about it? I'll be forty-five, old as my mama, and little girls at church will still point at me and talk about it."

Maggie knew she was right. A stigma was hard to drop in a small town.

The door swung open and Webb entered. "Hey," he said and set a Dairy Queen cup in front of Sue. "I brought you a milk shake."

"Must be Christmas around here today." She took a slurp and laid her head back on the pillows. "It's what everybody thinks, isn't it, Maggie?"

Webb probably thought she meant something about Christmas, but Maggie understood. Sue wanted to know if Webb thought about the rape every time he looked at her too. "Hard to say, Sue. If I were a mind reader, I'd have brought some base coat." Maggie picked up her pocketbook, noticing how much flatter it was without the nail polish, with just a small billfold and tissue inside. She looped it over her arm and touched Webb's hand as she passed by. "See you later."

She knew he and Sue needed to talk. She wished she could become invisible and stick around to hear what they said.

Not too long ago she *had* been invisible.

Chapter Twenty-Six

SHE WOKE THE next Saturday with one message clear: she needed to talk to Dixie's mom again. Of all the adults she knew, Mrs. Chambers was the one who could help her sort through her emotions. Maybe she couldn't talk with her about Sue and the whole rape issue, but Mrs. Chambers could help her figure out how to deal with Andrea in her life.

Mrs. Chambers came to the door. "Dixie is still asleep, hon, but you can wake her up if you like. She needs to get started on her chores, anyway."

Maggie examined her toes. "Actually, I came to talk to you."

"Well, come on in. I was just having my morning cup of tea."

Maggie followed her back to the kitchen and took a seat at the table. "You were so right about Tony, I thought maybe you could help me with this other matter."

Mrs. Chambers set a cup of tea in front of her, placed the teapot in the center of the table, and took her usual seat beside her. "Certainly. I'll try anyway. Sometimes it helps just to talk."

Maggie explained what had transpired. "It was bad enough when she started buying stuff for the house. I mean our stuff is really old, so in some ways it was great getting new things, but it has gone way beyond that now."

"Like how?"

"Like she's buying the groceries now and planning our meals. I'll be in the kitchen, and she shows up and rearranges what we're going to eat and how it's supposed to be cooked. She made Tony replace the air conditioner filters and trim the bushes out front. She has a list of chores for Billy tacked to the fridge."

"Chores? Really? Like what?"

"Watering the flowers she planted by the mailbox. Walking his dog and cleaning up the piles in the yard. Washing the car every Saturday."

Her laughter said it didn't sound all that drastic. "How does your dad feel about all this?"

"I don't know. He doesn't say much. He's too worked up about the other stuff."

"What other stuff?"

"The renovations she's plotting. She has new tile picked out for the bathrooms and some plans for expanding his closet, and she wants to tear down the wall between the kitchen and family room, and install new cabinets so the kitchen will be *more efficient*."

"You aren't serious?"

"Oh, yes I am. Daddy keeps putting her off, but she has this whole floor plan sketched out, and she works on it at night, picking stuff out while Daddy is watching television."

Mrs. Chambers set her sights on something in the hallway, maybe searching out small ears that might be lurking nearby. "Has she moved in?"

"No! She hasn't even spent the night. You know Daddy wouldn't do that. If he did, I would scream till the roof caved in, but . . ."

"But what?"

Maggie swished the tea in the bottom of her cup and watched it slosh against the sides. "I did notice a new set of sheets in the wash."

"You're kidding!" Mrs. Chambers's eyes widened.

"I threw them in the trash."

She laughed heartily. "You didn't?"

"I did too. Stomped them right to the bottom of the can."

Mrs. Chambers held her hand up. "Give me five, girl!"

Maggie obliged, slapping her hand against Mrs. Chambers's thin palm and long fingers.

The glee didn't last. Maggie leaned back and crossed her arms across her chest. "Could you talk to him?"

"I'm not sure I would know what to say."

"But you know him. Or at least you used to know him. Please? Just say something."

She sipped her tea and gazed out the window at the brightening day, deep in thought, before she finally nodded. "Okay. Sure. Is he home?"

"Yes, but I didn't mean right now."

"Is Andrea there?"

"She's at a conference in Atlanta this weekend."

"Good. No time like the present. Let's go."

She hollered for Dixie and Cindy to get up and put clothes on, and they all set off down the road for what looked like an early morning walk through the neighborhood, but Maggie's heart pounded, knowing they were on a mission much more purposeful than anyone looking on would have guessed.

Maggie's father was watching a football game on television when they arrived. "Hi, Daddy," Maggie said as she rushed through the door and ran to give him a hug. "Look who's come to visit — Dixie's mom."

He turned with a surprised look on his face, and Maggie saw in him the embarrassment he must have worn as a teenager when a girl flirted with him in the halls at school, or a teacher called on him for a question when he hadn't been listening. She looked from him to Mrs. Chambers and back again, and realized he was good looking, something to which she'd never given much thought.

He muted the television and stood to greet them. "Jessie. Wow. How are you? I'm sorry I haven't stopped in to see you. I should have, I know. It's so hard — "

She gave him a hug and laid her hand on his arm. "Really, it's okay. I didn't want company for a long time. You know how that is. You've been there."

"That's why I didn't call. How are things?"

The question held much deeper meanings about life and death and all that joined the two, all that neither of them wanted to put into words. Maggie had seen the dance many times before.

"Getting easier. It's been two years. . . ."

"It hasn't been that long."

Maggie pulled Dixie and Cindy away toward the kitchen door and watched the exchange from a distance. Her father's eyes followed Mrs. Chambers's every movement, an attentiveness she'd never seen him display toward Andrea.

Mrs. Chambers nodded. "I think we're okay. We've pulled ourselves together. We've started to move on as best we can."

It was his turn to nod, and with unspoken agreement, they both sat on the sofa to talk further. Mrs. Chambers noticed the girls by the kitchen door and indicated she wasn't pleased they were still standing there.

Dixie took Cindy's hand, and they followed Maggie upstairs.

"So what brings you over? Not that you have to have an excuse or anything."

Their voices faded as the girls reached Maggie's bedroom. She opened her closet and rummaged in the corner until she found what she wanted—a plastic box full of Barbie dolls and all their paraphernalia. She plopped it on the center of the bed and pulled off the lid. "Here Cindy, play with these."

Dixie reached for a red velvet dress with white trim. "I remember this dress. It's mine. You never returned it."

Maggie rolled her eyes. Dixie could be so obtuse at times. "We have more important things to worry about than Barbie doll clothes. C'mon." She crept back down the stairs to where the wall met the railing, where she could listen without being seen, not bothering to see if Dixie followed.

Mrs. Chambers was talking. "I think the problem isn't so much that Maggie doesn't like her, you understand. In fact, she says Andrea has done a lot for her."

Maggie peeked around the wall to watch her father's face. He was still concentrating, not halfway paying attention while really watching television like he did with Andrea when she talked about her plans for the house.

"I don't want to talk out of turn here, Frankie, so stop me anytime."

Maggie turned to Dixie, who had finally joined her on the step, and mouthed the name at her. *Frankie?* It brought to mind a guy in a leather jacket with a pack of cigarettes in his shirt pocket, not her daddy at all.

Dixie snickered silently.

Frankie said, "I thought after all this time it wouldn't bother her. Her mother has been gone for twelve years. How long am I supposed to wait?"

Maggie blushed deeper than he did at hearing it, especially the way he said it.

Mrs. Chambers folded one leg across the other knee and fiddled with the hem of her jeans. "That's not it. It's not that she resents Andrea trying to replace her mother."

"What then?"

"She thinks Andrea is replacing her."

"Huh?" The reply came across like a giant question mark that took his whole body to express, from his quirked eyebrows to the shifting of his posture.

Mrs. Chambers laid her hand on his leg. "Maggie has been the mother in the house for as long as she can remember. She's decided what you eat for supper and when. She's done the laundry, bought the groceries, signed the boys up for soccer and baseball, fixed their lunches, and changed their sheets. Now, Andrea is trying to do all those things."

"But I thought she'd be glad not to have to do that stuff anymore."

Mrs. Chambers picked up a square pillow that had fallen on the floor beside her and held it to her chest. "Don't hit me when I say this" — she braced the pillow out like a shield — "but Maggie feels like she's been the wife for the past twelve years, and now you're cheating on her." She hid behind the pillow.

Maggie's mouth fell open. Dixie poked her and hissed in her ear. "You do?"

Her father almost lost his seat. He pulled the pillow down from in front of Mrs. Chambers's face. "Did she tell you that?"

She threw the pillow at him. "She didn't have to. Don't you see it? She does all this stuff for you for years without so much as a thank you, just like any wife and mother, and then you bring home some other woman who starts in on her job, encroaching on her space, and making her feel like she's expendable."

"Not expendable. I want her to feel freer, you know, so she can be a kid while she still has time."

"She's way past that, Frankie."

He looked away.

"Remember, her mother married you at that age."

"And she wanted to go back to being a kid. That's what I started to see. On Maggie's sixteenth birthday I woke up and saw it, and I thought, *Here I am doing it all over again, this time to my daughter.* I didn't want that."

"Maggie isn't her mother. She's much stronger."

He nodded. "I know."

"She doesn't want to give up her place. She might want a little help, but she doesn't want to be pushed off the lifeguard stand and told to go play in the shallow water with the other kids."

Maggie twirled a lock of hair. How had Mrs. Chambers known what she felt? She hadn't said anything like that.

Maggie watched Mrs. Chambers appraise the room, seeking out signs of the changes Maggie had described. "I hear Andrea has all kinds of plans for the place."

Maggie's father frowned. "Yes, she does."

"You don't sound too happy about it."

"She wants to totally renovate. Take walls down. Rearrange the rooms. I'm not ready for that."

"You don't have to, Frankie. You're not married to her. It's still your house."

He didn't respond. He looked into his lap.

"You're not engaged, are you?"

He laughed an odd, short chortle that started in his belly but never made it all the way out. "No. But it's long past time."

"God's timing is always perfect; you know that. Maybe she's just not the right one."

He rubbed his scruffy, unshaven chin and spoke quietly. "No, she's not."

"Then end it."

"I'm not sure I know how. It's been a long time since I played this game."

She touched his face, and the magic pixie in her lit up around both of them. "It's been a long time since I played this game too."

Some of her pixie dust radiated to his face, and he smiled. He took her hand in his. "Thanks, Jessie."

"It could be that God had some other reason for things taking so long, you know." She let the words settle before she pulled away. "I better get the girls. I've distracted you from watching the game."

He picked up the remote. "No rush. Seems to me you always liked football. Why don't you stay and watch it? We'll order a pizza for all of us in a while."

Mrs. Chambers glanced toward the steps as if she knew they were there and was dismissing them. "Sure. I know the girls won't mind." She retrieved the pillow and settled beside him with her legs crossed in front of her and the pillow in her lap.

Maggie hurried Dixie back to her bedroom. She could hardly contain herself, and Dixie seemed about to burst too.

"Wow. I wouldn't have believed it if I hadn't heard it all myself, " Dixie said.

Maggie twirled euphorically and hugged Dixie. "I'm guessing they dated a bit more than once!" She grinned so big it divided her face in two as she settled beside Cindy on the bed. She picked up a pink ball gown and dressed her favorite Barbie. "She looks like a fairy godmother, don't you think?"

Dixie joined them on the bed. Maggie hummed to herself and relaxed into the past, into being a kid for a couple hours while a new game played out downstairs.

In the days after Mrs. Chambers visited, the house became amazingly quiet, almost reverting back to how it had been prior to Andrea's arrival in their lives, except for the new decorating. Andrea had showed up only on Thursday evening, and that was for a walk around the neighborhood with Maggie's father and Whizzer. Whatever was said between them left her father subdued.

"I broke up with Andrea," he announced to them when he turned off the television for the night.

The boys stood and shrugged, offering little comment besides a sincere "Too bad, Dad," from Tony. Maggie had told them she thought it would happen soon, so they weren't all that surprised.

Maggie thought *breaking up* was a rather juvenile expression, as if her father were still in high school, but then she realized he hadn't had much practice talking about such things since those days, and it endeared him to her. As much as she was glad to see Andrea out of their lives, she saw how forlorn her father looked and understood what a powerful presence Andrea had been in his life. Andrea's absence left a gaping void that she couldn't fill.

Maybe it had been as selfish for her to wish Andrea out of her father's life as it had been to wish for popularity.

She wrapped her arms around him and laid her head against his chest so she could hear the beating of his heart. *If my daddy needs someone, Lord,* she prayed, *please lead him to the right woman.*

On Friday, Dixie decided to spend the night at Maggie's house for a change, but her mother wouldn't let her walk over by herself, not even with police reassurance that the attacker was probably hundreds of miles away and in hiding. She drove Dixie down in the car and walked her all the way into the house.

Maggie pulled Dixie into the kitchen to help her finish making the macaroni, then peeked out the swinging door to see what transpired between her father and Dixie's mother.

Mrs. Chambers came all the way in with Cindy at her side and greeted Maggie's father with a swat on the arm before he could get up, then took a seat beside him while Cindy wandered around the room looking at pictures and knick-knacks. "So, did you get things straightened out?"

He sighed. "I guess so. Kind of."

"Good. Glad I could help." She started to stand, then changed her mind. "Hey, Maggie was telling me you have *Cinderella* and wouldn't mind us borrowing it. She said no one watches it anymore."

Maggie did a double take and stayed by the door, keeping it ajar just enough to hear what else transpired. She hadn't said a word to Mrs. Chambers about that movie. She'd mentioned it to Cindy one day, eons ago, when the one they rented tore up.

"Oh, sure." Her father's face lit up as if he hadn't considered that Cindy was only seven and watching a Disney movie would be a great way to keep them around. "You know what? I haven't watched that movie since Billy was a tiny fellow. How about we put it in and watch it right here together?"

Mrs. Chambers smiled like a child. "We won't be keeping you from anything?"

Maggie grinned. What Mrs. Chambers meant was whether or not he was expecting someone else to occupy his time.

"Not at all."

As they busied themselves getting the movie started, Maggie closed the door. "Now I know where you get it."

"Get what?" asked Dixie.

"The way you smile at people when you want them to do something for you." Maggie had noticed Dixie perfecting that sweet smile ever since they'd moved into a larger circle of friends, especially with Elliott. But right now she didn't want to think of all that entailed. She was glad Dixie was spending the night and they could chat and carry on just like they had for so many years without thoughts of Heather and Tammy or anyone else.

Some time later, after they'd all had their fill of macaroni and the dishes were washed, Maggie pushed the kitchen door open but stopped halfway out, causing Dixie to collide with her back. Maggie pointed. Cindy was stretched out on the floor watching the movie. Their parents were on the sofa with the chessboard between them, idly playing and chatting in soft tones.

Maggie let the door close softly. "Maybe we'd better not disturb them."

"What? And spend the rest of the night in the kitchen?"

They peeked out again just as three hard raps sounded at the front door and Andrea strode in. Maggie held her breath as Andrea's face registered the scene in the family room.

Mrs. Chambers took her time standing up. "Oh, I see you do have company after all."

Andrea recovered and went into sweet mode. "Am I interrupting? I had no idea." Obviously Andrea wasn't ready to toss in the towel yet, but she hadn't realized she had competition waiting in the wings.

"No," Mrs. Chambers said. "Frankie and I are old friends. He was kind enough to let Cindy watch one of Maggie's Disney tapes."

Andrea's smile stayed plastered to her face as she jiggled keys in one hand. A bag of Mediterranean food from Andrea's favorite restaurant dangled forgotten in the other. *Nothing with MSG*, Maggie thought. No Chinese food or takeout from a steak house that used meat tenderizers. Nothing good.

Mrs. Chambers turned to Maggie's father. "We'll just take it home and finish watching it there, if that's okay."

He scrambled to get away from between the two of them, practically tripping over the coffee table to get the tape out of the machine.

Mrs. Chambers followed him to the cabinet. "I see you have a whole set of Disney tapes."

He nodded.

"Maybe we can come back and watch another one sometime."

He nodded again, looking past her to Andrea, whose smile had turned sour.

Dixie pushed past Maggie through the door to her mother. "Are you leaving, Mama?"

"Yes, honey. You call me when you're ready to come home in the morning. I don't want you walking up that hill alone."

"I'll bring her," Maggie's father said.

Maggie crossed behind Andrea and met Dixie's mother at the door to give her a hug. "See you tomorrow, Mrs. Chambers," she said.

Mrs. Chambers winked. "You're a big girl now, Maggie. I think it's time you started calling me Jessie, don't you?"

Maggie grinned, knowing the trail of pixie dust ran all the way back to her father. Andrea would have to battle pretty hard to win this challenge.

Chapter
Twenty~Seven

MIDWEEK, MAGGIE WAS practicing her speech for the big presentation when Billy appeared at her door and waited there until she reached a stopping point.

"So who is it in our family?"

"What, baby?" she asked distractedly, realizing too late that he'd asked her not to call him baby anymore. It was a hard habit to break, especially when he'd come to her door with his baseball glove hanging from his hand and looking so dejected, like he'd just struck out at the most important game of the season.

Even as the thoughts flew through her head, she wasn't really thinking about Billy. She was practicing her speech and kept mixing up paragraphs in the middle, making the flow sound disjointed. She intended to repeat it again and again until she got through it at least once without an error before quitting for the night.

"You said one out of four."

She nodded. He must have been listening from his room.

He continued. "There are four people in our family, so which of us is it?"

"It doesn't mean exactly every fourth person. It's a statistic, a number some researcher devises to show how widespread something is in our society."

He stuck his fist into the glove and rocked back and forth on his feet like he was gearing up for a pitch. "But if it was someone in our family, for instance, who would it be?"

She hadn't thought about it, really. "It doesn't have to be any one of us. I'm not trying to frighten you, Billy. It's not really about us. It's to help other girls keep from getting in trouble like Sue, so they know what to do if someone tries to hurt them that way, and teach them things they can do to help prevent it, like not walking places alone."

He plucked at his ear, a sign he was deep in thought, and then turned away, back to his room.

She felt like she ought to go to him and wrap her arms around him, apologize for scaring him. He was still a little kid even if he didn't want to be called baby anymore. But she had to get the speech right. She would plan something special, one on one with him, when it was all behind her.

She decided it wasn't just Billy that needed some attention. The whole family needed something fun and lighthearted to break the somber mood. A cookout. She mentioned it offhandedly to her father the next evening. "I thought we'd cook on the grill this weekend. It's supposed to be warm."

"That sounds good. I'll check to make sure there's enough gas in the grill."

"We could invite Webb for Tony, and Jasper, that new boy Billy's age who's moved in down the road, and Dixie and Mrs. Chambers and Cindy."

He weighed her words a moment before nodding. "If you're sure."

"Of course I'm sure. We all need friends, Daddy."

She found Billy in his now usual spot — reclined on his bed, reading comic books. "Hi, bud. Daddy said we could have a cook-out. Would you like to invite a friend?" She hoped he would think of the new boy without her having to suggest him.

"Who's coming?"

"Dixie, Cindy, and their mother. And Webb. And whoever you invite."

"I don't want to invite anyone."

"Not even that new boy down the road?"

"No."

She sat beside him on the bed. It smelled like urine again. Something was terribly wrong. "Billy, tell me what's bothering you."

"Nothing."

"Andrea thinks you're upset about seeing Smokey . . . well, cut up. That's why we got you a dog, but Whizzer hasn't seemed to help. Are you still upset about Smokey?"

"No."

"Then what?"

He wouldn't look at her. "Nothing."

"Come off it. Brad has been your best friend for two years and suddenly you never want to see him. Did you get in a fight?"

"I just don't want to go to his house anymore."

"You went to the zoo with him and spent the night with him when I went to that party with Dixie."

He turned away.

"What happened, Billy?"

He pushed at her. "Go away and leave me alone."

Mr. Dweller's face rose before her again, his intent look at Smokey, and in the crowd at the crime scene, and then all the horrible questions he asked her that day in his living room when she stopped to pick up Billy. She thought of the times she'd found Billy's bed wet, of his recurring nightmares, and of his refusal to play with friends anymore, and wondered how she could have missed the very things she was trying to teach other kids about. No wonder Billy had asked who in their house might be the victim! "Has Mr. Dweller hurt you?"

Billy's face crumpled.

"What did he do, Billy?"

Billy started crying.

Why hadn't she seen it before? "Did he touch you, Billy? Did he make you touch him?"

His voice cracked between sobs, small and frightened, more like a six-year-old than a growing twelve-year-old boy. "He said we were all so upset over Smokey that we needed to comfort each other in special ways to help get over it. He said I had to do it or he would tell Dad it was our fault Smokey died."

"What he did was wrong, Billy. He was abusing you."

"I didn't want to do it."

Maggie took him in her arms. "I know, Billy. I know. He's a pervert."

She sat there with him for a while before whispering in his ear, "We have to go talk to Dad."

"No!"

"Shh. Billy, it's okay," she said, stroking his head. "You're not in trouble. But Mr. Dweller is, and we're putting a stop to it right now."

Her father's face turned hard as Maggie explained about Billy, his jaw clenching as tight as his fists at his side. "I'll call Andrea. She's an expert," he said. "It just makes sense to get her involved."

Maggie paced the room, wondering if involving Andrea in Billy's confession would mean her sliding back into their lives again, but when she arrived, Maggie quit worrying. Andrea took a seat beside Billy on the sofa, while her father sat on the edge of his recliner, leaning in to hear everything Billy had to say. Her father and Andrea hardly even looked at each other until Andrea finished taking notes and promised to pass them on to the authorities, and even then, the look in her father's eyes was gratitude, nothing more.

"Do you think he's the one that raped Sue too?" Maggie asked.

"We'll leave that up to the police to investigate."

"He was there at both crime scenes. Remember what you told me about the rapist coming to watch the investigation? Mr. Dweller came when we found Smokey and again when I found Sue."

"That's not enough to convict a man."

Billy went up to his room again after Andrea left, and Maggie followed her father into the kitchen. "It's still okay to have the cookout on Saturday, isn't it, Dad?"

"Sure, I think it'll be good for Billy to socialize. He needs to know life must go on." He poured more coffee into his mug. "Did Jessie say if she's coming with the girls?"

Maggie grinned. "Yes, they're coming." She kissed his cheek and skipped up the steps to her room. Her father was looking forward to having Mrs. Chambers visit!

The sun hung just over the trees on Saturday afternoon when Dixie arrived with her mother and sister.

Maggie led them all into the kitchen, where her father was gathering everything for the grill. That was one area of cooking where he took over.

Jessie glanced around at the lime green kitchen. "You told me Andrea made some changes, but I never imagined her picking out such a happy color."

Maggie laughed.

Her father joined her. "Andrea painted it white. The kids repainted it lime green."

Jessie offered Maggie a high-five. "Good for you."

They all moved outside to the back patio, still laughing at the audacity of redoing Andrea's decorating job.

"By the way, that reminds me" — Maggie's father turned to her — "speaking of redecorating, I bought myself a new set of sheets a few weeks ago, but you never put them on my bed. Where did they go? I'm sick to death of getting my toe caught in the hole in that old set."

Maggie paled. "I thought Andrea . . ."

Jessie laughed and laid a hand on Frank's arm. "I think you'd better buy another set."

"I'll find you some new ones, Daddy," Maggie said and walked away, sure that Jessie was going to have a good laugh explaining about Maggie's suspicions and how she'd disposed of the last set.

Dixie and Cindy had joined Tony in a game of croquet on the far side of the yard, so Maggie headed toward Webb playing with Whizzer in the back corner.

Webb tossed an old tennis ball for the dog to chase. "I think your dad has the hots for Dixie's mom."

Maggie glared at him. Why did he have to put it that way? Her mind was still on the sheets she'd thrown away and her own assumption of what her father had been doing with Andrea, and how far off base she'd been. "Why is everything about sex? Maybe he just likes her as a friend. A guy can be friends with a woman without it meaning sex."

Webb's voice sounded contrite, like a little boy. "I didn't mean it that way. I just meant he thinks she's good looking."

Maggie blushed. "Oh."

Webb sank to the ground and pulled the dog half onto his lap to scratch his ears and rub his belly. "I've been reading that book you loaned me. Seems like there used to be more love in the world back then."

"Not just more love," she said. "More respect. More morality. It mattered what people did. They were responsible for their actions. It just seems like they thought more about their relationships. They didn't just jump into bed on a whim."

"Maybe. Or maybe they just weren't allowed to write about it back then."

Maggie sprawled out beside them on the grass. "I don't think so. The world was different. Everything was more formal. There weren't freaks on every corner. The girls were held in higher esteem. They were guarded and cherished."

"Girls couldn't have jobs. They got married and had babies, and that's it. Is that what you want?"

"Well . . ."

"That's what I thought. Some things are worse, but some things are better. Look at all the things you can do. And look at all the technology we have."

"Exactly. Guys your age were out working jobs and proud of what they were doing. You and Tony lie in front of those video games like lumps, swilling stolen beers and telling stupid stories. Where's that ever going to get you? What's that going to do for the world?"

"We're still kids. We're supposed to have fun."

"You're not a kid. You're almost grown. You graduate in two years and you don't even have a life plan yet."

"Do you?"

She pulled her knees up to her chest. "I've been thinking about it. I used to want to be a teacher, but now I'm thinking of being an EMT. When I was in the woods, I wanted desperately to know what to do for Sue, but not as a doctor with patients and rounds and all that. An EMT seems so immediate, so on the edge."

He nodded. "Maggie, the girl with a plan."

"I want to get married someday, and have a family of my own. I feel like I've been a mother all my life, yet I still want my own babies, but not until I find the right guy. I want a real relationship with a guy based on love, not sex after a movie. Unfortunately, I think it will be a long time because I don't think there's a teenage boy out there who's ready to give out as much love as I require."

Webb didn't move an iota, but his expression flattened just enough that she knew her words had registered.

Tony hit a croquet ball into the bushes, which drew Whizzer's attention. He galloped across the yard in pursuit.

Maggie gazed after the dog, but her thoughts were on the real question, the thing weighing on her mind, hanging there in the balance. She knew Webb wouldn't volunteer the information. They sat there in the last rays of waning sunshine, letting time slip away between them as the sun turned to an orange ball behind the trees. Webb leaned back, plucked a long piece of grass, and nibbled on it. She finally said what was on her mind.

"Did you sleep with her?"

He arched one eyebrow, then flopped onto his back in the grass. It reminded her of how she used to find shapes in the clouds with her brothers when they were kids. She had done that with Tony so many times, but she wasn't sure if she'd ever done that with Billy, and she wondered with a pang if it was too late. Would he scowl at her with that twelve-year-old attitude and act like looking at clouds was babyish?

Webb pulled the piece of grass out of his mouth and rolled over onto his stomach so he could rest his head on his hands. "What makes you think I should answer that?"

She had to ask because it was connected to all the other questions, all the thoughts that swarmed in her mind every time she closed her eyes at night, echoing in her head during all the hours she couldn't sleep, when she relived the episode over and over again. She had to see it through someone else's eyes. She had to see it through his eyes. "I was wondering if it makes a difference. If you look at Sue and think, *I touched her there. I made love to her,* and then think of that pervert touching her in those same places, and whether or not that bothers you, if you think of that when you look at her, or if you could ever touch her in those places again without thinking of what he did."

He put his head facedown on his hands. Maggie remembered lying that way at the soccer field when she was tired of watching Billy chase a ball around. Her nose had been so close to the ground that she smelled dirt as if for the first time, the pungency of it bringing to mind the worms and moles that burrowed down so far that they probably hadn't ever experienced air without the smell of dirt. It made her want to scoop some up in her hand and hold it out like Scarlett O'Hara, like some glorious prophecy of future times.

Webb rolled onto his back again and sighed. A leaf drifted down and landed on his T-shirt. She watched it rise and fall with his belly as he breathed. She thought maybe he was waiting for her to say something else, but she was done. She didn't really expect an answer from him. She wouldn't answer if she were him. But the question was there between them like a map to some secret they'd never acknowledged until now.

She plucked some grass and tried to braid it into a chain. She had always wanted hair that could be braided, long brown locks, but with just a bit of a wave so the braids wouldn't fall apart at the nod of the head like Dixie's silky hair tended to do. She wouldn't have fixed it with two long plaits, but a bunch of tiny ones all around her head so that they would wave along her neck like a horse's mane at a show.

He turned his head to look at her.

She couldn't meet his eyes. She didn't want to look in case she didn't like what she saw. Instead she watched a bird fluttering along the ground and a squirrel scampering along a branch, then coiling up as he reached the fine point at the end so he could spring across the open air to land in another tree, making her ponder how such a small animal developed such courage.

She felt the same gap between her and Webb. She'd brought him to the end of a branch.

He placed another stalk of grass in his mouth, stuck it between his lips again where it could sway back and forth with the movement of his words. "I don't think that's any of your business."

Maggie had expected that reaction, but it still felt like a slap in the face. She was trying hard to deal with it all, to get life back into perspective, and talking about it with Webb, hearing his side of it and how it affected him, would have meant a lot to her, but he wasn't willing to cross the line. She was still walking the path alone.

She unhooked Whizzer's leash from where it hung on the side of the pen and clipped it to his collar. Without a word more to Webb, she led Whizzer from the yard. "I'm taking the dog for a walk, Dad," she called. "Back shortly."

Her father waved and kept talking to Jessie.

Out on the road, the same deputy's car that had been patrolling every few days approached from behind and slowly cruised by. He looked more at Whizzer than at her, but she waved anyway. She wondered how any deputy could devote so much time to one neighborhood. Probably someone with a little pull had asked that they keep the neighborhood patrolled. Maggie was glad. It made her feel safer to have him driving around all the time, even if he was kind of scraggly looking.

Whizzer pulled her toward the hill. She hadn't walked him anywhere except along the road within sight of their house, but she let him have his way this time and trudged up the hill with him tugging at the end of the leash, pulling her up step by step. How dangerous could it be with a deputy on duty and a dog at her side?

Halfway up the steep grade, Whizzer pulled her toward the path into the woods. "How do you know about the path, boy?"

He whined.

"If I find out Billy has been bringing you here, I'll give him a whacking he'll never forget. He's not supposed to play in these woods anymore."

Whizzer licked her hands, then tugged at the leash again, whimpering and finally barking at her.

The dark entrance into the trees loomed in front of her. The path wasn't as well worn as it used to be, but she knew someone had been coming and going because the grass and weeds were flattened. Maybe the other families had relented and allowed their children to run through the woods again. Maybe it was time for her to step into a new future too. Isn't that what Webb kept saying? And Andrea too. Move forward.

Maybe if she walked back there and looked at the rock she could face it all head on and come to terms with it. Maybe that would shake her loose from her prison of fears and let her get over it, get on with life. She could quit dwelling on Sue. She could quit worrying about what Webb did and didn't do, or what future he and Sue had together. Things could get back to normal.

She took one hesitant step toward the path, and then another. Whizzer hurried her forward.

The woods were dark, the last of the sun's rays not able to penetrate the thick trees. It took her eyes a moment to adjust as Whizzer pulled her down the path.

Every step relived that day. The stillness of the air reverberated with the leaves and sticks crunching beneath her feet. Tension crawled up her spine as she strained to see what lay ahead.

By the time she could see the boulder, she realized someone was sitting on it. For a moment she thought maybe it was the deputy. Maybe he'd gone to the upper path, the one near Brad's house, and walked down that way, but there hadn't been enough time for that. Who was it?

She hesitated, then turned away, yanking Whizzer as hard as she could.

The figure stood up, his face hidden by the shadows. "Maggie McCarthy. I knew you would come. I've been waiting for you."

His words caught her off guard, and she paused. The voice sounded familiar. Was it Mr. Dweller? Had the authorities told him she had turned him in? Of course, if he knew it was Billy making the claims against him, he would know it was her fault.

What would he do to her? She didn't think of Sue. She thought of Billy. Would Mr. Dweller try to do perverted things to her the same way he had with Billy? Would he try to coerce her, or would he be violent? He couldn't begin to think she would fall as easily as Billy. He couldn't say anything to make her touch him.

She tried to imagine being Billy with this man approaching her, telling her it was all in the name of love. How stupid! How could he believe that? How could he have convinced her little brother of such a lie?

Whizzer growled deep in his throat as the man took a step toward her.

Panic raced through her body.

She would never let him touch her.

The man took another step. His features became clear. It wasn't Mr. Dweller. It was Mr. Smith.

"Have you seen my cat?" he asked.

She relaxed. It was just Mr. Smith looking for his cat. "No, sir."

He took several more slow steps toward her. "Liar. The Garlens told me they saw you carrying her around."

Whizzer pulled at the leash.

"That was weeks ago, Mr. Smith. I carried her back to your house for you one day, but she jumped out of my arms and ran off."

"You were trying to steal her from me, weren't you? She's been living at your house, hasn't she?"

"No, sir." Maggie took a step back. "She's come up there a couple times, but she doesn't stay. Maybe she has a litter of kittens somewhere."

Mr. Smith was only a few feet away.

Whizzer's growl rose to three sharp yaps, and then back to a growl. "Why did you bring that dog? Planning to let him go after Cleopatra like that other dog did?"

"No, sir. He won't hurt anything."

His hand slipped to his back pocket and flashed silver as it came back around. A knife.

Maggie gasped and turned to run just as Whizzer pulled from her grip and jumped at Mr. Smith. The sound of leaves crushing seemed to come from every side of the woods as Mr. Smith moved toward her. In three steps Mr. Smith knocked the dog aside and flattened Maggie to the ground.

Maggie screamed. She knew without a doubt it had been him. She could see the crazed expression in his eyes and everything about Sue rose before her. The slash marks across her face, the bruises and wounds, all that he'd done to her.

Please God, save me.

As he held the knife to her throat, the stench of his breath gagged her. "If you're good, I'll let you live."

Whizzer jumped on his arm and sank his teeth in. Mr. Smith shook him off and stabbed at him with the knife, giving Maggie a chance to crawl a foot away before he was on her again. "Don't move again or I'll kill you."

Suddenly Webb was there, a shadow over her, his voice screaming out, his foot rising and hitting Mr. Smith in the chin. Mr. Smith took the kick and came down with the knife flailing, catching Webb across the ankle, leaving a bloody gash. Maggie screamed and clawed at the dirt, trying to free her legs from under the weight of him. Webb kicked at him again, but Mr. Smith grabbed his leg and pulled him down. Maggie scrambled away from them, screaming and crying as Webb and Mr. Smith rolled and fought on the ground.

Maggie didn't hear the other figure approach from the upper path till he was right upon them. The deputy stopped ten feet from the struggle with his gun cocked and aimed. "Hold it right there, boys. I've got a gun on you."

The two continued to fight.

Whizzer attacked Mr. Smith again, this time sinking teeth into his calf. With a shriek of pain, Mr. Smith let loose of Webb just long enough to swing his blade at the dog. Webb jabbed his knee into Mr. Smith's gut.

The deputy was flashing the gun from one to the other. "Get up now or I'll shoot you both."

"Not Webb. Him. It was him!" Maggie screamed.

Webb jerked out of Mr. Smith's grasp and scrabbled backward to his feet.

The deputy trained his gun on Mr. Smith.

Whizzer attacked his leg again, sending Mr. Smith thrashing backward. "Get off me, you mutt."

"Stand still or I'll shoot you," the deputy said.

"Get the dog off me." He kicked hard and knocked Whizzer in the ribs, then stumbled.

A shot rang out.

Mr. Smith fell to his knees with blood gushing from his thigh.

"Stay put, or I'll put one through your back," the deputy said.

Maggie called Whizzer and grabbed his leash.

Webb was at her side. "You okay?"

She nodded, gasping for breath.

"I had a feeling if I hung around this neighborhood long enough I'd catch you, you scumbag." The deputy pulled the radio off his belt and talked to the dispatch, then began reading Mr. Smith his rights as sirens wailed in the distance.

All vestiges of daytime had vanished by the time the ordeal was over. Maggie's statement to the police had been pretty simple and brief, but they made her go over it three times to make sure they had every detail.

Finally, the family was back in the yard again, heating up the grill, getting ready for a very late supper. "We could skip supper and call it a night, Maggie," Jessie said, after the Grahams had been over to see if everyone was okay before finally departing to tuck Kimberly into bed.

"No. I'm starving," Maggie replied. "And I feel better with everyone here. I really don't want to be alone."

Jessie smiled and took over pouring the iced tea. "You sit. I'm waiting on you tonight."

Her father sat down beside her and held her hand for a long while. Maggie knew he was imagining what could have happened. Finally, she kissed his cheek and assured him she was okay, just as Mr. Childers, the elderly widower from up the road, ambled into the yard.

"What's all the commotion going on around here?" he asked. "Sirens, and people yellin', and now the smell of that grill filling the air. I figured I'd better check on you young-uns and that new dog of yours."

Maggie grinned, glad she'd thought to add an extra portion for him, hoping he would show up, and doubly glad they hadn't put up that fence.

Maggie's father waved the old man to a chair. "Come and join us, Mr. Childers."

"I brought my kinfolk. I hope y'all don't mind. This here's my nephew."

A man stepped into the light. Maggie gasped. It was the bearded man.

"He don't know a soul 'round here, so I thought I'd bring him over to meet y'all. He's been a missionary in South America till he come home about a month ago. My help quit, ya know, and he's been comin' to check on me now and again till we get someone new hired."

Maggie's father stood and pulled up another chair. "He's more than welcome."

As the bearded man took a seat, Maggie could see the light in his eyes and his kind smile, and she was glad her paranoia hadn't gotten the poor man arrested as a suspect when it was Mr. Smith all along.

She moved to the park bench Andrea had added to the corner of the yard opposite Whizzer's kennel and stared up at the stars. *Thank You, God. I know You were with me. You've been with me every step of the way, haven't You? You've had a plan all along. I have to be me, don't I? I have to walk the path You've laid out for me, even though that doesn't mean being popular. It means something much, much more.*

Webb walked over and joined her. "What're you doing?"

"Thanking God. And now, thanking you. I could have ended up like Sue."

"It's my fault you took off up there."

"How do you figure that?"

"Because I wouldn't answer your question."

He was right. That was why she had stormed off with the dog, but it wasn't his fault. "It was my choice. You didn't make me leave in a huff. It's my Irish temper."

She looked at the bandage Jessie had put on his ankle. "How's your leg?"

"I'll live." He pointed up at the stars. "Look. The Big Dipper."

She followed his gaze. She could believe in eternity when she looked at the stars. She could feel God and heaven and knew that there was much more at play than the smallness of everyday life. Everything seemed more like pieces to a huge puzzle, just as individual stars made up the constellations.

Webb continued to stare at the stars. "I never touched her that way, Mags." He closed his eyes. "Not everyone at school is having sex. Not even all the ones who say they are."

"Not everyone at school is having sex." He made it sound so simple, something she hadn't expected from him. No ego, no pompous false story.

His voice continued, very quietly. "But I do think about it. I think about what he did to her, and it fills me with so much anger I can't sleep some nights. Then I look at her and wonder what she's thinking. She hasn't talked about it once. I can't ask her about it, but I never stop thinking about it."

Tears filled her eyes. She swiped at them, determined not to become emotional. "She's not the only one who's been abused. Billy and I talked last night."

Webb was quiet, waiting.

"Mr. Dweller had been molesting him."

That made him sit up. "No way."

"Yes way. I told you I had a feeling about him."

"Billy must be making it up on account of your speech and all."

She knew that was coming. Webb had heard her practicing and had seen her notes. Everyone was going to react that way. She pressed on. "I saw Mr. Dweller standing in his front door one day, early in the morning. When he saw me, he undid the tie of his bathrobe and let it fall open. There he was in all his glory."

"Really? Mr. Dweller?"

Maggie nodded. "I knew right then he was weird."

"Why didn't you say something?"

"Everyone else thought he was such a great guy. If I'd said anything, you wouldn't have believed me. Like now. You would've said I was nuts."

He laughed at her. "You are nuts."

"You're right. I probably am nuts. But I think I'm getting better now."

He turned from the stars in the sky to the ones twinkling in her eyes, and she knew he understood how seriously she meant it.

Jessie's voice rang out through the dark. "Supper's ready, kids."

Chapter
Twenty~Eight

HER SPEECH TOOK on new meaning with all that had transpired. As she peeked around the curtain at the students settling in their seats, she thought of Billy and wondered who else had been a victim. She had to reach out to those kids.

When Andrea learned that Maggie was going to give her speech to her entire school, she stepped up to help despite everything that had happened between her and Maggie. She explained that an adult trained in counseling victims needed to be present to field questions and handle whatever else might happen. As promised, she showed up right on time and found Maggie behind the curtain.

Maggie approached her with apprehension. "Thanks for coming, Andrea."

She nodded. "To be honest, I've had reservations, but this isn't about you or me. It's about helping kids that need help, just like Billy. I can't turn my back on such an opportunity."

There was so much stretching between them. "Look, Andrea, I'm sorry for how things worked out with my dad. I know he still likes you a lot."

"Don't patronize me."

"I don't mean to. I just . . . I want you to know I appreciate everything you did for me. You were there when I really needed you. I think that was God at work, really. He knew what was coming and He dropped you into our lives. I couldn't have gotten through this whole ordeal without your help."

She nodded and smiled slightly, almost wistfully. "I know, Maggie. And I would do it again in a heartbeat. You're a great girl. You have a lot going for you. You just need to let go of your dad and your brothers a bit. You need to stand on your own and be comfortable with that." She swept her arm through the air. "All this, the speeches and standing up for what you believe in, this is a step toward that, toward being a complete you. You're starting to get to know yourself. Even when you were pushing me away, standing against me and undoing the decorating, you were actually growing and becoming a stronger you. I respect that. I'm still a bit pissed, but I respect it."

"I didn't mean to make you mad. I just couldn't take you invading my space anymore. Home is all I have. Can't you see that?"

Andrea grew thoughtful. "I guess I didn't consider that. I've never lacked confidence in who I am. I'm comfortable wherever I go. Maybe too comfortable. But looking back, I guess I can see how I may have been too headstrong. I didn't think of it that way. You're growing past that, though. This time next year you won't feel married to that house. You'll be a complete person, a real teenager. I'm sure of it. You're just a Johnny-come-lately, newly arrived at figuring out who you are, and with a cause to fight for. Now, enough of this. On with the show."

More like a Maggie-come-lately, she thought and breathed a sigh of relief, glad to have things aired out between them.

Principal Pompey walked to the podium. Student voices roared in the high-ceilinged room as they chatted and laughed among themselves. He called them to order, waited for silence, and introduced Maggie.

She stepped up to the microphone, her body shaking, her palms sweating. She tapped one finger on the edge of the podium, a trick she'd learned from Mrs. Newell, and the shakes subsided. With a deep, cleansing breath, she began with mention of what Sue had been through and her own close call, then continued with how faith and courage were helping her through it. That had everyone sitting up, listening. They all wanted to hear the details of what happened, and who better to hear them from than Sue's rescuer? Maggie managed to satisfy their hunger for the inside scoop without revealing anything too personal about Sue.

After a pause, she went on. "The hardest thing to face is that the type of rape and abuse that Sue suffered represents the minority. The most prevalent cases of rape aren't by strangers. They're by your dates and family members and people you thought you were supposed to trust, even people from church."

Everyone knew she was talking about Mr. Dweller. Whispers rippled across the room, but she continued. "The truth is that one out of every four people in this room has been date-raped or molested. The sad thing is that only a few of you will admit it or seek help."

Again, voices swelled throughout the auditorium. She gave them a moment. Those numbers were hard to accept. "We need help, all of us who have ever been, or are being, cornered into doing something we know is wrong. If you've been molested or raped, or if someone is trying to take advantage of you, there is someone here in whom you can confide. She'll help you get out of the situation and work through what happened. May I present Andrea Ford from the Crisis Center."

Andrea took over with her part of the presentation, and Maggie receded behind the curtain, glad to be done.

Most of her classmates had heard her first speech, so the presentation didn't bring much reaction from any of them, but she noticed more serious glances from some of her upper and lower classmen, and from other tenth graders who weren't in her English class, like Webb.

"That was brave of you," Webb said in the hall afterward. "You did a good job."

Others said so too. She'd quit hanging out with Heather and Tammy a while back, and she didn't plan to go to any more parties, but she wasn't invisible either. She and Dixie were still friends, but more in their off time and not so much at school when Dixie was being escorted by Elliott or hanging around Heather and Tammy. Instead, Maggie was starting to spend more time with Clarissa and getting to know Jeanette, the quiet girl. She decided she was okay with that and didn't hold a grudge against Dixie. Their friendship went too far back to let go completely. Sometimes it made her sad, but Dixie was enjoying the popularity she'd always sought, while Maggie had found a new path, one that meant leadership. The health teacher had already asked her to start up a girl's club to stay on top of issues like abuse and date rape. Mrs. Newell suggested she run for student council. And Mr. Baire said he considered her speech top-notch and asked her to assist with a special history presentation he had planned for the spring.

All the changes and attention filled her with new enthusiasm for life, even if she wasn't popular. And even if Webb was still Sue's boyfriend.

Chapter
Twenty~Nine

ON HER WAY home from Dixie's the next Saturday evening, Maggie stopped at Webb's to have Tony walk her the rest of the way home. Not that they weren't allowed to walk the neighborhood now. With Mr. Smith behind bars, they had their freedom back, but she hadn't fully recovered from all that had happened. She could manage walking from Dixie's house to Webb's, but she couldn't go the rest of the way on her own.

She found Tony on Webb's bed, playing a stupid video game, as usual, but Webb wasn't in the room.

"We have to go, Tony," she coaxed, hoping the gradual mending of their relationship would make him comply without a fight.

He continued working the game control, his gaze steady on the screen. "In thirty minutes. I'm on the last level, and I'm not leaving till I beat this game."

She wouldn't walk back down the hill by herself, especially not in the dark. Tony ought to see that without her having to say so. It didn't matter that Mr. Smith had been arrested. She couldn't go alone.

"And then you'll look up and wonder why supper won't be ready until eight o'clock tonight." Too late she realized she had reverted to being bossy, but she couldn't take back her words.

He shrugged. "I'll eat a sandwich."

She regretted putting up the wall. Couldn't he see she was scared? Couldn't she admit to being vulnerable? "We're supposed to stay together."

"How many times do I have to say it? You're not my mother. Get over yourself."

She sighed. She had to learn to watch her tongue.

Of everything that was changing in her life, mending her relationship with Tony was one of the hardest obstacles, some-thing she hadn't expected. In other areas, things seemed to be falling into place. Andrea had called in a favor with a friend and arranged for her and Billy to start seeing counselors. Her father was enjoying Jessie's company but taking things slowly. And Billy had spent some time with the new boy down the road. She'd already seen a glimmer of the old Billy.

If only she could keep things on an even keel with Tony. She decided the best course was to be honest. "Tony, I'm scared. I don't want to go down the hill by myself. I need you to walk me home."

Webb walked into the room with a textbook in his hand. Maggie hadn't noticed his desk lamp was on, and papers were strewn across the tabletop. He was studying? Tony was playing the game alone?

Webb looked from her to Tony and assessed the situation. "C'mon," he said and set the book down. "I'll walk you home."

They walked in silence, their feet plodding to the ground as they progressed down the hill, past the awful spot in the woods without looking toward it. They skirted around a huge rain puddle and then stayed along the edge of the road.

Webb slowed his pace. He kicked a stone. "I broke up with Sue."

Maggie came to a stop. "Really?"

He nodded.

"After all she's been through . . ."

"It wasn't that. It was, well, I've been thinking about what really matters to me, what I really want in life. Me and Sue, it was just superficial. We don't really have anything in common."

"She's changed."

"We all have. We didn't really know each other before, but we've talked a lot lately, and we both realize we're good friends, nothing more. She wants time to sort things out. Her family might even be moving away. Fresh start and all that."

"I don't blame her."

"I'm starting over too. New priorities. Goals. Plans for the future. Life is short."

Everything about his demeanor suggested he was being sincere. "Plans for the future?"

"Yep. I'm getting a job. And I'm thinking about college, studying for the SAT, and working on getting my grades up. I'll be a junior next fall. I've got to decide what I'm going to do with my life."

She felt like he'd swallowed one of her speeches and recited it back to her. She could hardly believe it. "You're serious?"

"Yep," he said. He moved closer and draped his arm gently across her shoulders.

She wasn't about to fall for one of his advances. "What're you doing that for?"

"I thought we could hang out together. You know, talk about our futures."

The weight of his arm hung on her shoulders. How long had she dreamed of his making just such a move? Things had changed. "I'm not easy, you know."

"Sure, like I haven't figured that out listening to you all year."

Maybe he really had listened to all her spiels and taken her ideals to heart. She had made an impression on him. She had influenced his life.

She cast him a squinty-eyed grin and lifted his arm off her shoulder to clasp his hand in hers. "Good. So you won't be offended when I tell you that you can start by just holding my hand."

He laughed. "Exactly what I expected." He squeezed her hand, and they continued up the smaller slope to her house.

She stopped halfway and turned her Claddagh ring around.

ACKNOWLEDGMENTS

EACH BOOK TRAVELS its own road of creation, but always with the invaluable help of others along the way. To my friends, A. H. Jackson and Sylvia Roller, thank you for your input and enthusiasm, and Wendy Toy, for your comments.

I am deeply grateful to Margaret Crites of the Rape Crisis Center who shared her experience and knowledge on many points in the story.

I extend great appreciation to Lesa Bethea, MD, for clarifying medical information, and to Laura Power, for being my teen reader.

Jeana Ledbetter and Nicci Hubert, you're both wonderful; I owe this one to you.

Laura Wright, thank you for all your hard work and long discussions.

To all the folks at NavPress, my sincere thanks for pulling it all together.

Most especially, my deepest love and gratitude goes out to my family. Your love, patience, and encouragement sustain me.

In the end, I am naught without God. All glory be to the Father and to the Son and to the Holy Spirit.

If you have been raped, molested, or abused, there are counselors at RAINN (Rape, Abuse and Incest National Network) ready to help. To be directed to a local crisis center, and for more information and assistance, call 1-800-656-HOPE (twenty-four hours a day) or visit www.rainn.org.

ABOUT THE AUTHOR

MICHELLE BUCKMAN LIVES with her husband and children near the Carolina coast, where she enjoys spending her free time walking the long stretches of sandy beaches. She shares news and welcomes comments from readers through her website: www.MichelleBuckman.com.

AVAILABLE OCTOBER 2007

THE PATHWAY
COLLECTION

My Beautiful Disaster

MICHELLE BUCKMAN